the trouble up north

travis mulhauser

GRAND
CENTRAL

New York Boston

Copyright © 2025 by Travis Mulhauser

Cover design by Sara Wood. Cover images by Getty Images and Shutterstock. Cover copyright © 2025 by Hachette Book Group, Inc.

Grand Central Publishing
Hachette Book Group
1290 Avenue of the Americas, New York, NY 10104
grandcentralpublishing.com
@grandcentralpub

First Edition: March 2025

Grand Central Publishing is a division of Hachette Book Group, Inc. The Grand Central Publishing name and logo is a registered trademark of Hachette Book Group, Inc.

The publisher is not responsible for websites (or their content) that are not owned by the publisher.

The Hachette Speakers Bureau provides a wide range of authors for speaking events. To find out more, go to hachettespeakersbureau.com or email HachetteSpeakers@hbgusa.com.

Grand Central Publishing books may be purchased in bulk for business, educational, or promotional use. For information, please contact your local bookseller or the Hachette Book Group Special Markets Department at special.markets@hbgusa.com.

Library of Congress Cataloging-in-Publication Data

Names: Mulhauser, Travis, 1976- author.
Title: The trouble up north / Travis Mulhauser.
Description: First edition. | New York : Grand Central Publishing, 2025.
Identifiers: LCCN 2024045056 | ISBN 9781538767986 (hardcover) |
    ISBN 9781538768006 (ebook)
Subjects: LCGFT: Thrillers (Fiction) | Novels.
Classification: LCC PS3613.U435 T76 2025 | DDC 813/.6—dc23/eng/20241007
LC record available at https://lccn.loc.gov/2024045056

ISBNs: 9781538767986 (hardcover), 9781538768006 (ebook)

Printed in the United States of America

LSC-C

Printing 1, 2024

For my mom

the trouble up north

part I

rhoda

Northern Michigan.
Sometime in the middle aughts.

T he morning of the fire I was sitting on the porch with my husband, Edward. The sky was just beginning to blue above the trees, and the air was cool and snapped with pine. It was the sort of moment I did not want to ruin with business, but to talk about anything else would have been a lie.

"Jewell is going to set Van Hargraves's boat on fire," I said. "Tonight."

Edward looked off the porch. There was still mist above the grass in the field, and through the mist was the bend of our dirt road and the vervain along the shoulder. I waited a beat, but he did not respond.

"Van pitched her on it. It's an insurance play. I don't think she was going to tell me, but I found her in the shed last night, wrapping rags around the end of a broom handle for a torch."

"Good Lord," he said.

"I know."

"She better get paid up front."

"He gave her a thousand down. Nine more when the deed is done."

"What do you think?"

"I think we need the money." I paused. "And that I couldn't talk her out of it if I tried."

"All you Sawbrooks," he said. "You start out assuming nobody will ever change their mind and avoid all sorts of hassle."

"I do see that as an advantage of our hereditary stubbornness," I noted. "But in this instance, I also know that I'm right."

"You've never been wrong in your life," he said, and smiled.

It was a joke, and I was glad for it. He had color in his cheeks and seemed contented. He was having a good morning, which is a relative term.

Some days he can walk to the porch and other days he needs the chair. Some days he needs the oxygen with the chair, and some days he doesn't need either. That morning he was in the wheelchair, without the tank, and I was sitting beside him. We both had coffee. He sipped from his and then went on.

"Is she working with Van outside of this?"

"He's a drunk and she's tending bar, so in that way there is a professional relationship, I guess."

"No more games, though?"

"No," I said. "I don't believe Van is allowed to host social functions anymore. I heard Franklin put his foot down on that front."

My daughter plays poker and plays it fairly well. Van used to run games in his garage, and he'd give Jewell a seat at the table for a small cut of her winnings. Those games were for his buddies from Harbor North, the resort where wealthy Detroiters and Chicagoans spent their summers blocking everybody else's view of Lake Michigan with their beachfront homes and condos.

Van is a resorter himself, but he lives in the newer construction along the Crow River. Harbor North wasn't happy with just the coastline, of course. They had to move inland, too, and connected their two sprawling locations with a brand-new bike path.

The path is plenty pretty. Even I can admit that. There is a tall canopy of shade trees and tasteful cuts in the foliage where you can catch a gentle bend of river, but none of that changes the fact that it shouldn't be there in the first place.

"I'm not sure this boat thing is the best idea," said Edward. "Matter of fact, I'm sure it's a terrible idea, but I am glad you told me."

"Of course."

I said it matter of fact, but I'd debated the matter plenty. The last thing Edward needed was something else to worry over, but it was also a boat fire on the Crow River. If Jewell did it right, and she would, he'd see it from the very porch where we were sitting.

"I'm going to walk the bike path this morning," I said. "Make sure there's no sight lines we don't know about."

"Shit," he said. "You really must be worried."

I avoid that path like poison, on principle and because there is not a more insufferable population on this earth than cyclists. I wish I could say it's all tourists, but there's plenty of locals zipping around that thing, too—all of them in their too-tight shorts and space helmets. They do group rides and then drink beer after, standing at the bar in their Lycra suits with their privates all bundled up like cinnamon buns and we're all supposed to just sit there and take it.

"Wait a minute," he said. "Is she going up the resort side?"

"No, no. She's going up the east bank. I just want to make sure there's no gaps in the trees from the other side."

"She's going to wait until dark, isn't she?"

I told him she was.

"She'll be fine, then," he said. "You're just being one of those helicopter parents."

"I'm sixty years old," I said. "And she's a full-grown woman."

He wagged his finger in my direction. "That's what makes it funny."

"Well, I'm glad you're getting a kick out of it."

"I get my kicks where I can," he said. "It's my one defining truth."

I worked my rocking chair slow. I could hear the floorboards sighing and there was birdsong in the trees.

Edward used to ride his chair like a mechanical bull and it drove me crazy. Now he sat silent and hunched slightly forward, and the quiet he left was so much worse.

"You look good today," I said.

It was a note to myself, more than anything. I was trying to stay positive.

"I'm dying of lung cancer," he said. "I'm shriveled up to nothing and look like a goddamn Muppet."

"You do not look like a Muppet."

"I'm one of those old-men Muppets. Up in the balcony."

"You look great and I don't want to hear another word about it."

"You look great," he said. "Better than the day we married."

"Now who's lying?"

"I'm dead serious. But I'm also going blind, so that may be a factor."

"I'll take it," I said.

He took a gummy from his shirt pocket and popped it in his mouth. I try not to count, but it was the second one I'd seen him take that morning, which meant he was likely on number four.

"What about Luce?" he asked.

Lucy is our oldest, and the park ranger at Crooked Tree. It's a small park, but it sits across the river from the resort on the north end.

"What about her?"

"Does she know about all this?"

"Hell no," I said. "Absolutely not."

"Is she working tonight?"

I told him she wasn't. "She's downtown tonight, with her fancy friends."

Edward tilted his head, which is something he does when he's seriously considering—like his thoughts are too heavy to hold up straight. Like his spine may give out from the sheer weight of his deliberations.

"She'll figure it out," he said. "She's too smart."

"Well, I can't worry about what Lucy knows and what she doesn't. Not anymore."

"You worry about her constantly. I don't know who you think you're fooling with that."

"I worry about her some, but it's not in the way I used to. I used to worry like a mother does, now I worry what she's going to do to hurt us next."

Edward doesn't like when I talk about Lucy as an enemy, but I don't have time to pretend or pretty things up. The fact is, she sold us out.

I carved up three chunks of our land to give to the kids eighteen months earlier, strictly for tax purposes, and before the ink was dry on Lucy's deal, she had it moved into a trust with her conservation group. They gave her cash for the land and signed some papers that she claims protect that acreage from development or bank seizure.

I don't believe that for a second, and even if I did, it wouldn't change the fact that the first thing Lucy's group did was put in a "nature trail" along the river where we used to have pines. It's not as bad as the bike path, but that doesn't make it good. Now anybody in the world can park their car and stroll through what used to be our forest just as pretty as they please, and we get about half a dozen strays a week—all because Lucy went off to college, got some big ideas, and sold our land to the hippies. She might as well have shot me through the heart with a deer rifle.

She is not welcome on our property any longer, though I know for a fact that Edward sneaks her over to watch Tigers games.

Lucy is a bitter disappointment to me, but she is not alone. Buckner, our boy, is also banned from the property, though unlike Lucy, he does not sneak over to check on his daddy. Buckner is too selfish to do anything but think about Buckner because Buckner is a drunk.

He claims to be sober now, but I know how that ends. My sister was cursed with the same affliction, and I spent years trying and failing to help her. Wanda was my older sister and she put a pistol barrel in her mouth when she was twenty-two years old and pulled the trigger. I'll never forget the sound of that shot and how it rose from the pines and broke the stillness on a quiet morning. I'll never forget how the moment I heard it, I knew exactly what it meant.

I've tried to warn Lucy and Jewell both to be careful with their hearts, but Buckner's got them thinking he's some sort of triumph of the human spirit because he's managed to not get drunk for a little while.

Matter of fact, I heard Lucy was having a celebration for him in town. They were going to sit around and sing his praises and I wasn't invited because I am not considered part of Buckner's support group. That's a funny one, being that I raised the boy, but Lucy has read all the books and she knows best.

"Can I say one more thing?" said Edward.

"Could I stop you if I tried?"

"I don't want you anywhere near that fire."

8

"I won't be."

"I mean, at all."

"All I'm doing is helping her get rigged up and making sure the plan is solid."

"Aiding and abetting." He sighed.

"It's the least I can do."

He settled back into his chair. Took one of his thin, raspy breaths. He was worried about Jewell, but there was something else eating at him, too. Something besides the cancer.

"What's wrong?"

"Nothing's wrong," he said.

"I don't believe you."

"I mean, everything is wrong, but it's nothing out of the ordinary."

"Say it, then."

"I was just sitting here thinking about rich people, I guess. How nothing ever touches them. They set their own boats on fire and it only makes them richer."

———————

Van Hargraves was rich—there was no doubting that. He lived in a big, sprawling three-story on the outer edge of the resort and liked to call himself a summer resident. It's a contradiction in terms, if you ask me. I've never believed a person can have more than one home.

They try to, of course. They have second homes and third ones too and that's a big part of what's wrong with this world—the idea that more than one place can belong to a person without that person having to belong to any one place in return.

People say we cling to our land, but I like to think it grabs onto us a little bit, too. I like to think we protect each other.

The Crow is sourced out of Long Lake and runs southeast into town where it empties into Lake Michigan, and that was where the resort built first.

They cleared out the cement plant and put up summer mansions and condos and then added a golf course and a marina and erected tall black gates around all of it.

People said the economy was shifting. They said there was nothing to be done and that it was out of our hands, and then they all stood there on the beach and cheered when the wrecking ball swung and took half the jobs in Cutler County with it.

I'll admit the plant was an eyesore out there on the bay, but it was the last thing in this county that made something and sold something other than itself and I miss its long shadows on the water. I miss its air of defiance.

The casinos followed shortly, and after the casinos came the resort's expansion to the river in the form of a second golf course and a ski lodge. Then the tagalong condos and the sort of retail that nobody who actually lives here can afford.

They bought out the entire western bank, and most people sold fast and moved gladly. I don't blame them. It was more money than they'd ever seen, so of course they lunged at the bait and took it.

Or maybe it wasn't bait at all. Maybe it was exactly what they wanted, and they are living happier lives now in the suburbs and cities and far-flung towns where I occasionally hear reports of their lives through Edward and his Facebook account. Just the other day he told me the Hendersons, who lived on the river for thirty years, are in Tempe, Arizona, in the middle of a goddamn desert. I can't imagine.

The resort started building, and anybody who didn't sell was dug out with rising property tax. Meanwhile, they buried the eastern bank in so much sediment that some of those lots actually devalued. Connie Becker, Jewell's best friend, was trapped down there with her mother and three baby girls because their piece of the Crow had turned into swamp.

There was some good that came with it, I guess. Money for builders and tradesmen. The county coffers got stocked and they actually did some good with it, too. I couldn't believe it, but they fixed a few roads and maybe I could have learned to live with it all if they hadn't trained their sights on us directly. But they did. Of course they did.

My family has been on this river for close to two centuries and holds over five thousand acres of land. We're the one thing standing between the resort, a new exit off Highway 31, and miles of uninterrupted development.

The property taxes hurt, but when Edward got sick, things went sideways in a hurry, and to pay for treatments I had to take a bank loan he begged me not to get. He said he was ready to go.

"You're going to lose the land and I'm going to die anyway," he said.

"You're going to live," I said. "And we're not going anywhere."

I know there's times that Edward resents me for keeping him alive, but it's not half as much as I would have resented him for dying.

jewell

J ewell met Van a few summers earlier, when she became a sort of celebrity guest at his well-heeled poker games. Van didn't play himself. He said cards got in the way of his drinking, but he loved the chatter and the action, and every Tuesday night in the summer he'd have as many as three tables humming in his garage. Jewell heard about the games at the casino, showed up uninvited, and cleared twenty-five hundred in her first sit.

She figured that would be the end of it. You didn't get let back into games you gutted, but with Van it was just the opposite. He said he wanted 5 percent of whatever she cleared and that he'd stake her buy-in anytime she wanted.

She thought it was going to be some sort of hustle, and short-lived once word spread, but there were no secrets or setups in Van's garage.

If anything, her reputation brought more fish to the table. These were men who were more than willing to lose money if it meant they got to sit with a player of her caliber and take some stories back to their golf buddies.

The stories were provided by Jewell herself. She supposed it was a shtick, for lack of a better word, but she picked it up from the poker room at the casino and the fact was, it worked. Resorters loved local flavor and mystique so much they'd let themselves be charmed right off the table and barely feel bitter about it.

Mostly, she told family yarns. The Sawbrooks had bootlegged through Prohibition and those stories were always a hit, particularly once she name-dropped Al Capone, who may or may not have stayed some nights on the Sawbrook property when things got too hot in Chicago. Then she'd hit them with Kern, the long-ago great-uncle who'd fought for the Union and received the high honor of serving as Abraham Lincoln's body man after the war.

The interesting part was that Kern had been discharged shortly before Lincoln's death. He'd had a dream foretelling the assassination and began to unnerve the president and his staff by suggesting Lincoln go underground to live out his second term in a bunker.

"Kern knew that hit was coming," she'd say, then lean in to rake a pile of chips in her direction. "They had an article about it in the *Detroit Free Press*. Google that shit. The media got all caught up in the dream and the supernatural element of it, but Kern's basic point was this—have you met these Confederate assholes? Of course they're going to try and kill the president."

She'd wear a Detroit Tigers hat low over her eyes, her dark hair in braids or falling free over her shoulders. A tank top, blue jeans, and high-top Chucks. Pretty, but distinctly proletariat.

Van went so far as to claim that Jewell was personally responsible for the area's new, emerging tourist market—mushroom hunters. These were people who would spend entire weeks scouring the woods for a skillet full of wild mushrooms, and they came from as far away as New York and California and Texas and Italy and Spain. Van said he and Franklin had actually met a couple who'd come all the way from Moscow.

"Not Moscow, Idaho," he'd said. "We mailed them a Christmas card and addressed it, literally, to Russia."

One night Jewell had been talking about the chanterelle toast her grandmother used to make and apparently there was some food writer from New York at the table. He went out and found some for himself, did a write-up in one of the fancy magazines, and six months later the woods were filled with foraging tourists in floppy hats.

Van's games were a gravy train and she would have ridden it forever, but his husband forbade them after one of Van's stints in rehab and he never got them back off the ground.

He never stopped drinking, either. Jewell knew because she bartended at the Sailor's Knot and that was where Van spent most of his evenings. In addition to a few of his days.

The Knot was a burger-and-beer joint on the waterfront. It sat between the public beach and the gated edge of the resort and was the one place in town where the two populations regularly mixed—tasty burgers and a good beer list being generally unifying factors.

The night he pitched her on the boat scheme, Van was hunched in his usual spot beside the chalkboard where the daily specials were announced in vibrant pastels. She had a full bar and patio, but he kept pestering her to step outside.

"Step outside for what?"

"It's about business."

"A game?"

"Not that kind of business. This is far more lucrative."

She nodded to the door.

"Give me five minutes," she said. "But whatever it is, I'm probably not interested."

Jewell was interested, though. Not in whatever business Van was hinting at, but in the prospect that she might get him to host a game in exchange. She'd just returned from Vegas where she'd gone belly-up in the Under 30 Elite and she was desperate to get her bank-roll right.

The U30 was a hold 'em event with five million in prizes on a twenty-thousand-dollar stake, but it was also a stepping-stone. The tournament was only open to younger players, and past winners had ridden victories straight onto magazine covers and sponsorships. She'd gone to the desert convinced she was going to solve the family's financial issues in one fell swoop but didn't make it out of the first round. She barely lasted two hours. In Vegas, nobody cared about her stories. In Vegas, the only thing they cared about was the game.

She knew she wasn't going to go out there and sprinkle the pot with Sawbrook yarns, but what she hadn't expected was how wooden she would feel without them. There was no rhythm to her game. She played desperate and afraid and she lunged at hands—like maybe the stories were as much for her as the sunburned golfers who paid for them.

Outside, there were gusts off Lake Michigan and the bay was choppy beneath high stars. Van's white hair was wind-blown and he was wearing an Oxford shirt and khakis. He stank like aftershave and whiskey.

"So what's all this about?" she asked.

He slurped from the Manhattan she'd just mixed him. "It's a bit of a felony, actually."

"A felony?"

"Nothing too dire. Something I have some experience in, as well. I don't know if you know this about me, but I dabble in some areas that might be considered unlawful. All white collar, of course. And not the bad kind of white collar. I don't steal people's 401ks. I'm not Madoff, for Christ's sake. I just occasionally need to do things that aren't technically legal, to sort of stimulate my own economy. If that makes sense?"

"I guess it makes as much sense as anything," she said.

"My husband doesn't approve, so you cannot tell him. No matter what, Franklin cannot know."

"I don't really talk much to Franklin—"

"Right," said Van. "I'm just saying that's part of the deal."

Jewell leaned back and folded her arms across her chest. She was conscious of the stance and it bothered her. She couldn't help but notice body language and understand what it meant whether she wanted to or not. In this case she was in the defensive posture she so often found herself occupying when dealing with resorters. Except on the poker table. On the poker table she was never on her heels.

"What's the rest of the deal?"

Van took another drink. Drained the glass and then set it down on top of a small fence post and held up his hands, palms out. "Are you ready?"

"I'm on the edge of my seat."

He leaned forward and whispered it in her ear.

"I want you to set my boat on fire."

Jewell had never had any real interest in a criminal life, but Van's money was too good and he'd agreed to host a game in return.

"And I don't want to pay anything off the top," she'd said. "I want to keep everything I win."

"We'll do the game this fall," he said. "When Franklin is at his yoga retreat."

He paid her the thousand on the spot. Dug the cash right out of his pocket.

All told, she thought it was a good deal. Maybe even a great deal. Still, she woke up the morning of and knew she had to talk it through with Connie.

Jewell hadn't said anything to Connie about Vegas. She went alone on a whim and was nearly certain that Connie would have talked her out of the trip if given the chance. Jewell had gone rogue and paid the price and now she needed her best friend's blessing.

"So you're going to set Van Hargraves's boat on fire," she said. "And he's going to pay you to do it?"

"Correct."

They were in Connie's living room. Connie in a T-shirt and cutoff sweatpants, now fraying at the thighs where she'd scissored them. She wore a beanie and house slippers and sat with both legs folded beneath her.

She had always been so tiny. Five foot four and not 120 pounds and somehow she'd carried three babies and birthed them all in a tub right there in the room where they sat.

Connie was on the couch facing outside so she could see her girls, and Jewell was in the same blue recliner that had been in that very spot for the twenty-five years they'd been best friends. It was at the exact same angle, too. The chair faced the television in the corner, which was the one thing in the house that Connie's mom kept updated.

"Why doesn't he do it himself?"

"Because they've got these claims investigators," said Jewell. "They're like detectives. They'll come up and do an investigation and apparently they're pretty good. Most of them are ex-cops who got fired for stealing evidence or shooting somebody."

Connie asked how much, and Jewell told her.

"Shit," she said. "That's a lot."

"It's ten thousand we don't have, that's for sure."

Connie shook her head. She and her mother would have sold their land on a dime if they could. Connie thought Jewell was crazy, fighting so hard to stay on the river, but mostly she was glad that Jewell didn't want to leave.

"You leave me here," she liked to say, "and I might have to hunt you down and kill you."

Connie's girls were starting to run wild in the yard. They all looked alike but had different daddies. They were between three and seven and wore flashing, superhero sneakers. Their skin was pale and freckled and their blond hair was white as cornsilk from summer.

"Do it," she said.

"Yeah?"

"Tonight is good, too," she said. "According to Rick, there's a concert out in Harbor and they're going to have the entire sheriff's department working traffic."

Rick was Dot's daddy. He was a sheriff's deputy and the only one of the three fathers Connie still spoke with. Dot was the middle girl.

"What kind of concert would they be having in Harbor?"

"It's a Christian band playing at the church," she said. "They're basically like the Jonas Brothers, but without any talent."

"A Christian boy band?"

"Exactly." She put a finger in her mouth, like she was about to vomit.

Jewell heard a shriek and looked outside. The oldest, Rebecca, was driving a motorized Barbie monster truck and chasing the youngest, Christine. Jewell waited for Connie to react, but she didn't.

"That's just how they play tag," she said.

Jewell thought Rebecca was going to flatten Christine, but somehow the little one made it around the side of the house and lost her sister on the turn. Jewell was undecided on the matter of children, but her trips to Connie's were beginning to push her further from the idea.

"Where'd you get that Barbie truck?"

"It was a parting gift," said Connie. "From this dickhead I was seeing."

"When was this?"

"Pretty recently. I told you about it."

"You didn't tell me about any monster trucks."

"He didn't really get it for me. He bought it for his own daughter, but then his wife found out and threw a fit."

"Found out about you?"

"No," said Connie. "Found out about the monster truck. She's one of those that's opposed to Barbie on political grounds."

"This was the guy from the resort?"

"Tom Breckon."

Connie said his name with a British accent, though he was not British.

"What a prick," said Jewell.

"It's my own fault," she said.

Jewell agreed but didn't need to say so out loud. Every girl who grew up on the river had a *Pretty Woman* fantasy that involved some Harbor Norther whisking her off into another life. It was well-tread ground that always turned out the same.

Jewell didn't want to be whisked anywhere and had never wanted any life but the one she'd been given, right there on the river. It was why she'd put her land into Lucy's trust and taken the cash out west. It was why she was about to become an arsonist.

She stood up from the blue chair and stretched. Thanked Connie for the coffee and her counsel.

"Out of curiosity," she said. "What's their name?"

"Whose name?"

"The Christian boy band?"

"Oh God," said Connie. "Who cares? I can't remember. Some Bible verse, maybe? The point is, tonight is a good night to set a boat on fire."

lucy

O ver in town, nestled into a residential block between two Victorians, Lucy's bungalow was teeming with people.

There were guests in the kitchen for coffee and donuts, and even more in the backyard where there was lively chatter and the occasional roll of laughter.

Buckner's anniversary celebration was off and running, and turn-out was better than expected. There were at least twenty people from Buckner's home group, and a dozen more that had come from the Al-Anon meeting Lucy attended.

Al-Anon was where she'd met Franklin, whom she was talking with now.

"This is all so lovely," he said. "And I can't think of anybody more deserving than Buckner. He's an inspiration to us all."

They were standing on Lucy's porch, facing the lilacs and the big, towering maple at the back of the yard. She could think of literally a million people more deserving than her brother, and "inspiration" was the most wildly hyperbolic thing she'd heard in some time, but what was the profit in saying so?

"That's so nice of you," she said. "You two are friends?"

"I would say we're chums," said Franklin. "We both smoke on

the front steps before our respective meetings and I've come to really enjoy our chats."

Franklin was a small man in narrow sunglasses. He wore a white button-down polo, salmon shorts, and boat shoes. His hair was thinning on top, but there was enough raw material for a messy, wind-blown look she felt suited him.

"And six months is a long time," he went on. "I mean, look at my Van. He has all the money and institutional privilege in the world, and he can't put together so much as a week. Meanwhile your brother has managed to fight and claw his way to this accomplishment. He's pulled himself up by the bootstraps, as they say."

Lucy did not point out that Buckner had some advantages of his own—namely that he didn't pay a dime for his own treatment because she'd footed the bill herself. Ten thousand dollars in cash, which was exactly half of what the conservation group had paid for her piece of land. But mostly what she didn't point out to Franklin was that Buckner wasn't actually there. Buckner had not shown up for his own party, and she could think of only one reason in the world why that might be.

People had been asking after him all morning. He was the man of the hour and there were well wishes to be delivered, and she'd told some of the guests that he was at the party, somewhere. She'd point off in a direction, say she just saw him, and slip quietly away. Other guests were told that he already came and left, while still others were told the truth.

"He's not here," she said to some. "Because he's probably drunk in a ditch somewhere."

People who were told the truth would laugh uncomfortably, unsure if she was joking. She was not joking, and could have clarified, but preferred the awkward silence to further explanation.

There was no larger strategy at play in terms of who was told what; she was just bouncing too quickly between concern and outrage to focus. She hadn't told Franklin anything yet, because Franklin hadn't asked.

She could have used some help from Jewell, but her sister hadn't bothered to show up, either. Jewell had made all sorts of promises about helping with the e-vites and paying for the donuts, but Lucy never put any stock in it. She just kept telling Jewell that all she had to do was be there.

"Obviously," Jewell had said. "Totally."

Prior to the party, Lucy had felt real progress was being made with her siblings. Jewell had seen the light and put her land into the trust, and Buckner had gotten sober and she had imagined the three of them there that morning—finally outside their mother's shadow and moving forward, together.

Now she felt like a fool. She wanted to lock her doors and cry, but what about all these guests?

Lucy hadn't gone to Al-Anon for herself. She found the entire thing ridiculous but had forced herself as a show of solidarity with Buckner. The meetings were tiresome and a bore, but they had also introduced her to this entirely new group of potential donors she saw no purpose in squandering.

"Franklin," she said. "I've meaning to talk with you about something else, actually."

"Please," he said, and sipped from his paper cup of coffee. "I am so ready to not talk about Van. Believe me."

"Friends of the Crow," she said.

"Of course," he said. "Your group."

"Not my group," she said. "I'm on the board, but—"

"Oh, please." Franklin waved the comment away. "Don't be

modest. You started that whole thing and got it off the ground. And you are doing amazing work, I hear."

"Well, I am flattered," she said, and went right into the pitch.

She no longer hesitated or apologized when asking for money. She just smiled and maintained eye contact and her lines were so shop-worn and smooth that she didn't even hear them when she spoke.

Franklin was exactly the sort of vaguely environmental resorter whose money she both desperately needed and deeply resented. There were more of these river-friendly rich people than she ever would have guessed, though they were not so river-friendly as to not be there in the first place.

She explained to Franklin that there were tiers for onetime donors, but she hoped he would consider a recurring setup with the group. Monthly or yearly contributions would make him a full member, increase his tax write-off, and help provide the sort of stability that would allow the Friends of the Crow—the FOC, she called it—to strategic plan.

"Membership," she explained, "also comes with swag. Coffee mugs, bumper stickers, and T-shirts. Branded rain ponchos for those able to donate at the platinum level."

"So you're saying that if I donate money to help the river, you will provide me with things that I can display to make my friends aware of my inherent goodness?"

"That's exactly what I'm saying."

"I want my mug to be bigger than the NPR one. Can that be arranged?"

"Consider it done," she said, and took out her phone. "Where can I email you?"

Franklin input his information into her contacts himself, and she invited him to their social that evening.

"And what is a social, exactly?"

"It's really just a meet and greet. Hors d'oeuvres and drinks at the Grenshire. We hold them once a month in the summer and it's honestly one of my favorite things that we do. Really low-key but gives some of our most valued members the opportunity to network."

"Will there be mucky-mucks?"

"I'm sorry?"

"Bigwigs," said Franklin. "Important people. Politicians, captains of industry, that sort of thing. Will the governor be there, for instance?"

Lucy laughed. "The governor will not be there, but we do have a few congressmen that stop by on occasion."

"Lansing folks?"

"Correct. Not DC."

"Well," he said. "My Van, for all his well-established faults, has actually given me a bit of a treat tonight. He has a work dinner, and so he's bought me a ticket to see Billy Joel in Interlochen. Have you been?"

"To Interlochen? Absolutely. I saw the Cowboy Junkies there."

"Oh, I love them," he said. "How was it?"

She had seen the show in high school and would never forget Margo Timmins singing "Sweet Jane" in a summer dress. The sun had set orange-red above the water that night, and the stage was softly lit and it was all so beautiful and breathtaking. On the other hand, she had never been more acutely aware that she was a Sawbrook and did not belong in polite society.

She'd gone with her friend Ben and his parents, and she remembered wondering what it might be like to have a family that went to nice dinners and to concerts and did not spend their lives at war with the very institutions of American life. Banks and the IRS and the federal government. She couldn't voice the root of her alienation so precisely then, but that had only made the feeling all the more powerful and consuming.

"It was beautiful," she said. "And amazing."

Franklin handed her phone back.

"We'll go to a show sometime. Me and you. Van complains too much about the drive whenever we go and to be frank, I'm not even sure if the man likes music. You and I will go and we'll have dinner before. We'll talk about the river and all the wonderful things you're doing."

"That sounds perfect," she said, and it did.

Franklin put a hand gently on her forearm and then leaned in for a hug. He said how nice it was to meet her. Franklin said he had some things to do in town but wanted to say hello to Buckner before he left.

"Do you know where he is?"

"The last time I saw him, he was in the front yard."

This was true, but only because he'd stopped by two days earlier on his way to work. Lucy had been out in the flower beds, tidying the garden for his party.

jewell

J ewell met her mother at the south end of the property just before
sunset. Rhoda wanted to stripe her face with hunting camo and
go over the plan one last time. Jewell didn't think that was necessary, but if it brought her mom some comfort, then it wasn't too much
trouble. Certainly not in light of the hovering guilt and dread she carried
over the land she'd sold so quick and easy. Rhoda had a way of sniffing
things out, and Jewell sensed a reckoning was near on that front.

She had a gallon of gas in a rucksack strapped to her shoulders
and a stick roped to the top of the bag. The stick was outfitted with
old rags she'd doused in lawn mower oil and wrapped in twine, and
there was a book of matches in a Ziploc beside the gasoline. Her
mother had two tubes of camo resting on a fence post, and she was
alternating stripes of light green and loam.

There used to be a sandy little beach where they were standing. Jewell swam there as a girl with Buckner and Lucy, but the sediment had
eroded the land and turned the swimming hole shallow and brackish.

It was pretty even so. Reeds in the still water and gnats swarming
above the bull thistle and blue iris. The sun was low and it was the
exact moment of evening when the light somehow both paled and
deepened and turned the surface of the river gold without glaring.

"He tell you not to say anything to Franklin?" her mother asked.

Jewell nodded.

Franklin never drank with Van but frequently gathered him from the bar at close. Franklin always stuffed the tip jar, apologized for whatever his husband might have said or done, and then dragged him outside. Jewell didn't know Franklin well, but he struck her as being as sweet as his husband was crass. Rhoda knew of them both, because somehow Rhoda knew at least a little bit about everybody.

Jewell looked at her mother with her short white hair and sun-dark face. She was still so strong. Sixty years old and as sturdy as she'd ever been—all square shoulders and straight spine. She was in a red field shirt and blue jeans and wore aviator shades. She had helped Jewell plan the fire earlier that afternoon and asked her to walk through it one last time.

"I've got it," said Jewell. "I promise."

"C'mon," said Rhoda. "Humor me."

Jewell rolled her eyes, but only slightly.

"I go up the east bank and I don't cross until I hit Van's property line. The boat will be tied off and I'll douse the deck good."

"Then what?"

"Then I put the can back in the ruck and I light the torch—"

"Light the torch?"

"I get in the river," she said. "Then I light the torch and I toss it into the boat and take off."

"Take off where?"

"Back to the east bank," she said. "Through Crooked Tree Park."

"Good," said Rhoda. "What else?"

"Don't get caught up watching."

"Why not?"

"Because fire can be pretty and pretty is almost always dangerous."

"Leave your phone at the four-wheeler, but call me if there's trouble."

Rhoda put the caps on the camo tubes and then stepped back to look at Jewell's face in what was left of the light.

"It occurs to me," said Jewell, "that you sort of seem to know what you're doing here."

"How do you mean?"

"When it comes to setting a fire."

"It's not an overly complicated process."

"Still," said Jewell.

"Is there something you're trying to ask me?"

"I guess there is."

"I've never set any boats on fire, if that's what you want to know."

"Small buildings?"

"No."

"Then what?"

"Then nothing."

"C'mon, Mom," she said. "Please?"

Rhoda looked over Jewell's shoulder at the river. She was gauging how low the sun had fallen and how much time they had before dark.

"Fine," she said.

"I knew it!" said Jewell.

"I guess there may have been an incident involving a Ford Pinto."

"A car?"

"The Pinto would barely qualify as a car, but yes. It was a crime of passion, if you must know."

"Was it to do with Daddy?"

Now Rhoda glanced toward the woods. She was embarrassed.

Jewell lowered her voice but only slightly. Pressed on. "I'm obviously going to need the entire story, and I mean every last detail."

"It was a long time ago—let's start there. A lifetime, really."

"Like when, exactly?"

"Back in high school. It was right after I started dating your father and there was this other girl who was throwing herself at him like a squirrel in heat. Her name was Jody Pitowski."

"And you burned her car down for it?"

"That's an oversimplification, but yes."

"So what happened?"

"She was at the movies with her friends and somehow I caught wind. There wasn't much to it beyond that. It was kind of spur of the moment, actually."

"Was Daddy there?"

"Oh hell no. He still doesn't know about it to this day."

"You're shitting me."

"I am not."

"How does he not know?"

"Because I never told him."

"Why not?"

"Because he didn't need to know. Jody Pitowski needed to know, and believe me, the message was received."

"Was Aunt Wanda there?"

"She was. It was actually her boyfriend that drove us. Kevin Sharp. He wasn't much to look at if I remember, but he drove a Chevy Malibu that your aunt just adored."

"A Chevy Malibu?"

"Wanda was really into cars," she said. "And your grandfather wouldn't let either of us drive off the property. Your uncle Billy could, of course. Your grandfather was a real pain in the ass that way, so Wanda picked her boyfriends based largely on what they drove. Billy was gone by then or we would have had him drive us."

"Gone?"

"Just to the army. He was still alive, but it wasn't long after that he had his crash. I didn't know it then, but I was actually never going to see him again."

Rhoda grew quiet. Her brother and sister had both died young and within just a few years of each other. Billy's helicopter crashed during a training exercise and Wanda was in her early twenties when she shot herself.

Jewell didn't know much about her aunt or her uncle, but Rhoda had told her that Billy was the family favorite. Wanda was an alcoholic who suffered from depression, and neither affliction was uncommon in the Sawbrook line. Rhoda said Wanda had a good heart but that it got buried too deep to find her way back to.

"So you just drove over there and did it?"

"Pretty much," she said. "There was only one screen at the theater in those days, and the parking lot was nearly empty. I think it was a weeknight, actually."

"What movie was playing?"

"What does that matter?"

"I don't know," said Jewell. "I'm just curious."

"Shit, I can't remember. But I believe it was around the time of *Doctor Zhivago*."

"What happened after?"

"After what?"

"The fire."

"We drove away. What do you think happened?"

"I mean, did Aunt Wanda's boyfriend rat or anything?"

"He was in love with Wanda and just watched me set a car on fire. Hell no, he didn't rat."

"I still can't believe you never told Daddy."

"Your father loved me," she said. "But he was scared shitless, too.

His parents were schoolteachers and here he was with a Sawbrook."

"Daddy's kind of a badass in his own right, though. I mean, he ran the borders with you, didn't he?"

"He did," said Rhoda. "But it was after a time. He had to get used to me first and I couldn't have Jody Pitowski getting in the way. And the truth is, when he started doing the runs, he was terrified. The man did two tours in Vietnam and was afraid of a border run? It didn't make any sense to me, but he told me one was legal and the other wasn't. I said they had the wrong things legal in the world and he said that might be true, but it wouldn't matter if we wound up in prison."

"What'd you say?"

"I told him that Sawbrooks don't ever get caught. I told him it was the one thing he could count on."

"He didn't believe you?"

"Not at first," she said.

"I guess he had to see it to believe it."

"I think you kind of have to," said Rhoda. "It's not the sort of thing people like to take on trust."

rhoda

J ewell left the property at dark, and I watched until she disappeared around the first bend. I'll admit, I was proud of her.

Harbor North was just the latest in the long line that had come for our land, and we'd fought off the lumber companies and the government the same way we were taking on the resort. It was what the Sawbrooks had always done.

Alfred was the first of our name on the river and he arrived here in 1850 with nothing but his beaver traps and a dream. Little is known about his life before northern Michigan, except that he worked for the American Fur Company and was a trapper of some renown.

Alfred became far more than just a pelt man, though. He learned to speak parts of the native languages and could communicate and conduct business with both Indians and whites and was frequently used as a translator and go-between. He was what the French called a *courrier des bois*, or runner of the woods.

He married a local woman named Katherine Carver and when they wed, he began to purchase land as a hedge against rival woodsmen. The land was perfectly suited for Alfred's needs, but it was also rocky, densely wooded, and hilly. It was not suitable for farming and so the die was cast early—we Sawbrooks would need to rely on our own ingenuity and not necessarily be beholden to the narrow margins of the law. Not if we wanted to keep what was ours.

Alfred and Katherine had a mess of babies, but their best-known child was Mabel. She shoved a fire poker into a man's testicles, right before she shot him in the heart. That man's name was Bradley Beech and he was a lumberjack who'd made the mistake of trying to force himself on her one night in town.

Mabel killed him, lit out for home, and when the sheriff and his deputies arrived at the property to make an arrest, they were met with a hail of gunfire.

The legend is the law struck an unofficial deal with Alfred and Katherine. They wouldn't mess with Mabel so long as she didn't leave Sawbrook soil, and that's what led Alfred to become interested in increasing his already large holdings of land. Alfred wanted Mabel and all of his children to have space for families of their own, so he bought up every neighboring plot he could. As the land stretched wider, though, it became even more wild and unfit for farming.

Mabel's firstborn, Germain, is probably the most famous Sawbrook. He was a bootlegger who helped open the Canadian Corridor and did business with Al Capone. Germain married a Chicago prostitute named Angelina, and there are pictures of the two of them at the Cutler Historical Society.

Angelina was so beautiful. Tall and dark-haired. Mysterious. In the pictures, Germain is always beside her in a suit, copping a lean against some tavern wall. I think Jewell favors them both, but Edward says the resemblance is fleeting and based mostly on what I want to see.

Germain and Angelina were eventually gunned down by hit men. There was a special they used to run about them on television. It was an hour-long investigative journalism deal done by PBS. They called it something terrible like *The Bootleg Murders* and I remember there being too many interviews with historians for my liking, because I just wanted to see pictures of Germain and Angelina. I still watched it every time it came on, though, and Lucy and Buckner carry their legacy as middle names.

Our kids never really ran the borders, but it's still probably the closest thing we have to a family business. My daddy was the pioneer who branched out into cigarettes and small electronics after Prohibition, and when I was sixteen, he started teaching me the same routes that Germain himself had run.

We'd usually shove off from the northeast coast of Michigan, Daddy preferring to trailer to a little out-of-the-way landing we favored on Lake Huron. I remember the cold and the fog on those early mornings and cutting the still water as we pushed northeast toward Ontario. I remember looking out in all directions and seeing nothing but a soupy mist.

We had a twenty-four-foot cuddy cabin that could scoot pretty good but was also subtle enough for Daddy's nerves. The boat didn't look like much out on the big lake but you could stack a few hundred cartons of cigarettes in the cabin and we cut panels into every bit of boat that wasn't already fitted for storage and filled those with whatever Daddy might find the smallest bit of profit in—toaster ovens and cereal boxes and household cleaning supplies.

We had a few sellers up there and we bought and moved almost everything wholesale. Daddy could line up interested parties on the Michigan side for just about anything we could get our hands on, though I also remember plenty of bonfires. Every few months my mother would lose her patience for whatever boxes were cluttering the house and barn and we'd set fire to the perishables gone bad. We never had trouble moving cigarettes, though, and stayed afloat on those for a good long while.

Eventually, my daddy's hip started giving him trouble and I took the routes over myself when I was about nineteen. Ed came back from Vietnam a few years later, started riding copilot, and that's when I knew he was mine for real.

My God, I loved those runs. Edward in some frayed, blue-jean shorts and oversize shades. His blond hair sun-bleached and his big shoulders tinged red from the sun. Yeah, he was afraid of getting caught at first, but once that passed we had some of the best summers of our lives. The two of us hauling ass across Lake Huron with nothing in front of us but brightness and blue water.

Daddy always thought my brother would take over the routes, but when he left for the army, I was next in line.

Wanda was older than me by a full year and a half, but Daddy didn't think she could handle the money or the responsibility. It broke my sister's heart, but only because she knew he was right.

She and Billy are buried in the same field as my mother and father. It's only a quarter mile from the house and after Jewell set out, I decided to pay them all a visit. I was too nervous to sit around the house, anyway.

Our cemetery is really just a glade where I keep flower beds and lilacs and try to stay on top of the grass. The graves are between two hedgerows, and there was light from the moon that splashed across the headstones.

I still miss my sister. She did not come into this world broken and I prefer to remember her at eight years old, bounding through the wildflowers with a bushel full of freshly picked berries—her fingers and chin stained purple. I can hear her calling my name and asking if I wanted to swim or go fishing, and I remember her reading books by the fireplace in winter. I can see her eyes trained narrow on some novel and I can hear the snap of her turning pages over a crackling fire.

I felt her there in the field that night, too. Just like I felt my parents and my brother. I felt my obligation to them all and to the land where they were resting.

The lawyers and the bankers all think we're crazy. They think we're narrow-minded and afraid. They think we're clinging to the past, but only because they think the past and the future are two separate things.

———————

Edward was on the porch waiting when I returned. The night was a touch warm for my liking, but he was beneath a quilt. This man who'd been sweating like a bear our entire lives was buried beneath a blanket at the height of summer and it pained my heart to see it.

He didn't have the wheelchair or tank, though. He was in his favorite rocking chair and I sat down beside him in mine.

"I thought you were going to miss the show."

"I figure we've got at least another ten minutes," I said. "Maybe closer to half an hour."

"Really?"

"I sure hope so. She needs to be moving slow and careful."

"Slow and careful," he said. "Two words that have never been associated with a Sawbrook."

Edward stayed a Clark when we got married, but he never had any issue with our children bearing the Sawbrook name. He has an older brother with kids of his own, and generally speaking, the Clarks are a tepid and unremarkable line that I can't imagine anybody having much passion for extending.

People have credited Edward as modern and forward thinking, while others have assailed his manhood. I didn't listen to any of them on either side because he knew from the jump that my name stayed with me and went forward to my children. It was non-negotiable and he's always been smart about avoiding the fights he cannot win. So in that way, maybe he is forward thinking.

"You know what I was remembering just now?" I asked.

"What's that?"

"Those summers we ran cigarettes."

"The glory days," he said, and hacked hard into his fist.

I winced at the dry crack of that cough and watched him pull another gummy from his shirt pocket and pop it in. He stuck out his hand and offered me one, but I told him no. I told him I was on call for Jewell, but I don't care for those gummies anyway. They make my feet feel big and I worry that something will happen to Edward while I'm sitting there stoned.

"What was that song we were always blasting on the boat?" I said. "Do you remember?"

"We had a few we favored."

"I know, but there was one in particular."

"Sing it for me and I'll tell you."

"It was a duet. The woman had the most beautiful voice. She always went, *Oh-oh-oh-oh.*"

"'Take Me Home Tonight,'" he said, and smiled. "Eddie Money."

"That's it!"

"People used to call me that," he said. "Eddie Money. That's how I remember."

"Did they?"

"Just around town, when he was famous."

"You were both famous."

"Infamous, more like."

"It's the woman's name we should remember," I said. "She was the one that carried that song."

"Ronnie Spector was her name."

"How'd you remember that so quick? That's impressive."

"I think it's the gummies," he said, and tapped a finger to his temple. "They unlock certain powers."

"Those are some of my favorite days," I said. "I wish I could remember more."

Edward agreed. "We were so young. It's hard to believe how young we were if you really think about it."

"We didn't know a goddamn thing, did we?"

"We knew we loved each other, and we knew where we belonged. Don't kid yourself—there's plenty out there that never get either one of those figured out."

"We were lucky."

"Still are," he said.

I felt an impulse to argue the last point, but I let it go and reached out my hand instead. He took it in his own and we both went back and forth in our chairs.

"I had a thought," he said. "But I'm not sure I should share it."

"I'm pretty sure you should."

"The ship has sailed," he said. "So I'm not sure what good—"

"Just say it, Edward."

"I was just sitting here wondering if the price is too high."

"How do you mean?"

"Ten seems high for the job. Then he only gives her one down? That seems low, doesn't it? If the total is ten?"

"He's probably just broke. At least until the insurance pays."

"Van's version of broke isn't like ours, though. He's not going to ever have a day in his life when he's got less than ten just sitting around the house."

"You think he's going to stiff her?"

"I'm not saying that, necessarily. I'm just saying some things don't quite add up. The math is just slightly off on it."

"I think he just did a stint at the rehab in Traverse City, which you know isn't cheap."

"Another one?"

"That's what I heard."

"That could be it, then. Maybe he is bust."

"You'd have to imagine insurance isn't paying for somebody's third trip to rehab."

"Or fourth," he said.

"His husband doesn't know," I said. "So if he does try to stiff her, that's the play. I tell him I've got his man pulled up in my contacts and I'm ready to dial."

"Do you know the husband?"

"I know of him."

Edward nodded. "Okay, good. That's a good card to have."

That seemed to settle the issue, at least for the moment, and Edward turned his attention to the night. The crickets were humming in the grass, and I could hear the snap of the skeeters as they flew into the zapper—like kernels of corn popping. One wren called out, and another one answered. Edward's hand was so thin and so clammy and I was careful not to squeeze it too hard.

"Who called you Eddie Money?"

"I don't know," he said. "People."

"Like who?"

"Oh, for Christ's sake."

"It's just a question," I said, and smiled.

"Anyway, the point is that it was a good song. I don't care what people say about it."

"Do people not like that song?"

"You know how people are about music. Any song that's actually good, they have to hate it."

I looked off toward the river.

"I think she'll be getting there any minute now," I said. "It's just about time."

"You think she can pull this off?"

"I couldn't doubt that girl if I tried."

"She's the best of you," said Edward. "She's the sun shining."

"She's the best of both of us."

"She's a Sawbrook through and through," he said. "They all are. All I ever did was smooth over some rough edges."

"You need to get working on the other two, then. 'Cause both of them could use a serious sanding down."

"Lucy's doing just fine," he said. "Buckner, I'll grant you."

"We'll fight about Lucy later," I said. "I don't have the energy just now."

"Agreed."

I put my other hand beneath his and held it cupped there like a baby bird. Our chairs rocked slowly and in rhythm. The moon was above the trees, and beyond the trees I could see the black water and the stars that shined there.

jewell

J ewell moved carefully upstream. Walked low to the ground and stayed in the cover of the trees.

The river smelled like clay and churned earth and she could hear the drumming of the water against the big rocks. She was moving toward the falls, which was the dividing line between the resort and the rest of the river.

People called it the falls, but it was really just a single shelf that dropped straight into deep water. Still, it was a good twenty feet down, and every summer some jackass flew off it sideways and managed to find a rock bed and shatter something.

The falls were a rite of passage when you grew up on the river. Jewell was fifteen her first time. She and Connie split a can of Budweiser on shore, then jumped in the river and screamed like crazy all the way down. She still went at least once every summer, just to prove she could.

Her mother did it on her fifty-eighth birthday. It was just after Edward got sick, and he was still strong enough to come to the river with them and watch. This was before Lucy sold her land and during a brief, magical ebb in Buckner's drinking.

Her mother wore a black one-piece, and the lines and definition in her arms and legs were the same as they'd ever been. If anything,

Jewell had wondered if she might have been in better shape than she was in her forties. Her father straight-up ogled her as she walked away and it was one of those things that Jewell wished she hadn't noticed.

Rhoda had speed coming off the shelf that night. She disappeared inside the white water, and Jewell held her breath until she saw her mother emerge and straighten herself into a dive.

She dropped in a perfectly straight line with the sky bruised purple behind her and when her father gasped in wonder, she considered it the appropriate response.

None of them had taken a photo and she'd always regretted it. It should be a picture, framed on the wall. It should be something they could all point to and say, *That is our mother; that is who she is.*

Rhoda barely splashed the surface when she entered that night and then came up smiling. Her short hair was spiky wet and she reached up with two hands to flatten it to her head. Jewell looked at her father, who had his cane raised to the sky as he cheered—as if briefly her dive had given him the strength to stand unaided. Buckner whistled through his fingers and Lucy raised a bottle of beer to the sky and shouted.

Whatever she did in this life, Jewell knew she would never surpass her mother, and she took great pride and solace in the fact.

The golf course came on quick after the falls and the fairways wrapped close to the water. The sprinklers had cut on and made their *chik-chik-chik* sound and she watched the slow, arcing sprays of water. It was pretty, but mostly it felt empty.

There used to be dozens of families along that stretch of bank and they'd kept their Jet Skis and kayaks tied off on posts and the trunks of trees. There used to be kids running through yards, shooting water pistols and shouting while their parents sat in lawn chairs and drank beer around a fire. Jewell missed the sizzle and sudden burst of firecrackers in the summer and how she knew everybody's name and how they knew hers.

The resort had already cleared more land behind the course and the rumor was they were set to build another batch of condos in the spring. They weren't building yet, though, and she could still see the edge of Cutler where the town lights were a yellow line cut straight across the black.

A little farther upstream were the big private lots, and that's where Van's boat would be waiting. He called it a double-decker and said it would be tied off at the end of the dock.

"Right there at the edge of the property," he'd said. "It'll just be you and the pine trees. Her name is *True North*."

Between the resort and Van's was a final vestige of the river past—Scooter's Party Store. The Scooter family had sold bait and ice cream, rubber tomahawks and toy soldiers, baseball cards and candy bars. They sold Mrs. Scooter's homemade pies and kept rock candy in big glass jars on the counter. The storefront was built directly onto the family home.

John Scooter and her father had been friends and used to drink together in the evenings. The kids fished off the bank while their fathers cracked beers and listened to the Tigers on the radio. Ernie Harwell waxing poetic while everybody cast for trout.

Now the storefront was plastered with CAUTION and FUTURE CONSTRUCTION placards and the yard was overgrown and strangled with weeds. Jewell wished the Scooters were still there, but since they weren't, she'd just as soon not have to see the sad remnants of their lives every time she went upriver. It was rude, is what it was.

Crooked Tree came next. It was a small campground with hiking along the river, and she was cautious as she moved through the brush between the trails and the water. She didn't think there'd be anybody out wandering in the dark, but there was no point in taking the chance.

Van's place was kitty-corner from the park. His dock jutted into the water about half a mile north of the golf course and that was where she came off the bank and finally stepped into the Crow.

She was in jogging pants and water shoes. She wore a swimming shirt and everything was black and tight to her skin. The water was warm and only rose to her knees and she cut quickly through the slow current.

The boat was so big it blotted the stars from the river. It was dark where she gripped the edge of Van's brand-new aluminum dock and pulled herself up.

The house was towering at the back of the lawn and there were tall, glass windows that looked out on the water and shadows from the roof eaves. Everything was quiet and still and she quickly shook the ruck from her shoulders, took out the canister, and unscrewed the top. The gasoline had some bite as it wafted and her eyes were watering by the time she stepped aboard the boat and poured.

She was deliberate. Emptied most of the can onto the boat itself, then gave a few quiet knocks on the cabin door just to be sure it was empty. Nobody answered, and when she gave the door a little jiggle, it was locked.

She went back to the dock, put the canister in her ruck, then unclipped the broom-handle torch from the top. She strapped the bag to her shoulders and slipped gently back into the water.

She stepped away from the dock before she struck the match, and the torch flamed quick. She did not hesitate, entertain second thoughts, or mark her aim. She simply held the torch like a spear above her head, set her feet, and threw.

The torch lofted in an arc and then dropped gently into the center of the deck where the flames did not wait to gather but took with a *whoosh* and a blast of heat and light.

There was a moment before the boom, a single instant when she could see the fire swell like a big, rolling breaker, and she breathed in quick at its terrible beauty and power and then slipped beneath the surface of the silty water.

lucy

Lucy saw the fire from town. Black stacks above the pines on the eastern bank of the Crow and the wind pushing it north. The flames were on the resort side, but it looked far enough upstream that it might work its way to the park, and that meant she had campers to evacuate.

She was on the balcony of the Grenshire Hotel, seated with a state rep, the president of Michigan's Audubon Society, and a representative from the Ford Foundation—people who deeply impressed her but had not been enough to lure Franklin away from a Billy Joel concert.

The table had been discussing economic forecasts and the Democrats' prospects in November when Lucy saw the smoke and excused herself. She called her deputy and made her way to the door.

Deputy was a flattering term. D-Rod didn't have any real training and the state kept him at thirty hours so they didn't have to pay his insurance, but they put DEPUTY on his name tag so that's what she called him.

The call went straight through to voicemail, and by the time she reached the parking lot there was commotion on the balcony above—gasps and shouts as the fire grew and began to take shape in the distance.

She started her Silverado, backed out carefully between a BMW and Lexus, then punched the gas.

She sailed through two yellows in town and made good time to the river, but the cops already had a blockade set up about a mile from Crooked Tree. The city had two cruisers parked and they were blaring their sirens as they re-routed drivers off the water.

She thought about swerving wide and blowing the stop outright, but one of the cops came running when she didn't take the detour like everybody else. The cop was waving his arms like she was some-how confused—like she couldn't read the bright-orange signs and didn't know which direction the arrows were pointing.

Lucy thought she knew all the city cops, but they must have been recruiting the high school now because this one had flushed, rosy cheeks and a peach-fuzz chin. He might as well have been a Boy Scout.

"You got to take the detour!" he shouted. "There's a fire!"

She slowed to a stop and rolled down her window.

"Officer, I am the ranger at Crooked Tree Park and I need to get out there and you need to slide this blockade off the road. I can help you move it."

"I can't do that, ma'am."

"You're going to have to, because I've got campers to evacuate."

He cast a worried glance in the direction of the smoke. Lucy pulled her wallet to show her badge.

The badge granted no authority or extra privilege outside the park. Even within her jurisdiction the power she possessed was mostly ceremonial, but it was the one badge she owned and so she flashed it.

"Where'd you get that," he said, "a box of Froot Loops?"

This was a bit much, coming from the kid who looked like he should be on his way to a pinewood derby.

"This was supplied by the state of Michigan," she said. "You wouldn't know, since yours comes from the city."

He rolled his eyes. "I'll call this in and ask, but that's the best I can do."

The young cop stepped away to shout something at another cop. He clicked his walkie on next, and that was when she put her foot down and broke for the low, soft shoulder.

Lucy never meant to be a park ranger. She won an internship with the Department of Resources her junior year in college, worked on a soil study in the Hiawatha National Forest, and when the state offered her a full-time post-graduate position, she signed on the dotted line.

The DOR paid for her senior year, and after college she agreed to serve a five-year term at their pleasure.

She'd hoped her work would involve projects similar to what she'd done at Hiawatha. She would lead conservation research of her own, publish papers, and conduct workshops and guided tours of remote, exotic wildlands in the Upper Peninsula. She'd be a scientist who spent real time in the field and never had one day of work look exactly like the last. Instead the department had her spend a year shuffling papers in their Lansing office, then sent her to her hometown park and acted like they were doing her a favor.

In many ways, they were. She had boots on the ground near the river and used that opportunity to start Friends of the Crow. She organized and fundraised and spread awareness. She put together the trust that Rhoda hated her for, despite the fact that it was the best chance to save the land her mother loved so dearly.

The FOC was not just sitting on the property, either. They were planting native grasses to provide nesting and foraging opportunities for pollinators and birds and they were restoring eroded soils. Lucy was giving her mother butterflies and cardinals where there might have been a shopping center, and the woman had estranged her for it. And now, this fire.

The ranger station was still open when she arrived and she grabbed her walkie off the desk and clicked it on. Buzzed D-Rod.

"Ranger," he said. "That you?"

"I'm here, D-Rod."

"I was just about to punch out when I seen the smoke."

"Is everybody out?"

"Getting there."

"You check the beach?"

"Not yet."

"I'll take the four-wheeler," she said. "I'll do a sweep and then meet you back up here."

"That looks like a fire, fire," he said.

Lucy clicked off the walkie and holstered it. Pushed the station's screen door open and hurried back outside.

They kept the four-wheeler behind the station and she jumped into the seat, started it fast, and got low over the handlebars. There was a thick stand of trees that ran along the back of the park between the campsites and the beach, and she flipped on the vehicle's little speaker and rode fast along the narrow trail.

"*This is not a test,*" she said. "*Please move quickly to your vehicles and exit the park.*"

There was nobody in the woods or on the beach, but she rode up and down the shoreline twice to be sure. She could see the burn across the water, and the sulfur smell was hard in her nostrils. She couldn't tell if the flames had spread, but they were bright beneath the smoke and cast shadows across the tops of the pines.

D-Rod buzzed just as she was leaving the beach.

"Ranger," he said. "You should probably meet me back at the station, ASAP."

"I need to lock the back gate."

"I'd go ahead and put that off," he said.

"Why?"

"Because there's a situation."

"What kind of situation?"

"It involves your brother," he said. "And Ray Tomshaw."

"Buckner?"

"Yes, ma'am."

"What the hell is Buckner doing here?"

"I can't say what inspired the visit initially," said D-Rod. "But right now there's a standoff."

"What do you mean, a standoff?"

"Buckner has Ray's truck keys and is refusing to give them back. Ray, in turn, is refusing to leave without his F-150. They've both been drinking. Quite a bit, it seems."

She wasn't surprised. That was the one thing she refused to be. She was angry and she was brokenhearted, but she would not grant her brother the power to surprise her. Not anymore.

The truth was, she hated Al-Anon. She didn't like the readings or the slogans and found the ceaseless complaining of group members embarrassing. It was all a drag, but the one thing that bothered her the most was how surprised everybody was by the perpetual failure of their loved ones. They were always so wide-eyed and incredulous— constantly shocked by the one thing in their lives that was most reliable.

Buckner had humiliated her that morning and now he was drunk at her place of work and she simply did not have time for the luxury of disbelief.

She wasn't surprised that whatever foolishness was transpiring involved Ray Tomshaw, either. He was a bouncer at the Boogie Down Barn—a strip club across the river where the golfers liked to gather after hours. The barn did nothing but churn out noise and empty bottles for her to fish out of the river, and now Tomshaw was living at the campground to shorten his commute from the east county.

"Tammy Sharp is here, too," said D-Rod. "And also participating in this fiasco."

Tammy was Ray's girlfriend. She liked to walk around the park in her bathrobe and had frequent complaints about the condition of the toilet and shower facilities.

"And where is she?" said Lucy.

"She's hiding in the station and I'm down at the water pump as a sort of lookout."

"Is she hiding from Ray or from Buckner?"

"It's impossible to know. Apparently, Buckner believes Ray has some information that he is withholding. Buckner believes he is owed this information and stole Ray's keys as retribution. Currently, a quid pro quo is on the table. *Tell me what I want to know, and you'll get the keys back.* That sort of thing."

"What the hell does Buckner want to know?"

"I don't have any idea," said D-Rod. "It's complicated. There's a lot of moving parts."

"Is anybody armed?"

"Tammy says no. She says Ray had to sell his Glock to pay the truck insurance. She said it came down to the Ford or the firearm and he went with the vehicle."

"What about Buck?"

"Also unarmed, according to Tammy. Currently, Tammy wants to go home and I'm happy to give them all a ride, but Ray won't leave his truck and Buckner won't give Ray the keys until he tells him what he wants to know. Oh, and he's also demanding that Tammy apologize for something, which she refuses to do."

Lucy parked the four-wheeler outside the ranger station but left it idling. The smoke was blowing hard across the river and she wondered now if Buckner had ever really been sober at all.

"Apologize for what?"

"I couldn't tell you," said D-Rod. "There's a lot of layers to this onion, Ranger."

———————

Inside the station, Tammy Sharp was sitting bleary-eyed in a chair along the wall. Lucy went directly for the gun safe and turned to Tammy after she input the code.

"In school, Ray used to slice the tops off the girls' winter hats and store them in a giant box in his bedroom, like some sort of serial killer."

"I know that," said Tammy. "He did it to me, more than once."

"Which begs the question."

"Shit, Lucy. You think he was the first name on my dance card? You think I'm sitting around choosing whatever man I want? This is a supply-and-demand situation. This is basic economics. We're in a downturn and there is a drastic shortage of viable dating options. I'm doing the best I can."

"My God, Tammy. Ray Tomshaw is not the best you can do. That's the most ridiculous thing I've ever heard."

D-Rod came barreling into the station now, and he was breathing heavy. He'd run all the way from the water pump and leaned on the desk to gather his breath.

"You think maybe we should call the cops?" he said, finally.

There was a Taser and a shotgun in the safe and Lucy took them both out. Held one in each hand.

"If I thought we should call the cops," she said, "I would have already done it."

"Buckner could have a knife or something."

Lucy lifted up the shotty. "Push comes to shove, and I think I'd favor this."

"You going to shoot your own brother?"

"I'm not going to shoot anybody," she said. "This thing isn't even loaded."

"Then what's the point?"

"It's a deterrent. But if I need to, I will tase his ass."

"The thing is," said D-Rod, "the police are trained for exactly this sort of situation."

"I just ran a barricade to get out here, and now you want me to divert resources in an actual emergency because my brother is drunk and holding a truck hostage?"

D-Rod's shirt was untucked and blooming with sweat stains on the back and beneath the arms. He had his DOR trucker's hat turned backward, and his brow was glazed with sweat.

"The other option here," he said, "is to let them burn."

"That's paperwork," said Lucy, and turned to Tammy. "Any chance you could be persuaded to offer an apology to my nimrod brother and spare us some trouble?"

"If I wanted to say I was sorry, I would have already done it."

"And what's your transgression? Out of curiosity?"

"I called your brother's girlfriend the C word."

"Did you now?"

"I did."

Lucy paused.

"Buck's got a girlfriend?"

"He sure does," said Tammy. "It's the talk of the town. She's a dancer over there at the Barn."

"Buckner is dating a stripper?"

This came from D-Rod, who asked the question with a note of admiration.

Tammy looked at him with sad eyes. "Most of them have stretch marks, dude."

"What's her name?" asked Lucy.

"Her name is Sky. And when I called her the C word, I was being nice."

"Is that her stage name?"

"I don't know, Lucy. That's just what everybody calls her. I've never seen her birth certificate."

"I don't think it's ever appropriate to use the C word," D-Rod said. "That's just my personal opinion on the matter."

"Well, you and Buckner ought to start a club," said Tammy. "Maybe go on the speaking circuit and hold lectures."

"Enough!"

Lucy spoke and the room fell quiet. There was a fire burning and here she was wrapped up in Buckner's bullshit again. She passed D-Rod the shotty and kept the Taser for herself.

They made the short drive on the four-wheeler. Lucy had the handlebars with D-Rod perched behind her, and when they arrived at the campsite, they found Buckner slouched forward in a lawn chair.

He was a huge man, with broad shoulders and a square-shaped skull, and there was a bottle of whiskey lodged between his thighs.

Sober, he was all symmetry and muscle—like he'd been assembled from a stack of Lego bricks—but when he drank, it was like somebody severed a cord in his central nervous system and his whole body sort of dissolved into a loose-limbed pile. His head was lolling back and forth on his shoulders and he was mumbling something into his chest.

Ray was in a lawn chair of his own, directly across from Buckner. He was surrounded by empty cans of Stroh's but able to sit upright and stare at her brother straight-on.

"Look at this," said D-Rod. "It's a redneck stare-down."

"What do you want me to do?" said Ray. "I take a step toward him and he threatens to throw my keys in the river. Stands up and cocks his arm. It's goddamn childish."

Ray Tomshaw was a short man in a tank top and blue jeans. He wore a bushy beard, kept his hair trimmed close, and had his arms and neck covered in tattoos that generally coalesced around demonic imagery and racist political policy.

Lucy walked carefully toward her brother.

"C'mon, Buck," she said. "It's time to go."

"You want to wait in the station with Tammy?" said D-Rod to Ray.

"And leave my truck with this asshole? No, thank you."

Buckner slurred something, but nobody understood or cared what he said.

The flames had grown across the river, and she could see the orange glow through the trees. She did not think the fire would burn north around the river, but it was not out of the question. The sirens were in full throat but she still heard the rustling when D-Rod raised the shotgun. Her brother heard it, too, because his drunken eyeballs focused sharp on her deputy and his pointed weapon.

She didn't even have time to try to distract her brother. He was already up and walking straight for D-Rod because drunk or sober, he was the type of man that sees a shotgun pointed at his chest and is overcome with the impulse to approach its barrel. Sure, it wasn't loaded, but that wouldn't stop him from beating D-Rod to death with it once he snatched it from his hands.

She shouted for Buckner to stop, knowing that he would not. D-Rod took a step backward and she could see the whole thing now—the way D-Rod would stumble and fall and how her brother would take the shotty from his hands and come down with it on his skull. Michigan prisons were filled with the perpetrators of exactly these sort of pointless, tragic crimes.

She drew the Taser and put it to her brother's back. Shouted his name again, but he did not slow. Buckner didn't so much as break stride until she pulled and then it was all heat and crackle and rattling teeth. He stopped hard then, but he did not go down. He just kept twitching until she pulled a second time and dropped him.

Now he was in the dirt. He was flopping like a hooked fish and drumming the ground with his heels. He wasn't going anywhere, but she put one more into his chest that was just for her.

"Ranger!"

She heard D-Rod shout and then stopped and stepped backward. She dropped the Taser and watched her brother convulse, and she did not feel pride or shame or regret. She didn't feel anything at all.

Buckner had fumbled the keys and Ray had already scooped them up and was running for the truck.

"Tammy is at the station," D-Rod said as Ray passed.

"I don't give a fuck," he spat. "She bailed on me, anyway."

Buckner was thrashing less, but now she could hear his groans more clearly. His eyes were darting and Lucy stepped over him and gently put her knee against his belly.

"Are you okay, Ranger?" said D-Rod. "Is he okay?"

She didn't know how to answer either question, so she didn't.

"Go get some rope," she said.

They kept supplies in a toolbox on the side of the four-wheeler and D-Rod hurried off. She could hear him digging through the bin, the clank of the tools and the rustle of loose nails and screws. He returned quickly with a few lengths of rope and she told him to help her bind Buckner's ankles and wrists.

"Why?"

Lucy was already working a loop over her brother's boots and did not look up from the work. "Because I don't want him running off if he comes to. And you'll need to wait here with him until I get back."

"Where the hell are you going?"

"To lock the back gate. Then I'll get the truck and bring it over. You can help me get him into the flatbed and then I'll drive you back to your vehicle and we can all get the fuck out of here."

She tugged the loop tight over both boots, then pushed the loose end back inside the knot and gave it one more good pull through to cinch it fully. Her brother was breathing slower now, more steadily, but he was also sweating whiskey and he stank.

D-Rod turned to look at the fire, and then back at her. "What do I do if he gets loose?"

"He won't."

"But if he does?

"Then you should probably fucking run."

———————

Lucy took the shotgun when she left D-Rod with her brother and drove straight for the back gate. Lockup was the last item on the evacuation protocol and she wasn't going to start cutting corners and making mistakes because of Buckner.

The sun was long down, but there was still some light

downriver—just a smear beyond the churning smoke. The fire didn't look like it was spreading, but it was probably too early to tell. She could hear the pumper trucks across the water and the firefighters shouting as they worked.

It was a house fire, most likely. Probably bad wires. They put those houses up so fast and sloppy, they might just all go up in flames. She might root for it, too, except they'd further bury the river in silt, and then the houses would just be rebuilt bigger and faster and worse.

She idled the four-wheeler at the gate and was just about to snap the padlock closed when she heard some rustling in the brush behind her. She paused. It might have been a mink or a raccoon, but the sound was a little too heavy and when she turned around, she saw a woman standing between the trail and the river.

She was about twenty yards away. Tall and slender, with her hair pulled tight and her face striped in hunting camo. She wore black clothing and held her arms perfectly straight at her sides. She stared Lucy in the chest, but Lucy couldn't make out an eye color or any distinguishing features. Not at that distance.

The field where she stood was all sawgrass and milkweed. Gnats danced above the flowers and were backlit by the fire and she noticed the woman's leg twitch just before she turned and exploded into a sprint.

"Goddamnit," she said, and took off after her.

The woman was moving into a sprawl of pines and brush and Lucy would have taken the four-wheeler but there was no way through that mess on anything but foot. There were low-hanging vines and tangles of roots and sharp-edged rocks.

The woman was headed for the river and knew exactly how to get there. She wove between the pines and birch like she'd planted them there herself and disappeared into a blur between the trees.

Lucy ran as hard as she could but her lungs were clenching from the smoke and the effort and she was not gaining ground. If anything, she was falling farther behind. She came out into a clearing before the next patch of trees and saw the woman up ahead, angling toward the water.

The woman didn't slow, not even enough for a glance back across her shoulder. She just barreled straight for the muddy ledge of the river where she planted a foot before the ground gave way beneath her and she leapt.

She left the bank like it was a trampoline and sprang hard and high. She rose until she gathered herself at the top of her jump and everything around her was either dark with night or burning. That was when Lucy realized it was her sister.

Of course it was Jewell. She should have known it from her shape and speed, but it never occurred to her because the one thing she knew about her sister was that she loved the river and so she could not imagine that she would be the one to bring it harm.

There was light out there above the water, but more than anything it was the way she tilted forward into the dive and then uncoiled and made herself long. Jewell was a beautiful diver—it was one of the things Lucy most admired and envied about her, how effortless and graceful she was in her body.

Lucy watched her break the surface of the river with a splash, then heard the sigh of a nearby tree giving out. Then, the terrible thunder of its falling.

jewell

Jewell had been cruising through the park. The ruck was strapped tight to her shoulders and the breath steady in her lungs. She felt like she could run all night, right up until she hit the back gate and saw her sister.

Lucy was not in uniform, but she did have the park's four-wheeler, which meant she must have come from the dinner in town. The possibility that Lucy could have gotten to the scene so quickly had never occurred to Jewell, though maybe it should have—the event was on the Grenshire balcony and it was a clear enough night that the smoke was probably visible all the way in Cutler.

Jewell went for the river because Lucy would have no way of getting the four-wheeler into the thick brush, and no chance at all of catching her by foot.

Jewell had been an all-state cross-country runner in high school and still ran most mornings. Lucy was strong, but she was foot-slow and a weak swimmer, at least for a Sawbrook.

People said the Sawbrooks had fins for feet. In over 150 years on the river and working the Great Lakes, not a single one of them had suffered a water death.

Grandpa Harvard had probably come the closest. Harvard, who was not named for the school, but as hybrid of his own grandfathers—Harvey and Leonard—had a difficult stretch after World War II and used to get drunk and hurl himself over the river falls by way of canoe. Later, he would explain that he wasn't necessarily trying to kill himself, but was open to the possibility. Harvard had PTSD or, as they called it then, a bad case of the doldrums.

His father, Daniel, had been one of a handful of survivors of the SS *Carl Jenkins* shipwreck, a point of pride and later frustration when the *Jenkins* was usurped in the popular imagination by the *Edmund Fitzgerald* and the capable songwriting of Gordon Lightfoot. Germain, the bootlegger, had twice capsized in Lake Superior and floated to safety on the shards of broken rum barrels.

In any other family, Lucy would have been the star swimmer, but these were the Sawbrooks and she could not hang with Jewell in the Crow.

Jewell was not her mother, but she lifted high off the bank and would have nailed the dive were it not for the rucksack, which yanked her off line and forced her to glance the surface with a bit of shoulder blade on entry. She was turned around, but quickly unclipped the ruck and swung it in front of her to use as a buoy when the current took hold.

The sirens swirled. She could see them flickering blue and red through the smoke above the pines and there were embers swarming the bank like hornets.

She was in a steady patch of current and assumed she was alone until she heard shouting behind her and turned to see Lucy splashing like a fool upriver.

Now she considered swimming for the bank. She could climb to shore, hope Lucy didn't notice, and let her flail her way downstream. Then she could backtrack to the park, snag the four-wheeler Lucy had left, and ride it home to glory.

On the other hand, the last thing she wanted to do was head back in the direction of the fire.

The river had already gathered speed, but it would find another gear before she hit the falls. She couldn't imagine Lucy would be up for following her to the brink of the drop and so she held her breath and kept the ruck pushed out in front of her and kicked.

She kicked until her lungs grew tight and when she came up for air, she gulped it. The air had cleared around her. There were no more embers or shadows from the fire, and she could see the ski hills in the distance where the stanchions from the chairlifts rose toward the stars like some ancient, alien installation.

Lucy was still struggling behind her, though. She was no longer shouting, but her splashing seemed a touch desperate and that worried Jewell enough that she cut hard against the current and swam for shore.

She reached for a nest of low-lying branches and steadied herself in a calm patch and then turned and called for her sister. Lucy was still in the middle of the river, but she stopped flailing at the sound of Jewell's voice.

"Right here!"

Jewell waved and Lucy bobbed in the water about twenty feet away. Lucy had clearly seen her, but did not swim right over. Lucy couldn't just swallow her pride and bring herself to safety. No, she had to float a little farther downstream so she could pretend she had a choice in the matter before she finally gave in and broke for shore.

Jewell reached down to help her landing, but Lucy slapped her hand away and pulled herself out of the water. She was breathing hard and when she tried to talk, she coughed and spit river.

"Are you okay?" said Jewell.

Lucy slapped at the river in outrage, then finally turned to her sister.

"What the actual fuck, Jewell?"

"I can explain everything."

"I don't believe you can."

Even in the dark, Jewell could see the narrow squint of her sister's eyes and the hard line of her jaw. She could feel her anger, too— the heat and pulse of it. There would be no explaining anything. Not right now.

"You need to get out of this river, Luce," she said. "You look like you're about to drown. Just stay quiet and don't say anything to the cops. I'll come see you tomorrow and we'll talk."

"Tell me what you did!"

"Please, Luce. You have to trust me."

"I certainly do not trust you. Not one bit."

"Then don't trust me. The important part is not saying anything."

There was bramble around the branches between them and for a moment it felt as if Lucy was going to reach through the thorns and try to strangle her. Maybe she would have. Jewell would never know, because she dropped back into the water without a word and swam so hard downriver that she barely needed the current.

Lucy shouted her name once from behind her, but the sound was dulled by the rush of the river and if she called out again, Jewell did not hear it.

Jewell swam as fast and as far as she could. She swam until her lungs were tight, and when she came back to the surface and turned to look behind her, she saw Lucy had given chase. She couldn't believe it, but her sister was still right there with her.

"What the fuck?" she said, but it was more to herself than Lucy.

They were in the fast current now and Lucy was splashing even worse than before. She seemed truly panicked, but when Jewell tried to swim to her, the current would not allow it. Jewell was being flung forward and when she tried to call for Lucy, she was yanked beneath the surface and scraped hard against the rocky floor and the sound of her sister's name remained lodged in her lungs.

Jewell lost the rucksack in the pull and banged her knee and felt the pain knife in both directions up and down her leg. She did not reach for the leg, though. It was the bag that really mattered. The bag was a pile of evidence, a floating felony conviction, and she felt for it desperately as the river carried her toward the ledge.

The churn was as loud as thunderclaps and she was blindly reaching in every direction but the bag was gone and she could only hope it would come behind her in the fall.

The water went shallow at the last moment and she did not have time to ready herself. She could feel the cold, flat rock that formed the ledge, and then she felt its absence.

part II

buckner

A few hours before the fire, Buckner was bone-sober and leaning up against a wall at the Boogie Down Barn.

It was Delray Harper's place, a pole barn in a pine clearing that he converted to a strip club in the mid-1990s.

In the old days, the Boogie Down was primarily a funnel for Delray's small-time coke racket and a place for local dirtbags and crooked cops to pursue their mutual interests. Then the resort came along. It was like striking gold, except the gold was crinkled-up dollar bills from the bottomless pockets of men in khakis and brightly colored golf shirts.

The Barn itself was exactly the same as it ever was, though. Sawdust on the floor and birds nesting in the ceiling rafters. Buckner did not care for Delray personally, but he did respect the fact that he hadn't fancied everything up for the resorters. He'd stood his ground on that front, at least.

Buckner was there to speak to the man himself, but Delray was sitting at a big table near the stage with a bunch of his resort friends. Sky said Delray called them clientele, and they took clear priority over Buckner and his requested meet.

Buckner did not frequent the Barn, but he'd wound up there on the occasional Friday night and dropped more than one paycheck back in the private dance rooms. They were just plywood stalls with carpeting nailed to the floor, but Delray had put up a neon sign above them that said VIPS ONLY and that allowed him to charge a cover in addition to the standard cost of a three-song lapper.

The barkeep asked Buckner if he wanted a beer while he waited and he said that he did not. He did want one, vaguely, but he hadn't put together six months' sobriety by doing what he wanted. The barkeep nodded and filled him up a big, plastic cup of pop from the fountain instead.

Buckner was there on business, though he couldn't say exactly which kind just yet. Something had happened to Sky, but he didn't know what. Sky would not tell him, and neither would her mother.

Sky had not spoken to him since she went into work the day before and had not returned his calls or texts that morning. Buckner didn't forget about his own party so much as he lost the ability to think about anything else once he went to Sky's mama's house and she wouldn't let him in. Brenda, Sky's mama, had barely cracked the door when Buckner knocked.

"Sky can't see you right now," she'd said. "She'll call you soon, though. In a couple days, maybe."

Brenda was in a gray sweatsuit and holding a coffee mug. There was a hippo on the mug wearing a tutu, and the hippo was talking, but there were no other hippos in the scene. There were no people or other animals on the mug, either. Buckner supposed the idea was the hippo was talking to the mug's owner. The hippo was saying, A MOMENT ON THE LIPS, FOREVER ON THE HIPS. He found the mug off-putting, though he couldn't say exactly why.

"A couple of days?"

"It's nothing to do with you, Buckner."

"Then why can't I see her?"

"Because she would prefer not to, right now."

"Is she okay?"

Here Brenda paused. Clearly, Sky was not okay. Something had happened and he could see it all over her mama's face.

It was his instinct to force himself inside and demand to see Sky, to take stock of the situation and respond accordingly, but he was doing more than just putting the plug in the jug this time.

Buckner had scraped together some sober stints before, but he'd never done any of the real work. He'd never gotten into the underlying causes and themes. The nitty-gritty of who he was. They said at the meetings that drinking was just a symptom and he was willing to admit that they might be onto something with that. This time he was trying to change for real.

So he did not barrel inside Brenda's house. Instead he thanked her politely for her time and headed for the Barn. Buckner was a changed man, or trying to be, but that didn't mean he wasn't going to find out what had happened to his girlfriend. He was just going to be smarter about how he gathered the information.

Girlfriend wasn't quite the right word. It was more than that. Deep down, he knew that Sky was the love of his life and that he was going to marry her someday. Maybe someday soon.

Delray finally finished with the rich boys at the table and made his slow way over to Buckner at the bar. He asked Buckner what he needed, and Buckner told him he should already know.

"Is that right?"

"It better be," said Buckner. "Because it's to do with Sky."

Delray looked over Buckner's shoulder at the barkeep. "Me and Buckner here are going to have a little chat in my office," he said. "But let me know if the distributor shows."

Delray's office was a small box, barely bigger than the champagne rooms, but it did have a door and some drywall. There was a large desk, too large for the room, and a big leather chair that Delray made a show of settling into as he offered Buckner the metal stool across from him.

"So," said Delray. "Have you talked with Sky this morning?"

"She won't return my calls," said Buckner. "I went out to her house and her mom said she did not want to see me. Not right now."

"I called out to Brenda's this morning myself. Sounds to me like Sky is just resting up."

Delray had a big, bald head and a white handlebar mustache. He was badly sunburned across the cheeks and his T-shirt said, SURF NAKED.

"Resting up from what, though? That's my question."

Now Delray leaned back in his chair and put his feet up on the desk between them. It was a power move, which Buckner found tacky.

"I think the important thing is that Sky is okay and that we're going to handle everything from right here."

"Handle what?"

"It's just not something I can get into specifics on. You're going to have to trust me on that."

"I don't trust you on anything."

Buckner had an urge to emphasize the point by reaching up and pushing Delray's big, stupid-looking sandals off the desk. He might have done it, too, had someone not come into the room behind him.

The music grew briefly louder. Buckner heard a bass drop and some high-pitched horns and then the door swung quickly closed and there was a man standing at the wall beside him.

Some sort of muscle, it looked like. A big dude, north of six foot three and big across the chest. He wore his hair buzzed close and was in a bright-orange tracksuit with white stripes.

"Who the fuck is this?" said Buckner.

Delray pointed at the man, as if Buckner could have been referring to anybody else.

"That, is Bernard."

"And what's he do? Besides slink into rooms like a creep?"

"He's my new employee. Sort of like a bouncer, but for matters outside the facility."

Buckner looked the man up and down then turned back to Delray. "Why is he dressed like that?"

"Dressed like what?"

This was from Bernard, who leaned off the wall toward Buckner.

Buckner leaned right back at him. "Like you're about to get bronze in the bobsled."

"Hey, now," said Delray, and took his feet off the desk and straightened himself in the chair. "Bernard is on our side and he's only been here a few days. He's new in town."

"Who is this, Mr. Harper?" said Bernard. "Are we going to have a problem?"

"I don't know," said Buckner. "How long are you going to stand there looking like the world's biggest traffic cone?"

Buckner was mixing his metaphors now, but he didn't care. Each insult was appropriate and effective in its own way. Bernard seemed stumped, at least. He just stood there on the wall and stared at Buckner.

"Bernard, this is Buckner Sawbrook and he's just yanking your chain. We're all friends here."

"That remains to be seen," said Buckner.

"And why is that, Buck?" said Delray. "Why all this hostility?"

"Because something happened to Sky and nobody will tell me what it was, or who did it, and the truth is I'm starting to get pretty upset over the fact."

"Which I understand. That's why I brought Bernard back here and took the time to sit down and go over this in private. I want to make sure you're up to speed."

"Then speed me up, Delray. I'm sitting right here, waiting."

"Well, as you might have deduced there was an incident last night. It was here at the club and it did involve Sky."

"What kind of incident?"

"We had a customer get a little handsy with her."

"What the hell does that mean?"

Delray held up his hands. "It doesn't mean what you think."

"How do you know what I think?"

"Because you're her boyfriend and might be inclined to worry about certain things—"

"Tell me what happened, Delray. No more riddles."

"I would love to. Believe me, I would. The problem is Sky."

"How is Sky the problem?"

"Because the one thing she made me promise, Buckner, was not to tell you what happened."

"Fuck you."

"I'm dead serious. This is no riddle, and if you were smart, you'd listen to me right now because she's trying to protect you from your-self. And I promise you that what happened is not worth flying off the handle over."

"Then tell me what it was."

"I just did. We had a client get handsy with her, which is unac-ceptable, and we will deal with it swiftly and conclusively. Bernard is on it as we speak."

Buckner could feel his anger mounting, though to call it anger was slightly misleading. It was something wilder than that, some-thing more fundamentally dangerous and beyond his control. A world war, perhaps, or a sudden fluctuation in temperature at the earth's core.

"You need to tell me exactly what happened, and exactly who did it, or we're going to have a real problem, Delray. Me, you, Bernard, and whoever else."

Delray scooted his chair back, but just slightly. "Could you just stop being a hothead for one second and listen to me?"

"As soon as you say something worth listening to."

"Sky cares about you. I don't know why, but she's into you, Buckner. She talks about you all the time, drives everybody here crazy, to be honest. Frankly, I just don't think you're that goddamn interesting. You got lucky finding her and what you should do right now is respect what she is asking. You should let me handle this. And I'll tell you something else—"

Bernard moved to the side of the desk and stood next to Delray like he'd been waiting on a cue. Like the whole thing had been choreographed, which maybe it was—Delray was a showman and Buckner wouldn't put anything past him.

"Even if Sky wasn't so adamant about not dragging you into this," Delray went on, "I wouldn't tell you anyway."

"And why is that?"

"Because if I don't protect my girls, then I don't have a business anymore, do I?"

"I don't know anything about your business," said Buckner. "I've never owned a barn and called it a club."

Delray winced at that. He was sensitive about the Boogie Down, which was, of course, why Buckner had said it. Delray didn't take the bait, though. Delray just kept plowing forward.

"What you should do right now is go home and sit by your phone and wait for Sky to call. And when she calls, you should ask her what you can do to be helpful and supportive in her time of need, and then you should do exactly what she says. I mean, follow her instructions to the letter of the law. Write it all down and make sure you get it exactly right. Shit, you ought to be writing this down."

Buckner stood up. On the one hand, he knew that Delray was probably right. It pained him to admit as much, but the man was not unwise in his own way. He should go home and wait for Sky to call. That was what she had asked him to do and he should respect her wishes.

On the other hand, he did not want to go home and wait for anything because something had happened to Sky and nobody would tell him what it was. Yes, this was not really about Buckner, but that didn't change the fact that it felt, on some level, like it very much was.

Some nameless, faceless asshole had hurt Sky so badly that she could not talk to him, or so much as send him a text, and the thought of her lying up in bed at her mama's house suffering who knew what sort of physical and psychological trauma—well, it was more than Buckner could stand. It was more than he believed he should have to stand.

He had no idea what he was about to do next, but the hairs on the back of his neck had risen and turned stiff as bristles. Was he going to hit Bernard?

Bernard was packing, he'd noticed the bulge on the side of his ridiculous pants, but what was he going to do? Shoot Buckner dead right there in the club? Probably not, and that was if he even got to the gun in the first place. Which Buckner didn't believe he could. Bernard was big, but Buckner already had him figured as the oversize bully who'd just never had anybody stand up and punch him once on the bridge of his nose. He was a poser. He had to be, because who else wore a bright-orange tracksuit without so much as a hint of irony?

Also, Buckner wanted to punch Bernard. Separate of everything going on with Sky and Delray, he was just the sort of man that Buckner would not mind punching on principle.

He did not punch Bernard, though. He didn't even speak another word to the man. He just walked out the door into the club, into the noise and crush of people who had just begun to stream in from outside.

He could see the day's fading light through the door where a group of golfers were coming in. The sun was more orange than yellow now and dropping shadows on the grassy field where the SUVs were parked.

He did not ask for a drink but instead walked behind the bar and grabbed a full, unopened fifth of Jack Daniel's off the shelf and kept right on walking. The barkeep's mouth fell open, but what was he going to do about it?

Buckner strode for the door and nobody tried to stop him and he never once looked back. The barkeep shouted something, but Buckner couldn't have cared less. Buckner was already outside in the sun, cracking the thin paper seal on top of the bottle of whiskey. Buckner was twisting the cap.

rhoda

The fire had been burning for a bit, but I was still on the porch when Jewell called. Edward had gone in, but I was watching the show. We'd heard the explosion, the blast rippling out and rising into the hills, and then saw the columns of smoke.

Edward would have stayed out with me to watch it all, you couldn't have torn him away from the porch in the old days, but he got tired so fast now and I'd helped him to bed just before the phone rang in the kitchen.

There was a problem if Jewell was calling, and the second I picked up and heard her voice, I knew that it was serious.

"Mom?" she said.

I told her I was there, but Jewell didn't respond. She just breathed heavy on the other end and I made my voice low and calm—like I did when she was little and came tearing out of her room with a nightmare.

"Tell me what happened, Jewell."

She waited another long moment, and just when I was about to drop the calm act and start shouting, she finally answered.

"What happened was, Lucy spotted me."

"How did Lucy spot you? I thought she was in town."

"She was."

"What happened?"

"I don't know, but she was here at the park and she saw me and then chased me."

"What do you mean, she chased you?"

"She fucking jumped in the river is what she did."

"And she knows it's you?"

"Oh yeah," said Jewell. "She sure does."

"We've got to track her down right away. We need to keep her quiet."

"Mom, she's right here."

"What do you mean, 'here'?"

"She's here at the river."

"What's she doing there?"

"She's knocked unconscious, so not much."

"How do you mean, unconscious?"

"I don't know, is there more than one way to mean it? She's fucking knocked out cold. She chased me into the river and we both took the falls and she landed wrong."

"What the hell were you doing in the river!"

"I told you. She saw me at the park and I didn't think she'd be stupid enough to chase me into the water."

"But she did?"

"She mostly certainly did."

"And she went over the falls and landed wrong?"

"That's what happened, yeah."

"My God," I said. "Is she dead?"

"No. She's breathing."

"I'm on my way," I said, and hung up the phone.

I was, too. I flat sprinted to the truck.

Our road at night is dark, dark. It's like a tunnel cut through the canopy, and when I flipped my brights on, it was into a swarm of insects and a few darting bats. I lit the whole forest up around me, but we were so sealed in by the trees that my light only reached about forty feet before it hit the wall of black and was buried. If there were cops involved by the river, they could look right at me and see nothing but a smudge of pines.

Jewell waved me down from the spot where I'd striped her camo earlier and I slammed the brakes and let the truck slide sideways to a stop. I left it idling and stepped outside. We were still on our side of the fence and Jewell was already talking.

"She landed facedown, but I was worried about her drowning so I flipped her over and dragged her onto the bank."

"Leave the four-wheeler," I said. "We'll have to carry her."

"Why do we have to carry her?"

"So we don't get stuck in that soft ground. That's why."

I ran to Lucy while Jewell hobbled along behind me. She had hurt her leg, probably in the fall, but I didn't ask for specifics because we didn't have time for her to be injured.

Lucy was on her back where Jewell had left her. Her eyes were closed, but her shoulders were rising with breath. I hadn't thought to bring a flashlight, but I keep a little Maglite on my key chain and flipped it on. I shined the light in her face and Jewell gasped behind me.

"Oh my God," she said.

Lucy had a large swath of skin hanging off her left cheek, and beneath the skin everything was bright red and fleshy. There were mud flecks in the wound and she was going to need stiches right away. A good many stiches.

I'd felt a towering rage at Lucy for months, but it all dissipated now. My anger had been righteous and well earned, but it became a stranger to me in the snap of a finger. That's the problem with children, you can't hate them for long no matter how much they deserve it.

I squatted low and slid my arms beneath her shoulders. Told Jewell to get ready to help me lift.

Sawbrooks are skinny by nature, but Lucy was built like her daddy's side. Not overweight, but sturdy. Solid all the way through, and heavy enough that I had to set my boots hard in the mud before I lifted. Jewell had her by the feet.

"On three," I said.

The truck was a good fifty yards away and there were a few times I thought we might have to set her down like a couch caught up in a stairwell.

Jewell had moved from Lucy's boots to hold her beneath the knees and better balance the weight. She kept asking if I was okay and I kept telling her to walk faster. I needed a break, but I didn't know if I could lift her up a second time.

We managed to wrangle her into the back of my pickup and I told Jewell to follow me to the workshop.

"The workshop?"

My daddy did some taxidermy in his time, and we still have a nice space behind the house. I figured we could stitch her up there without waking Edward.

"You got a better idea?"

She did not. She just stared off into some point in the distance and looked like she was about to vomit.

"She's going to be fine," I said. "Focus."

"She grabbed my bag."

"What?"

"My rucksack. I lost it right by the falls and she had it hooked in her hand when I found her. She probably reached for it last minute and came off sideways. That's why she fell the way she did."

"Where is it now?"

"I got it. It's at the four-wheeler."

"That's all that matters, then," I said, and climbed into the truck.

There isn't a thing in this world more pointless than guilt, and I was not going to stand around and let my daughter indulge in it.

I put the truck in reverse and was starting to back into my turn when something came flying down the river trail. I saw the headlights first—like two tunnels in the dark—and then I saw the four-wheeler. Another four-wheeler, in addition to Jewell's. I thought for sure it was Lucy's idiot deputy, D-Rod, right up until I saw the outline of the big body behind the handlebars.

It was actually my idiot son and I knew it for a fact. I would have recognized that big, hulking frame anywhere. I thought he might be headed for the property, that he was caught up somehow in this mess with his sisters, but he did not make the turn. Buckner kept flying straight down the trail and I watched him until he disappeared into the high brush and was gone.

rhoda

Lucy was still unconscious when we set her on the table, which I viewed as preferable to the alternative. Jewell got some buckets of soapy water and a stack of towels from the house and stood beside me while I slipped Lucy's wrists through a bit of rope and looped the rope around the handle of a clamp on each side of the table.

Jewell asked me what all the rope was about.

"If I know your sister," I said, "she's going to come up swinging."

The big work bulbs clicked and buzzed and when they finally flicked on, they were bright as the sun in the ceiling.

Jewell gasped all over again when she saw Lucy's face in the full relief of the light. I might have gasped, too, if I didn't feel the need to try to stay strong for Jewell—to pretend like I knew what I was doing and that everything was going to be fine. Which is basically what parenting is—a whole shitload of pretending.

I'd say the flap of skin hanging off her cheek was roughly two inches wide and I held it with one finger while I started to clean the wound. Otherwise, I felt like the whole thing might just fall off and float to the floor.

Jewell gagged.

"Do not even think about puking, Jewell."

83

"I'm sorry—" she said, and gagged again.

She put her hands against the table to brace herself. Stared at the ground.

"Go outside."

"It's okay," she said. "I'm not going to puke."

"You goddamn better not."

I worked on Lucy for another moment and then heard Jewell sigh.

"I think I'm fine now," she said.

"Well, that's a load off. Thank God you're fine, Jewell."

"It's just a lot, Mom."

"Is it?" I said. "Is it a lot for you, Jewell?"

She pointed at Lucy, though I noted she still had her eyes cast downward. "I did this. This is my fault."

"Get off the cross, Jewell. We need the wood."

"What does that even mean?"

"It means stop whining," I said. "And get me a fresh rag."

Jewell's hands were trembling when she handed me the rag, and I could see that her eyes were teary. Maybe I'd been a little hard on her, or maybe I hadn't been hard enough when I'd had the chance. She was the baby, and I treated her softer than Lucy and Buck—at least that's what Lucy and Buck always claimed.

"She looks bad."

"You got to let me work, honey."

Lucy was breathing steady, but she started to twitch when I got more purposeful with the washing.

Jewell dunked the old rag in the pail and the water went dark with blood and dirt. She swears she saw pieces of bone when she emptied the buckets later, but I think it was probably just some little bits of river rock. Either way, I got the wound washed and then went for the rubbing alcohol.

"I think I'm going to pour, rather than dab. Just to get it over with."

"Is that the best way to do it?"

"I don't know the best way to do any of this," I said. "Just hold her shoulders down."

I unscrewed the bottle cap and winced. Had to lean back from the smell. Jewell got quiet for a moment, then looked up at me. "Did you see who was on the four-wheeler?"

"Yes," I said. "Did you?"

"No, but I saw it was from the park. It looked like the one Lucy had earlier."

"It was your brother."

"What?"

I nodded. "It was Buckner. I saw him clear as day."

"What the hell was he doing on a four-wheeler from the campground?"

"Well, I know he's not a park ranger, so I'd wager he stole it." I nodded at Lucy on the table. "Maybe this one left hers running when she went after you."

"Do you think he's drinking again?"

"Of course he's drinking again. That's what alcoholics do, Jewell. They drink."

"He was clean, though," she said. "For real."

"Well, you can see how that's going."

"He was just texting me about some girl the other day, too."

"Some girl?"

"He's got a girlfriend," she said. "I think he really likes her. He said she has a baby boy and that he likes him, too."

"Oh Jesus God."

"What? He sounded happy."

"Happy doesn't seem to be part of the equation tonight, does it? His, or anybody else's."

I was poised with the rubbing alcohol and I did not offer a countdown or tell Jewell to get ready or whisper any silent prayers. I just tipped the bottle and dumped what I could into the wound before Lucy shot up against her straps and screamed. Her eyes were wild with pain and fear and I didn't think it would do much good to try to explain what was happening, so I didn't. I just told Jewell to go and get a bite stick.

"A bite stick?"

"A stick for her to bite on while I sew her up."

Lucy dropped back down to the table, but she was screaming even louder now.

"Where are they?" said Jewell.

I looked at her stunned, but it was an honest question.

"What do you mean, where are they? You think I got a box labeled BITE STICKS somewhere? Go outside and get one! It's a fucking stick!"

Lucy was pulling against her arm straps and the table was starting to shake. She was making horrible animal sounds and I gave her knee a little squeeze.

"Just hold on, sweetie," I said. "You're going to be fine."

Jewell came back with a stick and told Lucy to open up. "I got a stick here for you," she said.

Lucy started to shout again and Jewell slid the stick in when she did and held it with a hand. Now Lucy's screams were muffled through the wood and I told Jewell to pin the flap of skin to the top of her cheek so I could start the needle and thread.

Lucy started to whimper.

"It's okay," said Jewell. "We're right here."

I poised myself above Lucy and waited for her eyes to calm just a bit. She saw me and grunted again and I talked to her low and quiet, like I did when she was a girl.

"Try and stay still," I said. "The more you move, the worse this gets."

Jewell had the skin held tight but the flap was still wide at the edges and when I pressed it back to her cheek so that I could start, Lucy flinched hard.

"You can't flinch like that," I said. "You just can't. Do you understand me?"

Lucy looked at me with drowning eyes, but I could tell she understood.

The first time I pushed the needle through I thought she was going to come right out of her body, but she held strong and did not so much as squirm. Jewell is the bravest of my children and Buckner is the purest of heart. Lucy is the toughest, though, and she just bit down hard on her stick and grunted while I worked. Before long, she was passed back out.

Small mercies will abide with you, if you let them.

jewell

J ewell woke up on the porch the next morning. Rhoda had dismissed her to get some sleep after they completed the makeshift surgery, and said she'd keep an eye on Lucy herself.

Jewell lived in what they still called Mabel's house. The one Alfred had built for his daughter, the murderer. The original had a pine tree nearly saw it in half during a lightning storm in the 1940s, but they'd rebuilt it right there and done plenty of renovations since.

Jewell had wanted to get home and snag a few hours in her own bed but was so tired she decided to take a few minutes in the rocking chair first. She smoked a bowl and must have drifted off because the next thing she knew the sun had risen above the pines.

Her neck was stiff as she blinked her eyes open and she could hear the floorboards creaking beside her.

"Daddy?"

She turned and saw him sitting beside her with a cup of coffee. He didn't have his wheelchair or oxygen and that was always good to see. Typically, the morning hours were his best.

"Hey, baby girl."

"It feels late," she said.

Her father nodded. "Seven forty-five. Give or take."

"I actually slept."

"Yeah, you did."

He was in a baggy sweatshirt and flannel pajama pants. He looked so small now inside of clothes that used to fit snugly at his shoulders and belly.

"How are you feeling?" she said.

"Compared to what?"

She didn't know how to answer that, so she didn't.

Her father brought his mug to his lips and told her there was coffee on. She wanted a cup, desperately, but a few moments with her dad always felt stolen these days and she wanted to savor them.

"I'll get some in a second. Thanks."

She sat up straight and started to work her chair slowly beside his. There was already a glare in the field off the porch, and there was no fog or dew. All told, she preferred a cooler, mistier morning. She liked to ease into the day rather than wake up to pure brightness, particularly when there was so much from the night before that still needed handling.

"I heard there was some drama last night."

Her father's voice was thin and rattled with phlegm, but at least he wasn't coughing.

"Little bit," she said.

"Mom came in for some pillows in the middle of the night. She slept out there, to keep an eye on Luce."

"Is she still out there?"

"Far as I know."

"I should trade her," said Jewell. "She needs to catch a few hours' sleep, I'm sure."

"We should talk first. Something came up while you were sleeping."

"Uh-oh. That doesn't sound good."

"Nathan Shipley was here this morning."

"The kid from the river?" said Jewell. "Molly's boy?"

"Yup."

"What the hell for?"

"He left this."

Her father picked an envelope out of his lap and handed it to Jewell.

"What the hell is this, Daddy?"

"Go on and read it."

"What's it say?"

"Open it up," he said. "See for yourself."

She reached into the envelope and pulled out a single sheet of paper and unfolded it. There was nothing on the page but two words typed in large, blocky font.

I'M SORRY.

She turned the paper over. There was nothing on the back and the envelope was not addressed or marked in any way. She looked back at her father.

"Is this from Van?"

"Kind of seems like it has to be, doesn't it?"

"Is he trying to rip me off?"

"I don't know," he said. "But whatever it is, it can't be good if he's so sorry he had to type it out on a sheet of paper and send that Shipley boy up here to say so."

Jewell looked out off the porch. Felt a roil of nausea in her stomach. Had Van skipped town? Even worse, what if Franklin had found out somehow and called the cops?

She heard a rumble in the distance and when she stood up from her chair, she felt a shot of pain ride up her leg and it almost felled her.

"Goddamnit," she said, and reached down to her knee. It was puffy and tender to the touch.

"What's wrong with your leg?"

"Nothing," she said. "I just scraped my knee."

The sound was probably a truck making its slow way up the hill, and Rhoda heard it, too, because she came hustling out of the workshop. Jewell handed the envelope back to her father and then watched her mother approach. She was still in the same clothes as the night before—her flannel shirt untucked now and loose at the neck.

"Who the hell is this?"

Rhoda pointed off toward the pines in the general direction of the racket.

"I don't know," said Jewell. "Van isn't supposed to be here until noon."

"That's not Van," said Edward. "That man drives a Volkswagen Jetta and this is a truck."

Jewell looked to both her parents. "Are you guys expecting anybody?"

It was a stupid question. The only one who liked houseguests was her daddy, and he'd stopped being interested in that when the cancer took hold. Rhoda did not bother to answer, just stormed up the porch steps and into the house.

Jewell leaned on the rail to take the weight off her leg and squinted into the sun. She heard her father sigh from the chair behind her and then caught the creak of the hinges when the screen door swung back open. Now her mother was standing beside her with a deer rifle aimed up the road.

The truck crested the hill and hit the open space and Jewell put her hand near the barrel. "Hold on."

"Who is it?" said her father.

"I think it's Connie."

"Are you sure?" he said.

"I'm sure," she said, and she was. "That's her Ford. Put it down."

"I can't tell," said Rhoda.

The truck had stopped about twenty feet from the house, but Jewell saw the right bumper hanging low and the sun glinting where it hit the paint between rust spots on the hood.

"It's her," she said. "I promise."

As Connie shut the engine off and stepped slowly out of the driver's side, Rhoda lowered the barrel.

The truck had kicked up some dirt but even through the cloud of dust Jewell could tell that something was wrong. She could see it in her friend's gait. The slow way she walked and the tight way she held her shoulders.

"What is it?" said Jewell. "What's going on?"

Connie stopped a few feet from the porch and Jewell put her hand to her forehead to block the sun. Connie looked stricken.

"Jewell," she said.

"Go on," said Rhoda.

"I don't quite know how to say it."

"Say what?" asked Jewell.

Connie turned off toward the trees. "Shit," she whispered.

"Spit it out!" Rhoda was shouting now.

Jewell put a hand to her mother's shoulder and spoke as clearly and as calmy as she could. "Whatever it is, Connie, you can tell me."

Connie turned back toward the porch. "They found a body on the boat. The remains of one, anyway."

Rhoda started shouting all over again, but Jewell didn't hear any of it. Not really. The only thing Jewell heard was the clear, singular sound of chickadees in the pines.

It was a strange, auditory break, but not entirely unfamiliar. It had happened to her in Vegas, too, the moment she went bust. Dealer flipped a diamond when she was waiting on a club and as soon as the card turned, the only thing she could hear was the slots ringing all brassy and bright.

She was outside of her body and would have stayed there forever if she could—the moment terrible and cold, but still preferable to whatever was coming next.

Finally, Rhoda screamed her name and Jewell came back to herself. Turned to Connie.

"Who was it?" she said. "Who was on the boat?"

"They think it's Van. But they can't say for sure. Rick told me this morning."

"Rick?" said Rhoda.

"My ex," said Connie.

"Which ex?"

"Dot's daddy."

"I don't give a fuck whose daddy it is," said Rhoda. "I'm saying is he the one at the sheriff's department?"

Connie nodded. "But they don't know anything else. It's not even official yet that it's Van. That's just what Rick figures and I drove up here as soon as I heard."

"Rick fucking Pico," spat Rhoda. "My God, I can't believe you married that man."

"We were never married. And he just came by this morning to get Dot for soccer. It was in the course of conversation that he told me about the body."

"Oh my God," said Jewell. "I killed Van."

"You didn't know." Connie took a step toward her friend. "It is not your fault, Jewell."

"I'll just tell them that, then. Sorry, Your Honor, I didn't know there was anybody in the boat I set on fire."

"I don't think they know it's you. Matter of fact, I'm certain of it. Rick wouldn't have been so casual about it all."

"Oh my God," said Jewell again. "I killed Van!"

Her voice cracked on "Van" and for a moment she felt as if she might cry.

"That sonofabitch," said Edward.

"Rick really isn't that bad," said Connie.

"Not Rick," said Edward. "Van Hargraves!"

"What?" said Jewell.

"The note! Now we know what he's sorry for, at least."

Jewell turned from the porch rail and looked at her father. "We do?"

"What note?" said Rhoda.

"What's happening right now?" asked Connie.

Jewell shook her head. "I don't know. I have no idea what's happening. What are you saying, Daddy?"

"I'm saying he killed himself and tricked you into helping."

"What goddamn note!"

Rhoda was right in Edward's ear, but he didn't even flinch. He just held up the envelope and let her snatch it from his hand.

"Life insurance doesn't pay out on suicide," he went on. "I've looked into it plenty, trust me."

Rhoda looked up from the note. "He's right."

"You're saying Van wanted to be on the boat?" asked Jewell.

"Yes," said her father.

"But he wouldn't do it that way," she said. "He would not be able to burn himself alive. He has no tolerance for pain, or even the thought of pain."

"He's a drunk," said Connie. "He probably just got hammered and passed out."

"I checked the cabin door. Before I did anything, I checked the cabin and it was locked. I even—"

"He was already dead," said Edward. "He probably popped a bunch of pills and drank himself under and then you came along and destroyed the evidence. He gave the note to the Shipley boy ahead of time and told him to bring it up here first thing this morning."

"Why would he do that?" asked Jewell.

"Because he loved Franklin," said Rhoda. "That's the one thing about that man you could count on. He would have done this for Franklin."

"That was the problem with the money." Edward was talking only to Rhoda now.

She pointed back at him. "That's exactly what it was."

"What problem with the money?" said Jewell. "What are you talking about?"

"You didn't kill Van," said Rhoda. "He set you up."

She didn't know if Rhoda was right, or if she only wanted her to be right so badly that she believed her.

"You really think so?"

Her mother looked at her quick and mean. "Why do you sound so happy about it?"

"Because it means I didn't kill him."

"Well, that might be good for your conscience, but it ain't going to matter to anybody else."

Jewell leaned back against the railing. Her knee didn't hurt, but that was only because she couldn't feel anything at all.

"What do you mean?"

"I mean they're going to charge somebody with murder," said Rhoda. "Whether it was a murder or not."

part III

buckner

Ten miles north of the river, Buckner was just waking up. He was fully clothed in an empty bathtub and remembered nothing from the night before. At least not beyond the parking lot of the Boogie Down Barn and those first few gulps of whiskey.

The blackout was absolute and while it might be difficult for some to believe, Buckner's memory, or its absence, was not affected at all by the gravity of the night's events.

He did not remember confronting Ray Tomshaw. His chest and back hurt terribly, but he had no idea why. He did not remember stealing the four-wheeler or driving it home or the river on fire or seeing his mama in her truck.

The only thing he remembered was the feel of the bottle in his hands and the whirring sound in his brain, the pure white noise and propulsive force of his compulsion. Then the sweet moment of relief when the whiskey first splashed his throat and landed gentle and warm in his belly. Drinking always felt good at first, which was why he did it.

Now he was left with this empty bathtub and the distinct sense that something terrible had happened. Actually, he knew something terrible had happened. He had gotten drunk for the first time in six months and then blacked out because everything they'd told him in the meetings about picking up where you left off had wound up, sadly, to be true.

The question was if another terrible thing had happened on top of the terrible thing he already knew about. In his experience, it was safe to assume the worst.

His dog, Harold, was curled up on the bathroom floor, whimpering. It was a whimper of concern and it hurt Buckner's heart the way his good boy looked at him. The righteousness of his worry and disappointment.

"Goddamnit, I know," said Buckner.

Harold barked and Buckner reached out his hand toward the dog and stroked him behind the ears. Harold was a pound mutt of unknown origin. He had jet-black fur and dark eyes and was likely some sort of pit-hound mix. Maybe some Lab in there, to boot. He whimpered one last time and then melted into Buckner's hand and Buckner knew that he was forgiven. He did not deserve it, but he was.

"I'm sorry," he said. "I truly am."

Buckner used to think that if you quit drinking for a while you got back to the good times at the beginning and reset the board. He used to think he could have a few years of quality drinking before things got bad again, which gave him a sense of hope in those hard, early days of getting clean.

Buckner had discussed this theory at the treatment center and it had not gone well. They jumped all over him about how his bottom would always be right there where he'd left it. He'd said something along the lines of, *I just need a few weeks to clean up and then I should be fine*, and it damn near caused a riot in small group.

People said his body would never be able to safely consume alcohol or any other mind-altering substances. They said once an alcoholic, always an alcoholic. God, they hammered that into his head—the "progressive nature of his illness." They hammered everything in the program. They were all a bunch of hammerhead sharks, sitting around saying the same shit off the same laminated readings at the same time on the same days and for some reason, to Buckner's utter disbelief, it worked.

Buckner didn't know why. Honestly, it was stupid, and he hated half the people there, but some of them weren't bad and maybe he'd even made a few friends along the way. Most important, the whole thing kept him clean and he stopped questioning it after a while and just went with the flow. It was kind of like a miracle, until it wasn't.

Twenty-four weeks out the window, just like that. What he should do now was call somebody from the program, but he didn't want to do that because of the terrible feeling he had about the night before.

The program was great if you needed support, but sometimes when Buckner got drunk, he got violent and he wasn't about to call somebody and start divulging potentially incriminating information. He did call Jewell, but it went straight through to voicemail. Then he called Lucy, but she didn't pick up, either.

On the positive end, he'd woken up in his own clothes and in his own bathtub. Those were two facts to build on, but it was also true that they didn't really eliminate any of the possibilities he most feared. Yes, he was still alive, but death was far from Buckner's worst-case scenario.

Harold crawled right into the tub with him and set his head on Buckner's chest. He was a good boy. The best boy.

———————

The next time Buckner woke, he was on the couch. He remembered being in the bathroom, but not leaving the bathroom to come to the living room. Sometimes blackouts were leaky. They cut in and out, like bad cell service.

His phone was on the coffee table and he picked it up and the picture of Sky on his home screen reminded him of whatever had happened to her, which was, of course, the reason he was at the Boogie Down Barn in the first place. *Sky*, he thought, and felt his chest crater when he noticed his stream of unreturned texts and calls from the night before.

Earlier, in the bathroom, he had thought of his sisters, and now, on the couch, he could only think of Sky. It was like the hangover had returned him to some base portion of his reptilian brain where Sky did not yet exist and so his initial thoughts were on his family of origin. Now that he was surfacing, so to speak, the full scope of the day before returned and he remembered why it was he flew off the handle and got drunk to begin with.

Actually, it wasn't why he flew off the handle and got drunk. He got drunk because he was an alcoholic and that's what alcoholics did. The meetings had taught him to accept responsibility for that fact and to stop blaming circumstance. He used to get drunk because the wind blew, so the triggering incident could have been anything. The important thing was that something had happened to Sky. Something so bad she was afraid to tell Buckner for fear of what he might do in response.

Delray said somebody had gotten handsy, which meant anything at all could have happened—Delray not being the type you trusted to tell you the truth, the whole truth, and nothing but the truth. Delray being the opposite of that. Delray being the type to use little bits of truth to spin his characterizations and outright lies into misleading blizzards of made-up horseshit.

Buckner checked Sky's MySpace, but she hadn't posted. Of

course she hadn't. Something horrible had happened, so why would she feel compelled to get on her computer and check in with the world?

God, she was pretty, though. He scrolled up and down her page for a minute and it pierced his heart clear through just to see her in her life and to see himself in a few of those pictures, too. He was the luckiest man in the world. To be who he was and to have a woman like that on his arm? It was something out of Hollywood. It was the feel-good hit of the summer, which was weird, because it was happening to him.

Her mama named her after her blue eyes, which was a risk considering lots of babies' eyes changed colors, though Buckner couldn't remember if they went from light to dark, or dark to light. Either way, it wouldn't have mattered because she had the Sky inside of her—she was love and pure light and in the end it didn't have anything to do with the particular hue of her eyeballs.

She had a way of laughing that was bigger and warmer than anybody he'd ever known. She laughed with her whole body, and claimed nobody made her laugh more than Buckner. He knew it was a compliment, and it wasn't the first time he'd been told he was funny. The bothersome part was that he rarely tried to be funny and so there was always part of him that wondered if he might be the butt of a joke he didn't realize he was making.

Then again, when it came to Sky, he couldn't have cared less. She could laugh at him all day long if she wanted—so long as he got to be there beside her while it happened.

She was long and skinny and smelled like exotic herbs and spices. She had curly black hair, pouty lips, and her cheeks were flecked with freckles and little baby acne scars. She loved Taylor Swift, the *Law & Order* universe of television programming, and playing games on the computer.

Buckner wasn't much for video games but liked watching her play and tried to be supportive of her characters. She liked games where you had to complete tasks, harvest resources, and keep your weapons upgraded. It was a lot to keep track of, but he did like the fighting parts and how she refused to pay for the shortcuts the games were constantly tempting her with. He believed that said something about her character.

The other thing about Sky, and it was the main thing, really, was her son. He was only a year old and the daddy was some resorter that was supposed to be sending money but never did. Buckner couldn't imagine leaving any baby, let alone one as precious as Frog, and he fell for the boy almost as hard as Sky.

Frog was not his Christian name, but it was what Buckner called him because the boy had a froggy way about him. It was hard to explain, but it was something about his scrawny legs and the way he sort of sat back in his little baby seat. He always seemed relaxed, but at the same time like he might hop up at any moment and start some shit. He had thin hair and big eyes and Buckner sensed he was bound for greatness.

His Christian name was Dashiell, which was a terrible name and likely to get his ass beat, but Buckner had not been consulted. Maybe the resorter had, though. Buckner didn't know a thing about the man because Sky never talked about him or even mentioned his name. Buckner didn't know for sure but suspected the resorter had never even put eyes on his son.

Frog was at Sky's mama's house, and what Buckner should have done was offer to take him out for a walk and to get some air. All he should have done was ask what he could do that would be helpful, but instead he'd run off to the Barn half-cocked and fallen into a bottle of whiskey. Jumped into it.

The one piece of good fortune regarding the night before was that Buckner had recently lost his job at Carter's Grocery. So he had not missed third shift, which definitely would have been noticed and potentially used against him in a court of law.

Buckner had not been fired for anything related to performance. In fact, it was just the opposite. He unloaded trucks and stocked shelves and his supervisor, Sanderson, had said he'd never had a more efficient or reliable man on the floor.

"I mean you get them boxes off the truck and on the shelves and broken down in record speed. I've never seen anything like it, but you were the last hired and now you got to be the first fired. It's a company policy."

"But why are you firing anybody at all?"

"On account of the economy," he said. "Supply chain. Inflation. Fuck, I don't know. They just sent me an email and this is the result."

"I guess that makes sense," said Buckner, and shook Sanderson's hand.

He didn't mean that he understood the effect of supply-chain issues on low-wage workers, he meant that he was not surprised to be losing a job that he was good at because of reasons that sounded made up. All that made perfect sense to Buckner. His only hope now was that he hadn't done anything the night before that couldn't be undone.

What he should do was fire up the Google search and see if there were any news reports that might pertain to him. Stories of sudden acts of tragic violence. A beating outside a bar or a home invasion. Historically, Buckner was capable of both.

The problem was, he did not actually want to know what happened. This was not a game of Clue or some cliffhanger TV show. More than anything, he wanted to crawl into bed and forget about everything—forget he'd ever existed at all—but at the same time the responsible thing was to be informed about his own actions.

He sat up on the couch. Held the phone in his hands and waited, though he couldn't say for what. His stomach was churning pretty hard, though, and it was possible he was going to vomit.

Whoever said ignorance was bliss was a privileged motherfucker, if you wanted Buckner's view on the matter. What kind of life might it be, to trust the things you did not know?

jewell

Rhoda left the property right after Connie dropped her bombshell. Told Jewell she was going to see about a boat and that Jewell should pack a bag in the meantime.

Rhoda didn't say what the boat and the bag were for, but Jewell didn't have to ask. Her mother was thinking Canada, and if they hadn't sold every watercraft they owned when her father got sick, she'd already be on her way. By kayak if she had to.

Rhoda had also said that Jewell and Lucy were to wait at the cabin until she returned. The cabin was on the farthest, easternmost edge of the property and right beside a bunker that had been built by her great-grandfather. It would be a long hike mostly uphill, but far safer than sitting around the house where the cops might pull up at any moment. The cabin had been built by Germain as a stash house for contraband and mobsters, and Rhoda said she'd meet them there by nightfall.

"That's the plan," she'd said.

The other part of the plan was that Jewell was not to tell Lucy that she was coming to the cabin, too. That part would have to come from their father, who was the only one that Lucy would mind.

In the meantime, Jewell headed to the workshop with some Advil and water and snagged a few gummies from her father's tin on the way.

Lucy was awake now, but just. She'd slept right there on the table with the pillows and blankets that Rhoda brought, and her face was even worse than Jewell had feared. The bruising was bright and held many colors—like gasoline in a rain puddle—and the swelling had nearly sealed her left eye closed.

"Buckner," she whispered.

"Buckner?" said Jewell.

Lucy winced. It looked like she was trying to nod, but even the slightest gesture appeared to hurt too much to execute. Jewell pulled up a chair to the side of the table and leaned in close to her sister.

"What about Buckner?" asked Jewell.

"Is he okay?"

"How do you mean?"

"I hit him with the Taser. Then hog-tied him and left him at the park."

"You tased Buckner?"

"I can barely talk," she said. "Don't make me say shit more than once."

"Sorry," said Jewell. "What happened?"

"He was shit-faced at the campground. He refused to leave and charged D-Rod, so I put him down."

"So he was drunk?"

"Very. I was supposed to come back and get him, but I didn't. And I had a dream just now that he got burned up in the fire."

"He didn't."

"Are you sure?"

"Positive. Mom actually saw him leaving the river last night."

"She did?"

"He's fine. Trust me."

"I dreamed the fire spread and he was just lying there, all tied up."

Jewell hesitated but decided to avoid the complicating and likely upsetting issue of the four-wheeler.

"Other than the drunk part, I promise he's okay. How do *you* feel?"

"I have two headaches. One is sharp and the other is blunt. The blunt one is everywhere, but the sharp one is just above my eye. My cheek feels like a water balloon."

"You took a tumble. There's no way around it."

Jewell opened the Advil and slid a pill into her sister's mouth herself. Lucy managed to get it down with some water through a straw. Jewell offered her the gummies and she said she'd love some but didn't think she could chew.

She was fully awake now, though. Jewell could see it in the clarity of her good eye—the hard way she stared off into the room.

"You missed Buck's party," she said.

"What?" said Jewell. "I thought that was today."

"It was yesterday."

"Are you sure?"

"I'm pretty sure, Jewell, but if you don't believe me, you could ask the other thirty people that showed up."

Lucy's tone managed to be so cutting and severe, even in a whisper. Actually, it might have been worse because it was whispered. There was an element of control involved—she wasn't losing her temper so much as deliberately applying scorn.

"I am so sorry, Luce. I totally mixed my days up."

"I guess you did have a lot going on. That fire wasn't going to set itself."

"That's not what happened at all. I just had it wrong."

"But you didn't mix up the days for the fire, right? That happened on the right day?"

"They're not related, Lucy. I am very sorry about missing the party, but those two things don't have anything to do with each other."

"Don't feel too bad. Buckner missed it, too."

"Buckner missed his own party?"

"You sound surprised."

"God," said Jewell. "How long do you think he's been drinking?"

"What's it matter?"

"I guess it doesn't. I'm just curious."

"He's also got a girlfriend," said Lucy. "Were you aware of that?"

"He told me about it the other day. He sounded good, too. That's why I'm surprised about all this."

"He didn't tell me."

"How'd you find out?"

"When he showed up drunk to my place of work and I was informed that the drama involved his girlfriend."

"That's weird."

"Is it weird, Jewell? For Buckner?"

"I guess not. No."

"Why would he tell you about his girlfriend, but not me?"

"I have no idea."

"'Cause now I'm wondering if he had something to do with the fire last night, too."

"No," said Jewell. "He didn't."

"Don't lie to me."

"I'm not lying."

"And why should I believe you?"

"I don't care if you believe me or not. I am telling you the truth, though."

"What'd you set on fire?"

"It was a boat."

"Whose boat?"

"Van Hargraves's."

Jewell said his name flatly and without equivocation. Didn't see any point in hiding the fact.

"Van," Lucy said. "I was just talking to his husband yesterday."

"What were you talking to Franklin about?"

"He was at Buckner's party."

"Why was he at Buckner's party?"

"Because he knows Buck. Franklin goes to Al-Anon because of Van and they smoke cigarettes before the meeting."

"Small world," said Jewell.

"Small town," said Lucy. "So why'd you do it?"

"Why'd I do what?"

"Set Van Hargraves's boat on fire, Jewell. Unless you did something else I don't know about in addition."

"Because he paid me. At least he was supposed to pay me."

"Who was?"

"Van."

"What was it, some sort of insurance play?"

"It was."

"My God, you're an idiot."

Her sister's judgment was earned, but it was also the one thing about Lucy that bothered Jewell the most—how unapologetically she looked down on her. Looked down on them all.

"We need the money, Lucy. In case you weren't aware."

"For what? I just gave you twenty thousand dollars."

"You didn't give me anything. You paid me for my land."

"The point is the money. Which was supposed to put all this bullshit with the bank to rest."

Jewell didn't answer. The problem was, Lucy was right. She'd had the money and then lost it. Then she doubled down on this thing with Van and got taken all over again. The whole damn thing was flat embarrassing.

Her first clue it was a setup should have been the money. Ten grand was too much for the job, but all she'd thought when she heard the number was to take it and turn her focus to getting that game set up. He'd bluffed her right off the table.

Van was a sonofabitch and she hated him. On the other hand, she'd known the man and was sorry he'd met such a gruesome and sudden end. She was doubly sorry she'd been tricked into helping him and might spend the rest of her life in prison for it. She was upset and she was angry, but the only person she was willing to blame was herself. Turned out, she couldn't see an angle to save her life.

"I don't have the money," she said, finally.

"What?"

"It's gone."

"What is?"

"The twenty K."

"What do you mean?"

"I mean I don't have it. It's in the wind. It's fucking *gone*."

"All of it?"

"More or less. But closer to the more side."

"Did you gamble it? Tell me you didn't gamble it, Jewell."

"I gambled it."

"You lost twenty thousand dollars at the Soaring Eagle?"

"No," Jewell scoffed. "I lost it in Vegas on a tournament stake."

"What the hell is a tournament stake?"

"In this case it was twenty thousand dollars."

"Unbelievable," said Lucy. "Actually, strike that. It's completely believable. Of course you lost twenty thousand dollars in a poker tournament and then came home and set a fucking boat on fire because that's what passes for logic in this family."

"A few minutes ago, you said it hurt to talk."

"That was before I got angry."

"I was trying to win the money for Mom and Dad. I wanted to pay the bills and take off the pressure."

"Let me guess," said Lucy. "You were going to get paid by Van, then take that money and turn it into twenty at the Soaring Eagle and re-up for the next bullshit tournament in Las Vegas. That sound about right?"

"Van said he was going to set up another game in his garage for me. Those were easy pickings."

"Casino, garage, whatever. Same difference."

It wasn't the same, though. Van's games were more money and less risk, but Jewell also understood that this was not a distinction that Lucy would find at all compelling and she was right about the gist of it. Jewell was trying to get her bankroll up so she could win back what she'd lost, and she found it deeply infuriating that her sister was so easily able to divine her plan and qualify it a failure.

"Holy shit," said Lucy. "You know what I just realized?"

Jewell did not know what Lucy realized, because unlike Lucy she could not read minds.

Jewell waited for her to go on, to answer her own question, but Lucy was distracted and no longer seemed interested in her sister. Lucy was staring at a trophy bird their grandfather mounted that had been in the workshop their entire lives—a giant black bird that had terrified them all as children.

The mount was nearly three feet tall on a wood pedestal, with a raised, rock base. The feathers were deeply black and the wings were arched like the bird was about to leap into flight and the beak still held the brightness of its original orange lacquer. The eyes were marbled green and as a child Jewell remembered catching glances through the workshop window and then taking off in a sprint—a shiver up her back like the thing was about to come to life and give chase. Jewell didn't know what kind of bird it was, but it was quality craftsmanship.

"Do you remember this thing?" said Lucy. "The way it terrified us?"

"Of course I do. It's creepy as hell."

"Well, it's a fucking cormorant. How did I not realize that until just now?"

"What does that matter?"

"Because it was endangered, that's why. This was a federally protected bird."

"Shit," said Jewell. "Really?"

"This family. Every time I think we can't stoop any lower, we manage to find a way. All the bullshit about protecting the land and here we are, plucking endangered species out of the sky and then building statues out of the bones."

"Are they—"

"Extinct?" said Lucy. "No, they are not. No thanks to us."

Jewell didn't know what to say about the bird that used to be endangered but was not extinct. The good thing was that it had allowed her to put off saying anything about Van being dead, at least for the moment.

Lucy was still turned toward the cormorant, but she was quiet. She seemed a little too upset about the bird in the context of everything else that was happening, but she was a bleeding heart and likely concussed on top of everything else.

There was a rumble in the distance. Not a truck this time, but something else. Jewell thought it might be thunder, but it was steady and too high-pitched. Lucy didn't say anything about the sound or the bird or anything else. Lucy seemed to be drifting off and it had come on as suddenly as her outrage at the cormorant.

Now the sound was closer and growing louder and Jewell stood up quietly from her chair and walked outside. She crossed her arms over her chest and squinted into the sun and when she looked to the south, she saw it above the stretch of pines where the Crow met Long Lake—a police chopper, flying low above the blue water and headed for the river.

buckner

B uckner didn't make it to the bathroom when he vomited. He didn't even have time to get off the couch. His guts opened up suddenly and violently—like a volcano or civil unrest—and he splatter-shot the room. Puked his brains out onto the coffee table and the carpet and the couch and even managed to hit the sliding glass doors.

It wasn't impressive, necessarily, but it did speak to the amazing potential of the human body and in that way needed to be acknowledged. Buckner had vomited plenty in his life, but he didn't know if he'd ever spewed ten yards across the room. The scientific term was *projectile vomit.*

Afterward, he stood up and staggered to the sliding door. Outside was closer than the bathroom, and he figured if he needed to puke again, he could do it on the cement pad that the rental office called his patio.

Buckner did puke again, but it wasn't as explosive as the first round. Some of it was just dry heaves and when he stood up afterward, he saw the four-wheeler parked in the gravel bed that the rental office referred to as his landscaped lawn.

On the hood of the four-wheeler, in white stencil lettering, it said RANGER. Below that, in smaller type, was CROOKED TREE PARK.

"What the fuck is this, now?" he said.

Harold was running in little circles in the yard and barking his head off. Harold was all hound when he barked. Long, plaintive vowels. Soulful and wise.

"It's okay, buddy," said Buckner, though clearly it was not.

Buckner lived in a single-bedroom cinder-block house in the middle of a clearing in the woods. There were a dozen exactly similar houses around him that had been the initial build of a housing development that never actually developed. The development was named Sleepy Woods, but now everybody in town called it Creepy Woods.

Buckner did not have a garage to stash the four-wheeler in but was lucky to be surrounded by mostly vacant homes. The few neighbors he did have were drunks or generally standoffish weirdos who always had their shades pulled and probably spent their days on the dark web. Buckner didn't know. He hadn't talked to any of them, ever. The point was, he didn't have to worry about anybody calling the cops if they saw him moving a stolen four-wheeler into the living room of his house—which was exactly what he was going to do.

The four-wheeler could not be returned to Lucy in its present condition. Both front headlights were busted, the side panels were scraped to hell, and there was a foot-long dent above the left rear tire. He'd need to hide the vehicle until he could repair it himself and the first thing to do was clear some space inside.

Buckner took a deep breath and held it, then braved the living room and moved his puke-soaked couch across his soiled carpet. Harold stood aside and watched. The general vibe was one of both concern and scalding judgment. He barked twice at Buckner, saying what he had to say, then started to lick up the vomit. Normally, Buckner would have shouted and shooed him away, but he was in no position to judge and the truth was, it was not unhelpful.

Buckner put the couch and the coffee table—they were the

room's only furniture—against a single wall, then pulled both sliding doors open and drove the four-wheeler inside. Afterward, he drew the shades and draped a comforter over the vehicle. It wasn't perfect, but what was?

"C'mon," he said to Harold, and led the dog into the basement.

Buckner needed a place to sit and think, and to escape the smell. Plus, he loved the basement. It was dark and musty, but it was quiet, too, and there was a pool where rainwater and runoff from the pipes collected and it felt like his own private little pond. He had a beach chair down there where he liked to sit and let his mind settle.

If Sky ever let him have Frog to the house, he thought maybe they could stock the pond with some koi fish. Koi fish were expensive, but they were hardy and might have a chance to survive. They could name them and then Buckner could teach Frog how to feed them and once Frog got old enough to talk they could have something to discuss. A common interest, so to speak. They were pleasant thoughts, but he wasn't sure if he actually believed that they could happen.

The fact was, he might never see Frog again. All of the sudden, Buckner had stolen state property in the living room and no idea at all how it had gotten there. There was at least one felony on the board at this point and it was likely to get worse the more he learned about the night before.

Harold had a spot he liked to curl up on the cement beside the chair and he gave a sigh as he dropped into his little pile at Buckner's feet. Buckner gave him a good scratch behind the ears and Harold tilted his head back, closed his eyes, and barked his long, sad bark.

"I know, buddy," said Buckner.

This was the kind of thing that would make the news. The headline would be *Drunk Man Steals ATV from State Park*. Then beneath it, in smaller type, *Drives It into Own Living Room*.

They'd get the context all wrong, of course. Make it seem like he crashed through the doors of his own house, or leave out the fact that he just didn't have anywhere else to put the thing.

Not that it would be a major news story. This would be an article people posted on Facebook that everybody would read and then pile on in the comments. Most people would just tease him, but others would probably say things about how sad it was and try to find a deeper meaning. Maybe bring up his past in the war and blame that. People loved to say you were traumatized once they heard you'd been in a war.

Buckner was in Iraq during the first big push, when everybody cared about the war and watched it on television, as a family. Buckner had always been a drinker but it really picked up after he got back from Iraq, which people liked to say was because of trauma. Buckner had not been traumatized, but after a while he stopped arguing and just let people believe what they wanted.

It wasn't like he'd been in Fallujah. He rolled into Baghdad after the fighting and the looting, and while everybody wanted him to be deeply scarred and a hero, he was neither. He had been there, then come home. He had not killed anyone, or held a dying man in his arms, and he most certainly had not been on the scene when they pulled down the statue of Saddam. No fewer than twenty people had asked him about that since he'd been home, while others had wanted to know if he'd been in any of those weird sex piles at the torture prison. Buckner didn't know anything about that mess. Vinyl hoods and barking dogs. Goodness grief that was some twisted shit. He was sure those people were traumatized, but he was not those people.

After Iraq he had a little bit of money in his pocket, and a whole lot of time, and those two factors, more than anything he'd seen or done in the war, contributed to the escalation in his drinking. It was the truth, but not the sort of truth that interested people.

Somehow, Lucy managed to get him into rehab. Drove him to the clinic herself, down in Traverse City. Buckner was passed out drunk in the passenger seat of her truck and didn't come to until they reached the parking lot.

He remembered the sound of her Chevy idling, and how he blinked his eyes open and began to take in his surroundings. He remembered the bright lights of the lobby and the alarming red signage. The generally bad vibes.

"What in the fuck?" he'd said.

The truck was in park, but Lucy kept her hands on the wheel and stared straight ahead.

"You're going to get sober, or I am going to kill you myself. You're breaking my heart, Buck."

"I'm sorry," he said. It was what he always said.

"Don't be sorry. I'm sick to death of sorry. Just get better."

"I don't know if I can."

"You can."

"I really don't know, Lucy. I'm not just saying that."

"Did I ever tell you about my buddy Ham?"

"Who the hell is Ham?"

"I worked with him when I was down in Lansing," she said. "He was the janitor at my building and we talked all the time. He was bad off. Way worse than you. He used to huff paint thinner and drink rubbing alcohol when he was hard up. He told me he used to give blow jobs for crack rock."

"Jesus, Mary, and Joseph," said Buckner.

"He was hardcore, is the point. Anyway, he came here to get sober and if it worked for him, it can sure as hell work for you. Ham's not just some janitor, either. He's an artisan now and makes chain saw sculptures. He's got one of a black bear they put in a museum somewhere."

Buckner didn't know what to say about Ham and his story of redemption. Buckner was still pretty drunk and didn't have much interest in the arts.

"I love you," said Lucy. "And it's time."

She filled out the admittance paperwork and the nurse said they were lucky there was an empty bed and that there weren't any referrals coming in.

"How much?" she said, and pulled her checkbook out of the inside pocket of her coat.

Buckner didn't know if he'd make it through a day, but he wound up graduating the rehab. They gave him a coffee mug and a medallion, and Lucy and Jewell came to the ceremony and they all went out to eat afterward. He said he was done drinking for good and had believed that to be the truth.

Now he stroked the top of Harold's head and waited for whatever was going to happen next. The dog sighed, and so did Buckner.

rhoda

All summer long, I knew something was coming. You hear about people getting bone feelings, ominous notes of dread that issue from some soggy recess of their soul, but I'm not a prophet and put no particular stock in the many twinges and pangs that might rattle around my body at any given moment.

I don't get vibes or pay any mind to the millions of whispers you might hear on this property—the early turn of a leaf, or the stray howl of a wolf. Edward was always the one that tuned into that delicate and subtle universe, like he was some sort of shaman and not the son of a roofer and a secretary. Edward invested incredible amounts of meaning into the glance of a doe or the sudden flit of a cardinal, but the only message I ever paid any heed was when one of my grandpa Harvard's land mines went off.

Grandpa Harvard, who was not well after the war, had built a bunker beside Germain's cabin and then littered the surrounding woods with land mines. Despite rumors to the contrary, Grandpa Harvard was not a survivalist. There were no stockpiles of food or bottled water. If the end of days arrived, Grandpa Harvard was primarily interested in killing as many people as possible on his own way out, and we've estimated he stuck north of thirty mines in those woods.

Daddy put up barbed wire in a wide berth around the area and we all knew to avoid that stretch of pines. Still, every few years we'd get an ambitious black bear that would work the fence down to get to some berries and then the blast would come.

I was close with Grandpa Harvard, who seemed to prefer me to my siblings. He was always stuffing my pockets with coins and hard candies, and every single one of those blasts has portended something meaningful in my life. Some good and some bad, but all of them significant. My first pregnancy, my brother's crash, Buckner getting shipped off to Iraq—three to six weeks before all those events one of Harvard's bombs went off and I've always believed it was his way of communicating with me, of telling me to be ready.

We were in the fourth week since the most recent blast, the first since Buck's, and, if anything, I'd say Harvard undersold the current drama and might have thought to give me an extra explosion for all that was coming my way. I needed to get my ass out there to fix the fencing, too. I'd been meaning to do it, but it was going to have to wait a little longer now.

The first thing to do was deal with Buckner. The cops would find out soon that he was at the park the night before and had an altercation, if they hadn't already. He'd become a person of interest and likely a primary suspect. They'd be at his house with a warrant and once they got Buck in a room and started asking questions, it could go any number of ways, and none of them good.

In the old days I would have already had Jewell on her way to Canada. Wouldn't have to worry about Buckner and his complications. Might even have been glad to keep him out there in the wind as a red herring.

In the old days I would have hitched up the Cutwater—we had a beauty—and taken back roads to the northeast coast of the county.

There's a little access there we favor and we would have launched and had Jewell safe by sunset.

We didn't have the Cutwater anymore, though. I sold it the second Edward got sick, and then I sold the old tin fishing boat that my daddy loved, and then I sold the kayaks and canoes. The Sawbrooks were landlocked for the first time in our history, and it was embarrassing, and a shame.

I saw the chopper the moment I left the property—hanging above the fields between the hills and the hardwoods. My God, talk about drama and a waste of tax dollars. I actually thought I was seeing things at first—some trick of the light and my sleep deprivation conspiring to make me a Christmas fucking fruitcake.

It was real, though. It was real and it was loud and low, and after it swooped above the fields it rose and turned sharply toward the river. They'll fall all over themselves, finding ways to spend your money.

The fire had left a nip of sulfur in the morning air, and the Crow was thick with silt and fallen branches. I could hear the first responders in the distance, too. The chain saws and sirens and the occasional order being shouted through a bullhorn.

I shouldn't have been surprised the golfers were out. I consider the sport itself fraudulent and without purpose, but I have no choice but to respect the obsession of its devotees, who are truly relentless.

They were out there by the dozens, chasing a little white ball through the ash and smoke and for the first time in my life the whisk of a swung club and the ping of a struck ball were a comfort to me—a welcome contrast with the histrionics of helicopters and sirens.

I crossed the river on the Benton Bridge, which used to be the Alfred Sawbrook Bridge before they stole it out from under him to honor the "service and sacrifice of John Benton." That was what the sign said, anyway, and they had one on each end of the bridge in case you missed it the first time.

They can put up all the signs they want, but John Benton is no hero. He was an independent contractor in Iraq and he died stateside of a heart attack ten years after the war.

I went to the city council meeting to speak against the change and everybody thought I was there because Buckner had been in Iraq as an actual member of the military. They said Buckner was a hero, too, but it was just that Benton had died and the sign was part of his legacy. I said if anybody thought Buckner Sawbrook was a hero, they'd clearly never met my son and that neither him nor John Benton was fit to clean the fur out of Alfred's traps.

I was gaveled off the microphone, and the resolution passed unanimously. Afterward, I was cited for some violation of decorum that they probably made up on the spot and I am no longer welcome at city council meetings and that is fine with me because it's the biggest collection of windbags I've ever seen north of the state capital. The fact is, the problems in this county go far beyond the resort—it's locals like the council and the Bentons who paved the way for Harbor North by avoiding our history to begin with.

Lucy likes to say everything we built ought to be named after the Indians if we're going to bring history into it, and I told her she might be right about that. I told her they could name whatever they wanted after whoever they wanted, and so long as they didn't fuck with Alfred's bridge you wouldn't hear one word about it from me.

The bridge dumped me onto the highway and I took that to Wentworth Road and drove east to Buckner's. He was staying out in Sleepy Woods, which was a tract of houses they'd built in a patch of pine forest for no reason at all.

Originally, the developers claimed they were providing afford-able housing for working families and put a community space in the middle—an outdoor basketball court and a playground and picnic benches. People said it was going to be urban sprawl, like northern Michigan was about to become a center of industry and technological growth and maybe it would have had I done what everybody expected and lurched at the resort's money when they waved it.

Now the houses were chipping at the foundation and that com-munity space was an open market for hookers and drugs. There were still families paying out the bank, and the developers had gone some-where else to spill more cement.

Buckner doesn't have a vehicle but I knew his place by the Mexi-can blankets he hangs in the windows for curtains, and then I noticed the tracks. Looked like he might have driven the four-wheeler straight into his house through the sliding glass doors.

Buckner didn't answer when I rang the bell, but it was no problem to pick the lock and let myself in. It wasn't even a dead bolt, so I just jabbed around with a paper clip I keep in my pocket for exactly such occasions.

Inside, the whole house stank like puke and sure enough, he had the four-wheeler sitting in the living room big as life. He had it draped in a comforter, too, because apparently one of Buckner's many remaining childhood qualities is believing that a household blanket can double as an invisibility cloak. I swear I never dropped that boy on his head as a baby, but there's times I wonder. I locked the door behind me and called out his name.

After a moment, he called back.

"Mama?"

"Boy, where are you?"

"I'm down here," he shouted. "In the basement."

———

126

Buckner looked like death warmed over—sitting in that musty basement and staring at a drainage pool. Even in the dark I could see how hollowed out and flat his gaze was. He was like Wanda that way. Somehow, when they drank, it was like the soul leaked right out of their bodies and left them all glassy and empty in the eyes. I told him he looked like hell.

"You should see how I feel," he said, and shot me a little smile.

He offered me his lawn chair and asked if I wanted to sit. I told him that I did not. "I'll only be a minute."

"Is everything okay?"

"You've got a four-wheeler you stole from a state park in the living room and the whole house smells like rotten death. You're down here staring at a fucking sewer pond so no, everything is not okay."

"I meant with you."

I shook my head. "I've got a few things going on myself."

"Are the girls okay?"

"Yes and no."

"What happened?"

"There's been a development," I said. "They're both at the property right now, but I need to get Jewell to Canada."

"Shit," he said. "That doesn't sound good."

"It's not ideal."

"Just tell me what you need, Mom."

"I need to get a boat, and in the meantime I need to get Jewell to the water. Problem there is they might be looking for her."

"You want to stash her at the cabin?"

"That's right."

"You want me to get the boat?"

"Can you get a boat?"

"No," he said. "Not really."

"Then you'll go to the cabin, too, because shit has gone sideways and there's cops everywhere. They've got a goddamn chopper up."

"I thought I heard a chopper," he said. "What happened?"

"Jewell set a boat on fire. Down on the Crow."

"On the resort side?"

I nodded.

"An insurance play?"

"That's exactly what it was."

"And they're making a big stink about it?"

"Well, there was a body inside. Probably dead before she burned it, but we can't say for sure."

"Who was it?"

"Van Hargraves."

"Shit, I know his husband," said Buckner. "Franklin's probably a mess."

"There's messes all around."

"What do the cops know?"

"I have no idea. They might have already made Jewell or they might not have a clue about anything. It's all dark right now, which isn't to mention the four-wheeler."

"Did somebody see me take it?"

"I saw you ride it."

"You did?"

"Right down the river."

"Jesus God. What about the cops?"

"We don't know and it sounds like you don't remember."

"I don't remember anything, but it's probably not good that it was down there by where the fire started."

"Exactly," I said. "And there were some witnesses to you being drunk and belligerent. Including your sister Lucy."

"I saw Lucy last night?"

"That's the rumor."

"What was I doing?"

"I don't know, Buck. I wasn't there."

"So you're thinking the cops will catch wind and come looking for me?"

"That's the general idea, yes."

"So I'll lay low at the property with Jewell. I promise, no drinking."

"You're still drunk right now."

"I mean after this one wears off."

"We need to deal with the four-wheeler first. We need to get rid of it."

"Why? I can fix it up and get it back to her."

"And what if she doesn't want to do that, Buckner? What if she decides she'd rather talk to the police?"

"Why would she do that?"

"I don't know, why would she give our land away to communists?"

"I don't know about the politics of all that," he said. "I had no idea those people were communists, but even if they are she's still my sister and she's not going to rat me out."

"She chased Jewell into the river last night," I said. "Took a tumble off the falls trying to catch her."

"Lucy did?"

"That's right."

"Is she okay?"

"She got beat up pretty good, actually. She's at the house right now because I had to stitch her up."

"Goodness grief."

"It's a whole to-do."

"I'll just drive it back to the park, then. No harm, no foul."

"They got roadblocks everywhere, Buckner. I'd say that's a uniquely terrible idea."

"So should we just leave it here and hope for the best?"

"When's the last time you hoped for the best and had it work out?"

"Then, what?"

"We got to get it off the board. Erase it altogether."

"How do we do that?"

It was something I'd been wondering myself, sort of on the back burner. "We could take it to the quarry and set the fucking thing on fire, I guess. Simple enough."

"That's not going to look good for Lucy at work, though, is it?"

"Trust me, it'll be fine. They'll probably give her a bonus. Government loves to burn up money."

"I really don't think she's going to bring the cops into this, though. I think we could just stash it somewhere and let her know. Then she can come get it later."

"We could do that, but let's walk this through for a minute first. What's the risk of hiding it?"

"The cops find it before Lucy gets it back."

"Then what happens?"

"I get arrested for stealing the four-wheeler and connected to the fire."

"You got money for lawyers?"

"No."

"You want to sit in jail?"

"Not particularly."

"And what's the reward? If you find some magic place to hide this four-wheeler and Lucy gets it back, no problem?"

"She doesn't hate me quite as much as she would otherwise, and she doesn't get in trouble at work."

"So are you willing to sit in a cell in Ionia and do eighteen months so Lucy can avoid a difficult conversation with her boss?"

Buckner stared at his sewer pond. Considered what I'd told him.

"Fine," he said. "Let's burn it, then."

I nodded. "I'll pick you up at the quarry in ten minutes."

"What about Harold?"

"Who the hell is Harold?"

Buckner nodded at the dog curled at his feet. He looked like a hound mix, but I hadn't paid him any mind until that very moment. "How long has he been there?"

"This whole time."

"He's quiet as a mouse."

"He's a good boy, but he's got anxiety and won't do well here on his own."

"Anxiety?"

"It's like when you're nervous all the time—"

"I know what the fuck it is, son. I've just never heard of any dog actually being diagnosed."

"They get diagnosed for it all the time. Dogs can get anxiety real bad."

I looked at Buckner and sighed. Knew I didn't have a choice but to take his weird little dog with me.

"Fine," I said.

"Mom?"

"What?"

"I'm sorry. I'm sorry for letting you down again."

I turned and started to make my way up the stairs.

"The one you're letting down the most is yourself, Buckner. That's always been the case and I hope the day comes you finally figure that part out."

lucy

Lucy was slightly less disoriented the second time she woke in the workshop and was able to catalog the events of the previous twenty-four hours as they returned to her.

Buckner had missed his own party and was drinking again. Jewell had also missed the party, but that paled in comparison with the fact that she had set the river on fire and was now holding Lucy hostage as an eyewitness. Her mother had been proven right about Buckner, and all the money was gone. Jewell had wasted her buyout on cards and Lucy had flushed hers on Buckner and while both bets were long shots, it struck her now that her sister's play had held considerably better odds.

She had tried to do the right thing, like always. She wanted to save the land and save her brother and to find a way to make the end of her daddy's life less painful. She wanted to make everything better for everybody, but all it got her was exactly where she was.

Briefly, she considered a dash for home. The problem there was she didn't think she could dash anywhere, and the cops would likely be circling to see if she'd seen anything at the park the night before.

She was so angry at Jewell she couldn't see straight, but that didn't mean she wanted her in prison. She decided the thing to do was steal a quick visit with her daddy and see if he had any thoughts on the matter.

Every movement she made toward the house was painful and

laborious. Her head still hurt in two separate places and the sun was so ridiculously bright that she actually whimpered when she faced it. She made her slow way forward, though. She squinted her good eye against the light and hobbled to the house. She pushed the screen door open and her daddy called out right away.

"Is that Lucy?"

"Dad?"

"I'm back here," he said. "In the bedroom."

She moved slowly through the living room and down the hall, then paused at her parents' bedroom door.

"Daddy," she said. "Please, don't freak out when you see me. It looks worse than it is."

"I won't."

"Promise?"

"Honey, there's not much in the world left that can startle me and even if there was, I'm half blind and unlikely to notice."

She stepped inside and while he didn't gasp or shriek, she could see the concern wash over him and that hurt almost as much as everything else.

"Oh, sweetie," he said, and patted the bed beside him.

She crawled in next to him and he handed her a pillow he'd had propped up against his side.

Her parents slept in a queen with a white, wrought-iron frame, and he was so thin and frail inside his pile of blankets that she thought he might disappear altogether.

"What are you up to in here?" she asked.

"Just looking out my window."

He nodded at the far wall where a single-paned window was open to the screen. There was a bit of air drifting over, and she could hear the chickadees and the rattle of a squirrel across a tree branch.

"It's nice," she said.

"I like it best in the afternoon. See how the light comes in through the skinny birch?"

She did see it, the long slants between the leaves and the way they dappled the grass with shadow.

Her father coughed, and she hated the dry sound—like a bundle of twigs being snapped—and the way his whole body rattled from the force of it. She put her hand to his chest and held it there, asked if he wanted some water. He waved her off, let the cough subside on its own, and went on.

"Mom asked me to talk with you about something," he said. "It's something we both decided, but she thought it would be better coming from me."

"Is everything okay?"

"Hell no, everything isn't okay, but this particular thing isn't bad in and of itself. You won't like it, but it's just something we feel needs to happen. We feel like you and Jewell should go to the cabin and lay low for the night is all."

"The cabin?"

"That's right."

"Why?"

"Just as a precaution."

"I can understand Jewell," she said. "But I haven't done anything wrong, Daddy. And I'm tired as hell."

"I know you are, and I'd like nothing more than for you to stay at the house to rest up—"

"Good," said Lucy. "Sounds like a plan."

"The problem is if the cops get a warrant and come up here sniffing around. The problem is them finding you here, the park ranger, all beat to shit. It's going to make for some uncomfortable conversations."

"And what if I say no?"

"We can't force you. All I'm doing is asking. I think it's best for you and for Jewell and I can also say that I would consider it a favor."

His tone was pleading and kind and it was clear that this was not just something her mother wanted. He was worried and he was asking her for help and that was the end of the discussion as far as she was concerned.

"Okay, Daddy."

"Yeah?"

"Yes," she said. "Of course."

Her hand was still on his chest and he put his own hand there over hers.

"Thank you," he said. "And look on the bright side, at least you won't have to sit here and watch the Tigers."

"Oh my God, Daddy, they are not that bad."

"Oh yes they are. It's the bullpen, but what I've been thinking is that if it's always the bullpen, then maybe it isn't the bullpen at all. Maybe it's the owner that never seems to care enough to try and fix the bullpen."

"What happened last night?"

"We lost nine to nothing, but it wasn't as close as the score indicated."

"How are you feeling, otherwise?"

Here he offered her a thin smile. "I feel like you look."

"That bad?"

"Worse, but I try not to let it bother me."

"You try not to let having cancer bother you?"

"Correct."

"How's that going?"

"Better than you'd think, actually."

"You don't have to put on a brave face with me, Daddy. You know that, right?"

"I'm not doing it for you," he said. "I'm doing it for myself."

He leaned away from her then, toward his nightstand. Slid the drawer open and groaned as he turned back to face her and held up a flask. Not any flask—Germain's flask. The Sawbrooks' most prized heirloom.

"I haven't seen that in years," she said.

"Your mother gave it to me when I got sick. Said it would give me strength and to keep it by the bed."

The flask was genuine silver with a working compass secured in an inset in the bottle's center. There were bears and beavers and wolves engraved on the edges and the story was that Germain had always sailed with it stashed in a pocket and filled with the family 'shine. The story was he used the compass to navigate because it was the only one he truly trusted.

"Does it give you strength?"

"If you go in the kitchen and fill it with some rum it will."

"Daddy, no."

"I'm not saying whiskey," he said. "I'm saying rum. Just something sweet and warm to sip on. It helps me sleep."

She sighed, but she would not be the one to deny her daddy a bottle of rum. Not today, anyway.

She pulled herself up off the bed and then made her way to the kitchen where she found some Golden Cane on the counter. It was gutter rum, but her father claimed to prefer it to the pricier brands he'd never even tasted.

She filled the flask and then held it up in a splash of light through the kitchen window. The compass sprang quickly to life and pointed east. She could see the engravings more clearly in the light—the careful work around the beaver tails and the wolves with their heads tilted back to howl.

They used to fight over the flask as kids and every Easter their mom would hide it with the eggs as the ultimate prize. Whoever found the flask got the biggest chocolate rabbit and got to keep the flask in their bedroom until the following year.

It had been a trophy, but now it felt like she was holding the weight of history in her hand. The flask was the Sawbrook family itself—all its mythology and loss and foolish, heartbreaking pride. It was a bottle full of rum to provide the thinnest veil of comfort to her dying father and she felt saddened and embarrassed by it all.

"Hurry up," he called. "I'm dying."

Her father had been joking about dying nearly as long as he'd been sick, but she'd never found it funny.

buckner

Buckner did not want to be out on the road in his plain face, so he put on a trucker's hat, pulled the lid down low, and slid on his wraparound shades. The hat was black with a dark, mesh back. The writing on the front was heavily shaded and difficult to discern, but he believed it said HERKY JERKY. Whatever that meant.

His mother looked at him and shook her head. "Where'd you get that idiotic hat?"

Buckner had no idea where the hat had come from, or the shades for that matter. He probably got them both from a gas station in a blackout. He shrugged and his mother half rolled her eyes and told him to hurry.

"Yes, ma'am," he said.

Buckner loved to ride a four-wheeler. It was good, honest fun, and he took off from home and left Wentworth Road for the two-tracks just as quick as he could. The trails were abundant in the north county and he could ride them clear to the quarry.

He was closer to still drunk than hungover. There'd been some question in his mind about that earlier, but out in the sun and air it was no longer up for debate. In many ways, this was good. He'd been buoyed by his mother's visit and now there was this little leftover buzz from the night before—it was like a warm pocket of air inside a chilly spring breeze—and he savored it atop the four-wheeler and rode the trail hard. Seventy miles an hour on a narrow path and the tall pines around him all blurred into a single emerald smear in the sun.

He'd given Rhoda a little gallon tank of gas he kept around the house. The plan was to set the vehicle on fire, which would be fun and not unwise, but there was part of Buckner that wondered if maybe he wouldn't be just as well served to drive the four-wheeler off the edge of the quarry. Let it tumble to its death below.

This seemed to be how Hollywood might handle it, and he had always wondered, and maybe even believed, that he would have made a helluva stuntman for the movies.

The one problem would be knowing when to make the leap. If you waited too long, well, that was a problem for obvious reasons, and if you jumped too soon then the four-wheeler would be hung up on the edge and you would have tossed yourself off a moving vehicle for nothing, which would be embarrassing.

In the end, it was best to set the thing on fire and stay in his mother's good graces. She'd made the plan and he needed to follow it precisely, lest she begin to doubt him more than she already did.

About half a mile from the quarry, he noticed something behind him. A white SUV. Not the police, but something. It was right there in the rearview, and gaining.

He was nearing the trailhead that would dump him into the quarry, then he'd be out in the air with about a hundred yards between himself and the line where the earth would crater.

He was almost there, but this vehicle was becoming an issue. It was right up on his back now, close enough that Buckner could see it was some snot-nosed kids playing chicken. The path was far too narrow to swerve to lose them, so he buried the gas as he neared the splash of light at trail's end.

Kids these days. It was more than just a saying, because they had clearly lost their way in the world. Why did they feel the need to harass a perfect stranger like this? From where did such a dark impulse arise?

Yes, he was an alcoholic and a criminal, but they didn't know that. Buckner might have been a law-abiding citizen who volunteered his free time to worthy causes and organizations and here they were trying to run him headlong into some pine trees. It angered him, is what it did, and he decided right then and there to teach them a lesson. It was up to them if they learned from it, of course. He couldn't be responsible for what they took away from the experience, but he was going to give them something to consider.

He caught air off the trailhead. The sun was bright in the open and even with his shades he lost a wide swath of his vision in the glare. He could see the side of his mother's Oldsmobile, though, and the warning signs that announced the approaching pit.

The kids were on his left now. Surely from the resort and probably in their daddy's vehicle. He likely paid their insurance, too. They were shouting and laughing and having a high old time and now Buckner would not be able to park the four-wheeler and calmly set it on fire, as had been the plan. Not in this day and age. The second he went for the gasoline they'd start filming.

Earlier, he thought he might like to launch the vehicle into the quarry, but now that he was being forced into the matter it felt onerous, like a chore. These little fuckers ruined everything. It was the hubris of it—running him into a chasm in the earth, just because they could.

It was nearly here. Buckner sharpened his focus and somehow through the dust and the dirt he could see the exact spot where the earth fell open, or at least he thought he could. The warning signs had grown larger and more exclamatory and the ground beneath him was softening and he kept his foot on the gas until the moment he felt the front tires lose touch with the gravel and he did not jump off the four-wheeler so much as he released his grip, leaned hard to the side, and fell.

He did not drop for long. The ground came up hard and fast and he hit it unbraced and skipped across the gravel like a stone on still water. He could hear the SUV's screeching tires as he dragged against the hard ground and finally skidded to a long, painful stop.

He tried to go from the ground to a flat sprint but stumbled and fell. There was a terrible ringing sound and it ran on a rail between the base of each of his ear canals. Finally, he set his feet beneath him and used his right arm to steady himself and stood. Then he ran.

He'd lost his shades and couldn't see through the dirt caked into his eyes, but his mother must have rolled down the windows because he could hear Harold barking and he moved toward the sound of the good boy's voice.

He reached out with his hands and when he felt the hard thump of the back door against his body he let himself fall forward through the open window and his mother gassed it while he crawled toward his dog—his feet still behind him and bicycling the air.

jewell

Out on the property, the sisters were standing on the front porch of Mabel's house. There was a rucksack at Jewell's feet and a nine-millimeter tucked in the hip of her jeans.

Jewell had showered and had her hair pulled back in a ponytail. She was wearing a black T-shirt and shades and she was as skinny as ever—all knobby knees and elbows as she handed Lucy one of their father's gummies.

Lucy chewed tentatively at first but was able to manage and washed the gummy down with a small gulp of water from Jewell's canteen.

"I washed yours out, too," said Jewell. "It's on the kitchen counter. I'll snag it for you here in a minute. We should probably head out."

Lucy handed back the canteen. "You know this is ridiculous, right? Hauling me to the cabin like this."

"I know it's a pain, but I think it's a good idea."

"It might be a good idea for you, but I'm not the one who set a boat on fire."

"I need to tell you something else, and if you still don't think the cabin is necessary after that, I'm fine with you staying here."

"There's something you haven't told me?"

"I'm afraid there is."

"Why am I not surprised?"

Jewell looked at her sister. Van's death was such a strange thing to consider, let alone say out loud. It didn't seem real yet, and maybe it never would. In some ways, that strangeness was what allowed her to say it at all—because it was still a surprise to her, it felt less like a confession.

"Van is dead."

"What?"

"Van," said Jewell. "He died."

"What do you mean, he died?"

"Apparently, he was on the boat when I burned it."

"What do you mean, apparently?"

"He was on the boat," said Jewell. "It is apparent."

"He died in the fire?"

"Actually, he committed suicide and then I burned the body unknowingly. So it's gone from an arson to a potential murder situation."

"A murder situation?"

"Yes."

"Murders aren't situations, Jewell. They're fucking murders."

"I didn't kill him, though. It just looks like I might have. I'm actually a victim here, in a way."

"So he got drunk and passed out and you set the boat on fire with him inside, but didn't know it?"

"No, he killed himself. He's trying to get the insurance money for Franklin so he set me up to make it look like a murder. Insurance doesn't pay on suicide."

"How do you know that's what happened?"

"Because he apologized for it."

"For what?"

"For everything. For stiffing me on the money and setting me up. He sent a note up here this morning with the Shipley boy."

"Where's the note?"

"Dad has it."

"Dad knows?"

"Dad is the one that figured it out."

"Why didn't he tell me?"

"I don't know," she said. "He probably thought you knew."

"I would have said something to him if I knew! I wouldn't have just not mentioned a fucking murder!"

"There again, that's just not how I prefer to frame it."

"He has to keep that note. To show the cops. That's evidence."

"I wish it were, but it just says *I'M SORRY.*"

"*I'm sorry?*"

"Yes. All caps."

"It's his handwriting, though, right?"

"He printed it."

"Am I imagining this? This feels a little like the dream I had about Buckner. Is there something more than usual to those gummies?"

"Sadly, there is not. This is real."

Lucy looked at her sister. Considered everything she'd just been told.

"Fuck!"

"I'm sorry, Lucy. I truly am."

"Sorry for what, Jewell? Killing Van Hargraves or making me an accessory to the murder?"

"There hasn't been a murder, there's been an accident."

"Most would call it arson, not an accident."

"You're not an accessory, either. You've got nothing to do with it."

"I do now! Now that you've told me!"

144

"That doesn't make you an accessory, does it?"

"Of course it does! That's exactly what it does!"

"How are people supposed to keep track of all this shit?" said Jewell. "About what's legal and what isn't?"

"Normal people don't have to. Normal people just hear about a murder and call the police."

"It's not a murder, though. I really don't mean to keep repeating that, but I do think it's important to remind you."

"That's why Daddy didn't tell me. At least that makes sense, I guess."

"I need to thank you for grabbing the ruck last night," said Jewell. "You saved my ass on that one."

"You are not welcome."

Lucy looked like she might scream again, or punch Jewell in the face. It was the same way she'd looked at her the night before, hung up on the river branches.

Lucy might have been the virtuous one, but she could also be violent. She'd punched Jewell more than a few times when they were children, and it was always a forceful blow delivered in an act of rage. Jewell was still afraid of her big sister in that way—maybe even more afraid than when they were kids. Just look at what she'd done to Buckner.

Jewell did not want to be punched, so she walked inside to fetch Lucy's canteen and filled it at the sink. Best to give her some space to cool off and some time to remember her more compassionate, sisterly impulses. Lucy was a hothead, but she was also protective.

In middle school, she punched Denise Garmond in the nose for calling Jewell a slut. Caught her in the hall after second period and knocked her clean off her feet. There was blood everywhere and while Denise writhed on the floor Lucy ripped off the cutout of John

Cena that Denise kept taped to her locker, wadded it into a ball, and dropped it on top of her. Everybody that had gathered around went, *Ooooooooohhh.*

Denise hadn't meant anything by calling Jewell a slut. They were friendly and tossed insults around affectionately in bio lab, but Lucy didn't know that and Jewell had always appreciated the gesture. Now she returned to the porch and handed Lucy her canteen.

"Water is all fine and good," said Lucy, and looped the canteen around her shoulder. "But what I'm really going to need is another round of those gummies."

Jewell patted her front pants pockets, then dug out two gummies and held them in her palm. "You want yellow or red?"

"I don't give a shit."

"Really? You're usually picky on the colors. Like how you don't like red Skittles."

"Why don't you give me both, then? I'll taste the fucking rainbow, I guess."

"Say no more."

Jewell dropped the gummies in her sister's hand, but Lucy didn't pop them quite yet. Lucy paused before she brought them to her mouth.

"What is it?" asked Jewell.

"Mom's not going for the boat. Eventually, she will. But not right away."

"What are you talking about?"

"She'll get Buck first."

"Why would she do that?"

"Because she can't have him on the loose. No more than I can be. Not after last night at the park. There were three witnesses, besides me, that saw him shit-faced around the time of the fire."

Lucy held up three fingers.

"D-Rod. Ray Tomshaw. Tammy Sharp."

"Shit," said Jewell.

"That's what I'm saying."

Lucy tossed in the gummies and then turned and walked down the porch steps. There was a long, gradual slope that led to Ellerbee Creek, where they would begin to move west toward the cabin. Jewell hurried after.

"What do we do about Ray and Tammy?"

"We don't do anything. The cops will talk to them and then go look for Buckner. As long as Mom gets there in time, it'll be fine. Aren't you supposed to be the one that figures this shit out?"

"I'm a card player, not a criminal."

"Right up until last night."

"Exactly," said Jewell. "This is all new to me."

They walked at a good, steady clip. Jewell's knee was deeply bruised and plenty stiff, but the twinge she felt with every step was nothing compared with the fear of getting caught. She had no choice but to move forward, so that was what she did.

Ellerbee Creek was named after Mabel's stillborn daughter, and they would follow it for a mile before they turned off and started to move uphill into the denser forest. This first part of the walk was the gentlest, but they were still shoving through a fair amount of brush and Lucy cursed the burrs and thorns.

"Good thing we didn't cut a trail," she said. "We got trails going everywhere on this property, but no sense in getting crazy and adding one more."

Jewell didn't know if her sister expected a response or if the statement was rhetorical. Lucy could be tricky that way. She might have wanted Jewell to commiserate or she might have actually not known why they hadn't cut the trail in. The second seemed unlikely, but Jewell couldn't be sure. Her sister was more difficult to read than any poker player she'd ever sat across from, and she supposed the problem was that she knew Lucy too well. When she looked at Lucy, she mostly saw her own feelings about her—all her fear and admiration.

She decided to answer, primarily because it was a long walk and there was nothing else to do.

"The whole purpose of the cabin is to hide things, so—"

"I know the rationale, Jewell. I'm saying it's stupid."

"It doesn't seem so stupid to me, being that it's the one place I can go to get off the board."

"Would you listen to yourself?"

"Is there a problem with the way I talk now?"

"'Off the board,'" scoffed Lucy. "You sound exactly like Mom."

"I'm just telling you the truth. I'm just telling you how I feel."

"There's no need to start telling the truth now. I'd say it's a little late for all that, Jewell."

Jewell pushed through a sprawl of ferns to draw even with Lucy, then stomped ahead a few more paces before she stopped and swung around to face her sister.

"I'm telling you the truth about Van. I had no idea he was going to be on the boat."

"Congratulations, you got played."

"I did get played. I won't argue it."

"Well, screw him, too," said Lucy.

Now Jewell was caught off guard. She'd been expecting further escalation, not this note of solidarity. She wasn't sure exactly how to proceed but settled on a thank-you.

"I appreciate you saying that."

Lucy took a long, deep breath. "I don't want you to go to prison, Jewell. I wouldn't be out here walking if I did."

Jewell felt like they might have arrived at a momentary cease-fire, at least that was her hope, but just as she was about to offer a final, conciliatory note, Lucy cut her off.

"Which kind of makes me even angrier about you not showing up for Buckner's party. I mean, how difficult is it, Jewell, to just do the bare minimum?"

Now it was Jewell's turn for a long, deep breath. "I told you I was sorry about that. And I am. But it wasn't deliberate. It wasn't about doing or not doing the bare minimum. I just got my days mixed up."

"I know you think that makes it better, but it really doesn't. Not to me, anyway."

"What do you want me to do? I've already apologized twice. I'm very aware that I've made my share of mistakes, Lucy. Don't think I don't know that."

"You and Buckner both. Certainly Rhoda, too."

"But not you and Daddy, right? You two are perfect."

"I'm not perfect and neither is he. But there's a difference between not being perfect and lying and stealing and burning the fucking river down."

"In Mama's eyes, you were the one burning down the river, Luce."

"What about in your eyes?"

"I don't know," said Jewell. "I honestly don't."

"That didn't stop you from selling, though, did it?"

"I only sold because I thought I was going to buy it right back."

"But why did you think that? That was never part of the deal."

"Because I thought I was going to win a million dollars in Las Vegas. That's why."

"You were that sure you were going to win?"

"Why wouldn't I be? In the long run, I always win."

"That's another thing I don't understand. Isn't this part of the long run right now? Shouldn't this be factored into the ledger?"

"It's a low point," said Jewell. "Not the destination."

"From where I sit, that sounds an awful lot like a justification. Like a lie you're telling yourself to try and feel better."

"Maybe so, but I can't help what I believe."

"But that's not true, either. You can help what you believe, Jewell. That's, like, the definition of what a belief is. It's something you choose, isn't it?"

"It's not something I choose, it's something I feel. Maybe that's the difference between us."

"Or maybe it's all just bullshit."

"So you think that everything I believe is bullshit, and everything you believe is a smart decision—is that what it boils down to?"

"I don't know," said Lucy. "Maybe I do."

"Do you have any idea how arrogant that is?"

"Kind of, but it doesn't feel like arrogance because I just honestly think I'm right."

"That's a closed loop if I've ever heard one."

"Closed loop?" said Lucy. "Now you're just saying words."

"This is already a tough walk. Maybe we should do our best not to make it even worse."

"You're the one doing most of the talking, not me."

Jewell turned around and put her back to her sister. Began to push ahead.

"Not anymore," she said.

rhoda

I 'm not much for idle hope, but for a moment I did indulge the possibility of a sudden and unexpected end to our troubles. I saw those resort dipshits fly toward the quarry and for a second I thought they might go ahead and launch themselves to a fiery death below. It was a Hail Mary, but if it landed, we might find a way to pin the boat fire on them and walk away from the whole mess unscathed.

Instead they pulled up short and the only explosion in the rearview was the tidy one left by Buckner's four-wheeler—a muffled burst and then a churn of coal-black smoke.

Buckner's endurance has always been for shit, but he's fast in short bursts and he sprinted through that dust cloud in the quarry and leapt into the backseat and we were gone. We flew down Wentworth Road and when it was clear the rich boys had lost their interest in high-speed pursuit, I pulled over so Buckner and Harold could get into the trunk.

"I thought you were taking me to the cabin."

"I am, but there's a highway between here and there and I expect they'll have traffic stops set up before much longer. I'm surprised they weren't out already, to be honest with you."

"Where's the truck?"

"At the property," I said. "I'm trying to keep a low profile while I can."

"I haven't seen the Oldsmobile in a long time."

"It was in the pole barn, gathering dust. You have anything else you'd like to discuss?"

"I guess I'm just wondering if it's really necessary to get in the trunk."

"It might not be. But there again, who can say? You feel that strongly about sitting out in the air, it's not my ass that was coyote-drunk at the scene of a boat burning last night."

I saw him take that in and nod as if I had just revealed some sort of startling twist to the plot. He is, without a doubt, the slowest of my three children, but that is also why his heart stays light. He just doesn't understand all the shit he should be worried about. It's true what they say about ignorance—it is oftentimes a blessing.

"Fine," he said. "Me and Harold will get in the trunk."

I told him that was probably the right decision, and reached down to pull the latch.

Once I dumped Buckner, the man to see about a boat would be Delray Harper. I don't think much of Delray and his house of ill repute, but he could be trusted on sensitive matters and I knew for a fact that he had at least two boats these days—maybe a third now that his ridiculous barn was all the rage.

It wouldn't be cheap, but he'd cut me a deal and get me outfitted quicker than any other way I could manage. The only thing that mattered now was getting Jewell out.

I was right about the traffic stops. They popped up as soon as we hit the highway and ground everything to a halt. They had us penned in like cattle and it seemed likely we were going to be stuck there awhile—two lanes at a standstill and the sheriff's department running everything.

The deputy in our lane was Rick Pico. Yeah, he had a girl with Connie Becker, but that was neither here nor there in my view. Generally speaking there is not a single identifiable difference that I've been able to locate between one Cutler County deputy and another. They're all just a bunch of has-beens that never were. Angry men with severe haircuts and little peckers. Or so I've been told.

There have been some good sheriffs in this county, men who could be reasoned with, but they have always surrounded themselves with the sort of sycophants who love nothing more than to stand at a traffic stop all day, peering into vehicles. Scaring people shitless and acting like they're some sort of detective on the television and not just a bunch of flunkies who went into county law when they couldn't hack it with the state.

I rolled forward, but slowly. There were cars pulled out on each side for full searches, which meant they were probably plucking one of every fifty from the line and tagging anybody else that seemed suspicious.

If nothing else, they figured they'd snag some other charges for their efforts—find a stray little cocaine baggie to ruin somebody's summer over.

Buckner and that goddamn Harold. I know he probably loved that mutt and he seemed like a good and decent dog, but what was this about anxiety? Could he be trusted to sit quiet for these next long minutes?

Were we going to get busted because Buckner adopted an emotionally fragile dog? Or was the dog emotionally fragile because he loved Buckner, and who could blame him if he was? It was the sort of idiocy I'd spend the rest of my life wondering over if this stop went the wrong way, and I made a note to myself to keep my hands light on the wheel—the last thing I needed to show Pico or anybody else was a raised set of white knuckles.

I should have set the boat on fire myself. If Jewell got caught and went to prison, we were through. We'd have to sell the land to get a lawyer who couldn't actually win but might save her from the very worst of the sentencing parameters.

We would lose it all and I would spend the last days of my life holed up in some apartment. My husband dead, Jewell in the penitentiary, and our land being stripped and bulldozed. My entire life and its purpose an abject failure.

If I'd set the fire, at least the land would go on to Jewell and I could tell them to let me have a state's attorney and tell the judge to do his worst.

It would be a nightmare, of course. I was under no illusions about that. I've always feared prison, almost as much as I feared losing the land. All those miles of concrete walls and dead air—it was enough to make me shiver.

I'd miss the winters most. That might surprise people, but it's true. The winter is dark and cold and the farmhouse gets drafty, but that makes for great fires over long mornings. You can sit and sip coffee and watch the snow fall and stack itself on the pine boughs and never pass a day in your life so peacefully.

In the winter, the clouds hang low and sit as dark as river clay. There's days you don't see the sun at all, but when the sky does break, the light hits the snow and ice and everything is crystalline and cold and bright to the core.

It is my favorite season, though the others are not far from it. The springs are short, but the lilacs always bloom in the field where my family rests and in the autumn the birch leaves there turn red-orange and spread around the pines like fire.

In the summer the sun might not set until a quarter to ten and you can live two days inside of one. I like to get up early to tend to the gardens and then take a nap after lunch and go out again with the chain saw and a wheelbarrow and fell one of the trees we'll burn for heat.

And then back to winter, when I like to sip my coffee and remember that day in July—the warmth and the wildflowers and how green the grass looks in the light. The explosion of dirt and dust when the tree drops and the dribble of the creek where it eases through the field.

On the land, each day connects to something larger than itself and the years stitch themselves together in ways that hold and feel solid beneath you. Take that away from me, and I can't tell you who I am. I wouldn't even know my name.

I was one car from the front now. Pico leaning in and haranguing some poor woman in a Ford Taurus about where she was going and what she was doing as I tried to level my breath.

I was nervous, but mostly I was angry. Angry at the hassle and the delay and the fact that Jewell was the one on the lam while men like Van Hargraves got to play the victim. Angry at Buckner, too, and Lucy. Angry at Edward for being sick and angry at myself for any number of mistakes—not the least of which was allowing Buckner to bring a neurotic dog that I just knew was going to start yelping at any moment and ruin all our lives forever.

The Taurus was finally released and I eased forward. Pico. I hated that man and I hated his face. The small, sparse mustache and the big wraparound shades. The domineering smirk. The way he motioned for me to roll down my window—like I was a bother to him for being there to begin with. Like I had the audacity to want my window up. The way he said my name, too.

Well, good morning, Rhoda, like I was supposed to be happy to see him. Like he didn't set my skin to crawl just by standing there.

"Where you headed this fine day?"

"Alpena," I said.

"What in the world for?"

"Edward's gummies."

"Why all the way to Alpena? They got that new dispensary in Gaylord, don't they?"

"I called Gaylord, but they don't have the kind he likes right now. I've learned to call ahead and check on the stock."

"What kind does he like?"

"Tropical Twist."

"What is it about the Tropical Twist he prefers, Rhoda?"

"I don't know, Rick. I guess they do a better job of helping him forget that he's dying."

Rick shot a glance over the hood of my car. I thought he might be signaling another deputy for help. I thought I was about to get tossed, but he just looked back at me and shook his head.

"I'm sorry, Rhoda. I forgot Edward was sick. Cancer killed my grandmother and it took its time, too. It was slow and mean and I hated every second of it."

"It's a rough go, Deputy. I won't deny it."

"I got a bumper sticker," he said. "One of those that says, F CANCER."

I told him I'd seen one of the stickers in traffic the other day. I told him that it gave me a little comfort to know somebody else out there was battling the same thing I was.

That was a lie. I'd never seen one of those stickers a day in my life, and the whole thing sounded ridiculous to me, but I could imagine the sentiment such a thing might provoke in those who are moved by trivialities like bumper stickers and cross-stitched poetry.

"You ought to get one," he said. "I enjoy mine."

"Maybe I will."

"I found mine on the internet."

"Did you?"

"That's where everything is these days."

"I'll tell Edward to give it a look, then. He's the one online."

I thought I might be off the hook altogether, but Rick held up a finger.

"Before I let you go, Rhoda, I'm curious if you saw anything suspicious over the last few days on the river. It's related to the fire."

"I saw the fire, but the only suspicious thing I've seen around here is that resort. They got a million people smushed in them condos and it would stand to reason one of them could be a firebug."

"You're saying a resorter did it?"

"I'm just telling you what I think."

"They're not all bad, you know," Rick said. "Some of them are pretty good people, I've found. We've got to get along in the world, Rhoda."

"I'll keep that in mind."

He smiled at me and gave the roof of the Olds a few friendly taps. Told me to call it in if I saw or heard anything suspicious and to take care of myself and Edward.

"I'll pray for you both," he said, and motioned me forward.

I didn't want his prayers, but I thanked him anyway and put the car in drive.

lucy

L ucy hadn't walked to the cabin since she was a teenager, but it was just as difficult as she remembered. There were the scrapes and the constant incline, the strangler vines and the mud and the gnarled tree roots that seemed to snatch at her ankles with every step.

But there was beauty, too. Almost impossible beauty that not even her blurred vision could conceal—meandering streams and vistas where the trees cleared suddenly to reveal lush fields all ripped through with blazing star.

She didn't know if she'd ever seen the wildflower in such quantity or brightness of bloom, and there were slants of light through the trees where she could see the asters and the butterflies floating in pollen mist.

There was the deep sound, too. It seemed like quiet on the surface, but it was birdsong and water on unbothered rock beds. It was wind-rustled leaves and the faraway scurry of some busy woodland creature, and it all sewed itself together in a pitch-perfect hum.

How anybody could look at this land and see stagnation and a barrier to progress was beyond her ability to comprehend. How anybody could want to change it defied understanding, just like it defied understanding that her mother would risk losing it all to keep it only for herself.

"So you're going to Canada after this?" she asked. "Is that the plan?"

"The plan is not going to prison," said Jewell.

"By way of Canada?"

"Correct."

"Like, where in Canada, though? And what happens when you get there? Are we just going to drop you off somewhere and then you write us postcards like it's summer camp? Tell us about all the friends you're making and the adventures you're having as a fugitive? Are you going to dye your hair in a public restroom, like they do in the movies? Will you change your name? How does this actually work?"

"I don't know how it works, Lucy. I've never done it before."

"Has Mom?"

"I don't know."

"'Cause you just seem to be going along with it, and now I'm wondering if maybe we're just making everything worse. I'm wondering if maybe the best thing would be to call the police and come clean."

"I know you're not serious about that."

"Actually, I might be," said Lucy. "I mean, he asked you to do it, didn't he?"

"And who is going to believe that?"

"I don't know, Jewell, but I do know that everything you're doing right now is going to make it worse if you get caught."

"I'm not going to get caught. That's the whole point."

"Because Sawbrooks don't get caught? Is that the idea?"

"It's not an idea, it's a fact. Not one of our name has ever done a day in jail."

"Or suffered a water death."

"Exactly," said Jewell. "Though you came close last night."

"But here's the thing. Mabel didn't go to prison, but she did have

159

to live her entire life right here, on this property, and Germain was, what, thirty years old when they gunned him down?"

"What's your point?"

"My point is there's more than one way to end up in prison."

"Honestly, if I wound up here forever, like Mabel, I'd probably be okay with it. I mean, there could be worse things."

"That's really sad, Jewell."

"Why do you keep saying my name?"

"What do you mean?"

"You keep saying my name. Like, I know you're talking to me. We're the only two people out here."

"I don't know," said Lucy. "I think I'm pretty stoned, actually. I'm sorry."

"You don't have to apologize. I was just making an observation. It was just something I noticed."

"You know what I've noticed?"

"I can only imagine."

"Health insurance. Every time I see Daddy I think about how much better things would be if he had just the slightest bit of help. Even just to take the edge off the pain. I've had insurance for three years now, since I started with the state, and I've got to tell you, Jewell, there's some real upside to it."

"There you go again, calling me by name."

"Not just health insurance, either," Lucy went on. "I've got a membership at a gym and a library card and it's all really kind of nice."

"We've always had library cards. Did you just happen to forget your entire childhood? Mom was just there the other day checking out some books for Daddy."

"Mom loves the library because it's free."

"So what?"

"So she just picks and chooses the parts of things she wants to believe in."

"I could have left you there to drown," said Jewell. "You were face-down in the mud and would have suffocated."

"Then where would you be?" said Lucy. "You'd have two dead bodies."

"And neither one my fault."

"Oh, it's not your fault you set the boat on fire?"

"It's not my fault Van was inside that boat, and it's not my fault you decided to chase me. And for what? What the hell were you going to do if you caught me? Tase me like you did Buckner?"

"It was just instinct at first. Once I'd been in the river awhile I thought better of it and tried to get out."

"When did you try to get out?"

"After we talked in all that bramble. I was going to pull myself to shore, but the branch I was holding on to snapped."

They were on a sharp incline. Jewell had stopped to let Lucy catch up and now they stood face-to-face, sweat stains on their shirts and dirt smears everywhere. Jewell pulled a blue bandanna from her back pocket, mopped her face, and then tied it off on her head, Rambo-style.

"Is that true? You fell off the branch?"

"Why would I lie about that?"

"I don't know. I guess I just assumed you were chasing me on purpose."

"Not at that point."

"What would you have told the cops, anyway? If it came to it?"

"I would have told them I saw somebody and chased them into the river, but they escaped. I would have stepped aside and let it all play out without me."

"Huh," said Jewell.

"You thought I was going to rat you out?"

"I don't know what I thought. I haven't had much time to think about anything."

The forest had darkened some. There were clouds above the trees and suddenly it felt a little bit like rain. People said that if you didn't like the weather in Michigan to wait five minutes. It was one of those sayings that was almost as annoying as it was true.

They both heard the vehicle at the same time. It was on the low ground to their east. Not close yet, but approaching.

Lucy thought it might be Rhoda with Buckner. There were no sirens and the sound was more Oldsmobile than whatever SUV the state might dispatch in this sort of scenario.

They could hear the chopper, too, and now it occurred to Lucy that they might have been spotted from above. Maybe the chopper had seen them and dispatched some sort of agile, tactical team to run them down. Either way, the instinct was to run.

The sisters did not discuss a plan or exchange a long, knowing glance. They did not hesitate or panic, but simply broke into a sprint toward their favorite childhood cave.

Jewell was out front quickly, though she was slowed enough by her knee that Lucy could keep pace and trail her through the trees. She didn't have to follow Jewell, Lucy knew exactly where they were going, but it did comfort her to keep her sister within sight—even if it was just the blur of her rucksack through the pines.

Actually, it was their mother's ruck. Jewell's was still soaked from the night before and back at the house somewhere. Or maybe she'd buried it, or burned it. Lucy didn't know and didn't like the fact that she was now thinking through the specific machinations of a cover-up.

Jewell was standing at the mouth of the cave and waiting when

Lucy arrived. They both stood there breathing heavily for a moment and listened for the vehicle and chopper.

"You hear anything?"

Lucy was straining to find her breath but shook her head. She couldn't hear anything over her own thumping heart.

The cave was clawed out of a stony rise beneath a stand of birch and Lucy braced herself against the rock wall. They'd spent hours playing inside as kids, and the limestone found her high in the nostrils—a musty-sharp echo of youth itself.

Their mother disliked the cave because she said Aunt Wanda used it for drugs and boys, but their father thought it was romantic, like something out of *Tom Sawyer*. The girls had both read Mark Twain, but Buckner was ten years old before he understood that Tom Sawyer was not an actual person that lived in the cave, and that realization had broken his heart.

They were still a long way from the cabin, but Jewell suggested they wait it out for a bit inside.

"Just until we're sure that chopper is gone."

Lucy didn't even have time to answer. The drone and whir of the chopper blades were back and they were louder and sounded much closer now—like it was flying a Z pattern over the river as it pushed north.

Jewell turned and hurried into the dark and Lucy put a hand against her sister's back and followed closely behind.

The cave was open and airy at first, but it narrowed quickly as it burrowed into the hillside. It was dark and damp, but there were breaks in the stone where light gathered and they could see dirt and vines and dead birch leaves wedged into the gaps. Eventually, the sides grew near enough that Lucy had to angle herself sideways as she trailed her sister, who was cursing the cobwebs.

The tunnel ultimately opened into a pool where the air was cooler and the dark more absolute. The floor around the pool was slick but there was a ledge where the sisters could drop their rucks, and they felt their way there slowly and then sat.

They listened to the water plunk and let their eyes adjust until walls emerged around them and provided some shape to the black.

"Can I ask you one thing?" said Lucy.

"Could I stop you if I tried?"

"Did Mom put you up to it? The fire?"

"Mom had nothing to do with it."

"You don't have to lie to protect her. I'm not going to say anything or do anything about it either way. I'm just curious."

"Van came to me. I'm the one that said yes."

Their voices were tinny against the wet stone walls, and in the dark Lucy trusted her sister's words. She knew she was telling the truth, the same way she knew it when Jewell lied. Jewell might have kept them all guessing at the Soaring Eagle poker tables, but Lucy could read her sister like a book—whether she wanted to or not.

"Well, if you do end up in prison, that trust is going to be the best thing that could have happened."

"Congratulations," said Jewell. "I'm sure that'll be a nice thing to hang over all our heads for the rest of our lives."

"That's not what I mean. I just mean, you don't have to worry about that part of it. You're not losing the land if this thing goes wrong."

"It's already gone wrong. We're hiding in the fucking cave, aren't we?"

"You love this cave."

"Yeah, when the cops aren't involved."

"I'm not sure it was the cops."

"Me either, actually."

"I mean, the chopper was the cops," said Lucy. "For sure."

"Maybe just flying over, though?"

"That's what I'm thinking. Or hoping, I guess."

"Then the car we heard was Mom?"

Lucy nodded, though she was unsure if her sister could see it in the dark. She was furious with Jewell, but there was gratitude, too, and she felt it there in the cave. This limestone would be quarried and squeezed for the slightest pinch of oil if it ever went to market and Jewell had done her part to protect it. Lucy was an idealist but she was also deeply pragmatic. Yes, Jewell had lost the money and set a boat on fire because of it, but none of that mattered to the cave where they were—for the moment, at least—sitting safely together.

Lucy wanted to say something to Jewell about all of it, about how she was not being snarky, or had not meant to be when she brought up the sale. She wanted to make absolutely clear how deeply she appreciated what Jewell had done, but her sister had shifted on the ledge beside her and was laughing quietly to herself.

"What is it?"

"Oh, it's nothing," Jewell said. "I was just thinking about Buckner."

"What about him?"

"Did I ever tell you what he told me once, about Tom Sawyer and what he thought he looked like?"

"No."

"Really?"

"I swear to God, I've never heard it."

"I can't believe I never told you this."

Her disbelief sounded genuine and now Lucy had to know. "What is it? What did he say?"

"It was just out of the blue, one day. Totally random. You know how he is. He just starts talking about the cave and Tom Sawyer and I realized before long that he was describing, and I mean in exact detail, the Lucky Charms leprechaun."

Lucy was building toward a laugh, but it still hurt just to smile, so she fought it off and just squeezed Jewell's shoulder.

"It hurts to laugh, but oh my God, that's incredible."

"It's weird, because Mom never bought the good cereal. I don't know how he knew about Lucky Charms, but I guess he got it from commercials. Either way, it was so sad when he found out the truth, wasn't it? It broke his little heart."

Lucy brushed some loose gravel off the ledge and listened to the soft plinks when they hit the pool of water. Yes, she hadn't been in the cave in years, but in the dark and musty wet everything was familiar and immediate—as if some part of herself had been preserved intact and could only be felt in this particular place. For a moment the world felt solid beneath her and she found it deeply reassuring.

"I used to think we might find some cave paintings back here," she said. "But Sawbrook ones. Like Alfred came back here and painted beaver traps on the walls. Sawbrook hieroglyphics. Trout lines and rum barrels."

"Could you imagine what Grandpa Harvard might have drawn?"

"To be honest, I'd rather not."

Lucy felt Jewell rest her shoulder against her own and they sat together in the quiet. The fear and the urgency outside felt so far away—the whole bright and burning world seemed distant and muted and dull. For a moment Lucy felt like she could stay this way forever, all sealed up inside.

Then a voice from the tunnel.

"Is that Buckner?" she whispered.

Jewell sat up off her shoulder and leaned toward the sound. The voice was drawing closer, and it called out their names. It was Buckner.

"Hey!" shouted Jewell. "We're back here!"

"Well, you got to come out! I can't fit back here any farther."

"How'd you find us?"

Lucy stood and gathered herself while Jewell and Buckner went back and forth.

"Mom saw you two running and said you were probably headed for the cave."

Jewell was already hurrying toward the sound of their brother's voice, her ruck hanging loose in her hands, while Lucy strapped her own bag on her shoulders.

Jewell asked Buckner if their mom had the boat and he said that she did not.

"She's going to get it now. We're supposed to wait it out at the cabin."

Jewell stopped at the entrance to the tunnel and turned back to Lucy.

"We were just back here looking for Tom Sawyer," she said.

"Ha-ha," said Buckner.

"We couldn't find him," said Lucy. "I'm sorry, Buck."

"I was hoping there might be a pot of gold, to boot," added Jewell.

The sisters wedged themselves into the tunnel and Lucy followed closely behind Jewell. The way out was always more difficult—it cut against the grain of the rock—but after a time she could see the broad outline of their brother at the cave's entrance.

"Tom Sawyer has been dead for years," he announced. "You both made sure of that."

"Don't be mad," said Jewell.

"I'm not mad," said Buckner. "But it was mean the way you both teased me over that when we were kids. He was real to me, goddamnit."

"Shit," said Jewell. "We're sorry, Buckner. We were just fucking around."

"Well, fuck around out here in the daylight. We've got a hike to make."

"He's still alive in our hearts," said Jewell. "If it's any consolation."

"It is not," said Buckner.

The sisters finally reached the cave's entrance and Lucy leaned forward and whispered to Jewell just as they were about to step into the light.

"If you can do a halfway decent Irish accent, now would be the time."

part IV

the siblings

The walk ahead of them was still long and mostly uphill, but at least they were together. Jewell was setting the pace in front, while the slower Buckner and Lucy paired off behind her.

Harold was yipping and tail wagging and running short laps between Buckner and Lucy. He'd sniff at Lucy's feet for a while, report back to Buckner with his findings, then repeat the whole process.

"He is a pistol, isn't he?" said Lucy.

"He's a good boy," said Buckner.

"What is he? Lab and pit?"

"With some coonhound in there, too, I believe."

"You could get his DNA tested if you wanted."

"Why would I want to do that?"

"Just to know what he is."

"I just told you what he is."

"They do the percentages and everything," Lucy said. "They map it all out. I think it's kind of interesting."

"He's got anxiety," said Buckner. "I do know that."

"Oh," she said. "Poor thing."

"Even so, he's the best dog ever. Not just my best dog. He's like the best dog in the history of all dogs."

It was late afternoon and the sun was high, but it was not too hot beneath the pines and birches. The trees were tall but skinny and they slalomed through them as they made their way. As much as she would have preferred to keep the focus on Harold, Lucy knew she had to switch gears before they went any farther.

"I need to apologize for something that happened last night, Buck. Something I did."

Suddenly, Jewell began to slow her pace in front. Lucy had nearly forgotten she was there, and would have been a little quieter and more subtle about things had she thought it through. She would have preferred to keep things between her and Buckner, but it was too late now and Jewell was not about to miss whatever happened next. For his part, Buckner looked confused.

"You did something to me?"

Jewell had stopped outright now and turned around to face them both. Lucy tried to stare a hole right through Jewell's forehead and then looked at her brother.

"I did," she said. "I tased you, is what happened."

"You tased me?"

"Yes, I did."

"Last night?"

"It was, and I'm sorry for it. I apologize. Well, I apologize about the third one, at least. The first two were not my fault."

Jewell unscrewed the top of her canteen and took a long, slow drink. Afterward, she wiped the corners of her mouth with a shirtsleeve and whistled. Made a sad trumpet sound, like an incorrect answer had just been offered on a game show.

"Oh, spare me," said Lucy.

"Was it in the back and chest?" asked Buckner.

Lucy nodded.

"Twice in the back, but only because you were charging D-Rod. The third was strictly for myself and I put that one in your chest. You were already incapacitated and that is the one I am sorry for. The first two bolts were in the line of duty. The third is where I may have crossed a line."

"May have crossed a line?" said Jewell. "What the hell is wrong with you, Lucy?"

"I was upset. It's not an excuse, but it's true."

"It's all good," said Buckner.

"It is definitely not 'all good.'"

Jewell dropped air quotes on the last line and while her gall was absolutely maddening to Lucy, she did not take the bait. This was not about Jewell. This was about Buckner.

"Are you sure?" she asked.

Buckner shrugged. "Honestly, I'm relieved. I got these little marks in my chest, they look like fang bites or some shit. So this actually makes sense. It's solved one of the mysteries I've been wondering on today."

"I think if I hadn't put you down, you might have beaten D-Rod to death. You might have woken up in a holding cell."

"You did the right thing, no doubt. And I was having some dark thoughts earlier. When you don't know where an injury comes from, it can be scary. It can be worse than the pain itself."

Jewell groaned and then turned away from them both and retook the hike. Buckner and Lucy followed and for a moment it felt like the matter was settled, but then Buckner went on.

"All day I was sort of wondering if I might have been abducted by aliens or something. You know how they do."

"How *who* does?"

Jewell didn't stop this time or even bother to turn around when Lucy asked the question. If anything, she began to walk more quickly.

"Aliens," he said. "They've run TV specials on it. They got a whole series I saw in rehab on unexplained phenomena. Those little fang bites might have been where the probes went in."

"Alien shows?" said Lucy. "In rehab? Is that what I paid for?"

"We had an hour of free time every night," said Buckner. "I spent mine in the DVD library and those shows were scientifically based. They were not for entertainment."

Buckner said this to Lucy as if it all made perfect sense—as if she would be reassured by the knowledge that he believed the alien movies he watched in rehab were based on "science." She did not know how to respond to such a statement, so she said nothing at all.

They were moving up a rock face now and briefly beyond the cover of the pines. They could see down over treetops that stretched clear across to Ellerbee Creek. The Crow was there, too, in the north—the wide blue push of the water and the faraway patter where it fell onto big rocks and was broken into mist.

The siblings had arrived at a familiar impasse. They had drilled down to the root of Buckner's addiction and found no satisfying answers, or even coherent questions. Buckner's addiction was Tasers and aliens and sudden acts of violence. It lacked meaning and substance and was a terrible, godforsaken bore.

Lucy did not want to talk about it anymore. She didn't want to regret the ten thousand dollars or the party she'd worked so hard on. She also did not want to think about Jewell in prison, or how much farther away the cabin was, or how much trouble she might be in herself. At the moment, the one thing Lucy wanted was a diversion.

"The other thing that happened last night, Buckner," she said, "was that I learned you have a girlfriend."

Jewell turned on a dime to face them both. "Oh my God! How did we make it this far without asking, Luce?"

"He was trying to distract us with the alien business," said Lucy.

Jewell was hiking backward now. She had her hands on the straps of her ruck and smiled at her sister.

"A red herring," she said.

"Oh for Christ's sake," sighed Buckner.

"Don't do that," said Jewell.

"Don't do what?"

"Don't start acting like it's some sort of inconvenience because we're interested in your life. Don't act like it's a hassle to have two sisters who love you and care about you."

"That was more of a general-life-situation sigh," he said. "It's not always about you, Jewell."

"I need to know why you told Jewell about this girl, but not me," Lucy said.

"I didn't tell you because I knew you would press me for more information than I wanted to give. I knew Jewell would be more chill about it."

"That's not fair," said Lucy.

"I don't know if it's fair or not," he said. "But it's definitely true."

"That is true, Luce," said Jewell. "You always have to know every little thing."

They were off the rock face now and walking on a short bit of flat ground. The trees were sparse but they would grow dense again soon and Jewell stopped the procession. They'd been walking steep and fast and it would be good to gather their breath for a moment in the sun.

"I want to know about her name," said Lucy.

"It's Sky," said Buckner.

"I know that. I'm curious how it's spelled."

"It's spelled S-k-y. Like the big blue thing above us."

Lucy smacked Buckner's arm with the back of her hand. "Don't be a smart-ass. I just didn't know if it was, like, some other—"

"Some other sky?" said Jewell.

"Some other spelling," said Lucy, and turned to her sister. "Like if it was a family name and spelled with an *i* or something."

"So, Ski?" Jewell smiled.

"Her name is Sky, after the sky," said Buckner. "It's spelled the normal way and she's the best thing to ever happen to me."

"Oh my God, that's beautiful, Buckner," said Lucy. "Is that really how you feel?"

"It's exactly how I feel."

"We're happy for you, Buck," said Jewell. "All bullshit aside."

Here the sisters exchanged a quick, surprised glance. They'd never heard Buckner say anything remotely approaching what he'd just confessed about Sky and they were entirely unsure how to proceed. Lucy felt like they had to say something, though. They had to keep the momentum rolling.

"Have you met her people yet?" she said.

Buckner toed the dirt beneath him and kept his eyes on Harold, who'd settled at his side.

"Her mom," he said. "And her son, of course."

"Well, quit being weird and introduce us all," said Jewell.

"I just got to figure what to say about Mom first. Once she meets you two the clock will start ticking and we got, like, two weeks max before Rhoda gets her alone somewhere and starts putting the screws to her."

"Just tell her Mom's crazy and get it over with," said Lucy.

"Can we just drop it?" Buckner pleaded.

"Absolutely not," said Lucy. "Are you worried Mom is going to say something about her working at the Barn?"

"Wait," said Jewell. "She works for Delray?"

Buckner looked up from Harold now. Nodded at Jewell. "She's a dancer."

"How did you know that?" said Jewell, and pointed at Lucy.

"Tammy Sharp told me."

Jewell turned back to Buckner. "Why didn't you tell me that?"

"I don't know. There's been a lot of shit going on, Jewell. I can't keep track of it all. But the thing is, the real problem right now, is that something happened to her out there the other night. At the Barn."

"Something happened to Sky?" said Jewell.

"Yeah," said Buckner. "But I don't know what it is because she won't tell me. Neither will Delray. Something went down, though. That's why I got all fucked up to begin with. Actually, that's not true. I got fucked up because I got fucked up. That was my decision and I need to be accountable for that."

"What do you mean, something went down?"

This came from Lucy, who asked the question as gently as she could.

"Delray said somebody put their hands on her, but he wouldn't say who. He's got some goon down there that he says is going to deal with it. He said Sky made him promise not to tell me because she didn't want me doing something stupid. She's laying up at her mama's house right now, but she doesn't want to see me."

"Somebody put their hands on her, meaning what, exactly?"

Jewell did not ask the question gently, and Lucy shot her a murderous glance.

"He just said he doesn't know, Jewell."

"I'm just seeking clarification, Lucy."

Buckner looked at both his sisters.

"Don't fight about this, please. You want to fight about something else, go ahead, but this is off limits. This is my thing and you two can't take it over just to have a fight."

"You used to like it when we fought each other," Lucy said, smiling. "That way we weren't ganging up on you."

"Right," said Jewell. "You used to start half our fights yourself."

"I've matured," he said. "And grown to see the error of my ways."

"While we're all speaking plainly," said Jewell, "I am sorry I missed your party, Buckner. I know you weren't there, either, but I just wanted to say that out loud. I just got the days mixed up is all."

"That's fine," he said. "Looks like we'll get to have another one in six months anyway."

"You can pick right up where you left off," said Jewell. "You got clean once and now you know you can do it."

"It doesn't work exactly like that, but yeah. I'm going to get it right. I've got no choice."

"I've been a wreck myself," Jewell went on. "This Van thing, Las Vegas, and all the land stuff."

"The land stuff?"

Jewell pointed at Lucy. "The thing she's been trying to get us to do."

"Where we give her our land?"

"You don't give it to me," said Lucy. "You get twenty thousand dollars and I put the land into a trust that protects it from the developers. It's a win–win."

"It's a win–nothing, 'cause I won't ever do it and neither will Jewell."

Buckner looked at Jewell in solidarity, but now she was the one staring at the ground beneath her.

"I sold mine three months ago, Buckner. I took the money for my stake in Vegas and lost it all."

"You did what now?"

"I sold it to Lucy."

"What the fuck, Jewell?"

"I'm sorry I didn't tell you."

"I'm sorry you did it at all! Does Mom know?"

Jewell quit staring at the dirt and looked up.

"Hell no, she doesn't know. I was going to win the tournament, buy the land back from Lucy, and pay off the bank before Mom even knew what happened. I was going to be a hero, right up until I went bust and had to get Connie to wire me money for a bus ticket home. Money she had to steal right out of the wallet of one of her baby daddies. I don't know which one, and I'm sure it's far less than he owed her, but that's not the point."

"You sold out."

Jewell took the canteen off her shoulder, but it wasn't to take a drink this time. She just needed something to do with her hands. She slapped the canteen with an open palm and looked her brother in the eye.

"You're right," she said. "I sold out."

"I know I'm right! I don't need you to tell me that. When are you going to tell Mom?"

"She isn't," said Lucy. "And as an aside, she was never going to be able to buy the land back. That's not at all how it works. She keeps saying that, but it's not true. Which she knows."

Jewell groaned and then dropped her head back and stared up at the sky. It was a bit dramatic, but it was how she felt.

"What I know, Lucy, is that if you have the money, there is always a way to get what you want."

"Actually," said Lucy, "there is no amount of money that changes the binding facts of the trust. I told you that and the lawyers told you that. You chose to ignore it, because you needed the comforting illusion that you were not going to break Mom's heart. That's all this is."

"You're telling me that if I went out to Las Vegas and won, I could not have come back here, dropped a big stack of cash on the table, and gotten that little bit of land back?"

"That's exactly what I'm telling you. It's what I've been telling you all along. Which isn't to mention the fact that you don't have any money!"

"I asked you when you're going to tell her!"

Buckner spat the line at Jewell so hard that she flinched.

"Jesus, Buckner," she said.

"It's a simple question."

"Fine," she said. "Lucy is right. I'm not going to tell her at all and just hope she doesn't figure it out."

"She's going to figure it out," said Buckner. "For sure."

"I know that, too," said Jewell.

"Holy shit, she's going to kill you," said Buckner. "She is going to skin you alive, Jewell. This is way worse than me being an alcoholic."

"It's actually not worse. It was the best thing she could have done and it might end up saving all of this." Lucy motioned to the vast expanse of forest around them.

"A lot of good it will do Jewell." Buckner laughed. "When Mom fucking kills her and cooks her on a spit."

"She'll be pissed but she's not going to kill her," said Lucy. "Jewell's her favorite."

"Buck is her favorite," said Jewell. "And it's not even close."

"Her favorite is Lucy," said Buckner. "And you're both too stupid to see it."

Lucy cackled and so did Jewell. Lucy being their mother's favorite was a ridiculous notion.

"She kind of hates Lucy," said Jewell. "You're the favorite, but if it wasn't you, it'd be me by default."

"No, it's Lucy. And that's why she pisses Mom off so much. Because she's the favorite and has the most potential."

"Why does Lucy have the most potential?"

"Are you kidding me?" Buckner said.

"Does it look like I'm kidding?" said Jewell.

"For one," he answered, "she's got a college degree. But even if she didn't, she's the toughest and the smartest of the three of us and it's not even close. Book-smart and people-smart. Look at all that shit she's done with her river club."

"It's not a club," said Lucy. "But thank you."

"How many times did she tase you?" said Jewell. "'Cause your brain seems just about scrambled to me."

"I mean, you have the second most potential. I'm the one in last in that particular category, so I don't know what you're so pissed about."

Jewell laughed again. "Potential, my ass. She went over the falls and almost died."

"You're good at shit like that," said Buckner. "For sure. You're the best swimmer and you can take the falls like nobody's business. It's kind of like how you could do cartwheels when we were kids, but Lucy couldn't. Like, yeah, cartwheels are cool, but what the fuck are you going to do with them? You can't go to any cartwheel college that I know of. I mean, maybe you could be in the circus or something, but Lucy was always reading books or in the woods studying shit. You remember she had those collections, the insects and flowers and all that?"

Lucy was greatly enjoying the conversation and did not want to disrupt the flow but also felt it important to clarify exactly what she had studied. "Butterflies," she said.

Buckner pointed at Lucy. "See. She was learning things. It's nothing to be mad about, it's just the facts."

"Fuck you, Buckner," said Jewell.

"Fuck me is right," he said. "I'm a drunk who can't protect the woman I love. I've been trying to get my shit together so she can quit the Barn, but you can see how that's going."

"Does she want out of the Barn?"

Lucy asked this question a little too quickly, and hopefully, for Buckner's taste.

"Hell yes, she wants out. You think I'm in love with a woman that wants to work for Delray her whole life?"

Lucy held up her hands. "I just meant that I'm sure some of them like it because the money seems good."

"Hell no, she doesn't like it! Nobody likes working anywhere, Lucy, let alone sliding up and down on a pole for a bunch of assholes in a barn that smells like piss. You know one of the girls got shit on the other day while she was dancing? They got birds in the rafters, Lucy, and they hit her with a wet steamer right on the shoulder. She was humiliated and ran off the stage crying."

"The trust could really help her get out from under Delray if—"

"Stop it, Lucy," said Jewell. "Not right now."

Buckner whipped around to face Jewell now. "What is it, Jewell? You get to take the money, but I don't?"

"Yeah," said Lucy. "What's that all about, Jewell?"

Now it was Jewell holding up her hands. "Do what you want," she said. "The both of you."

"Oh, really," Lucy snapped. "I can do what I want? 'Cause I'd really like to head home right about now and take a shower and crawl into bed. That's what I'd like to do."

Jewell gave the front straps of her rucksack a sharp tug. Turned to the side and spit.

"I never should have stopped walking. I thought it would be nice if we stood here for a moment in the sun and talked, but I can see now that I just need to get to the cabin and out of everybody's hair."

Lucy pointed ahead.

"Lead the way, Firebug."

"Fine," said Jewell. "But answer me this. What's police brutality called when it's done by a park ranger?"

Lucy answered the question by flipping Jewell off. Buckner retook his spot between his sisters. They all walked forward, and after a time Buckner looked down at Harold.

"This is what being a Sawbrook is all about, little buddy. You fight with each other all the time about nothing, but at the end of the day that's what makes us so good at fighting everybody else."

Harold barked.

"What I'm saying," said Buckner, "is that it's good to be home."

rhoda

I pulled into the Boogie Down at five thirty in the afternoon and Delray's shitty barn was already half full. Cars parked all mishmash in the clearing that surrounded the bar while music thumped from inside.

I've known Delray Harper my entire life and while I generally consider him a grade A certified piece of freeze-dried shit, I will acknowledge a begrudging respect for his business acumen. The man has more cash than he knows what to do with, and now he's bank-rich on top of it all. I don't approve of what he does, but I do admire the way he hasn't changed to appease his customers.

He keeps the roof patched these days, but otherwise he hasn't spent a red cent on renovations, and the brilliance of it all is that the golfers prefer it that way. They think it's organic and cultural in the way that rich people often find poverty an endearing part of other people's experiences. Edward says the golfers do this thing where they take a picture with Delray in his Hawaiian shirt and cargo shorts and post it to their Facebook pages like he's some sort of mystery on the mountain.

Delray is no mystery, though. He's just a survivor and for all his faults he was also the one person I knew I could trust to get me a boat without the police catching wind. It was going to cost me, but he wasn't a rat.

I parked the Olds at the back of the lot and made my way inside. There was a pink neon sign over the door that said ENTER above an arrow pointing down, and between the barn and the woods there were three trailers and a dirt walkway that was lit by tiki torches.

There was a picnic table near the trailers where a few women sat smoking cigarettes and looking at their phones. The official story was that the trailers were for anybody too drunk to drive home, but I'll let you do the math on that.

Inside, the whole place stank like sweat and stale beer and there were fog machines blasting pink clouds from just beneath the stage where I looked up and saw Jennifer Cart, Gwen's daughter, birth-naked and twirling on that pole like a top.

I've known Gwen Cart forever and while I can't say I'd allow one of my own daughters on that stage, I do admire the athleticism of it. If I remembered correctly, Jennifer had been a member of the high school dance team. They'd come out at halftime of basketball games and put on a show that was better than the game itself. They were called Rhythm Nation.

Delray was sitting at a table full of resorters near the stage and did a double take when he saw me. I nodded and then he excused himself from the table and walked right over.

He had on his usual Hawaiian shirt and his handlebar mustache was as gently arched as ever. He'd aged well, which I found irksome.

"Rhoda Sawbrook," he said. "What in the world?"

"I was hoping you had a minute."

"You want a job, don't you? If there was one woman our age I'd put up on that stage, it would be you—"

"Delray," I said. "I really don't have time for your bullshit right now."

"Okay, okay. Let's go have a sit in my office, then."

Delray cut across the room and I followed, the floorboards sticky beneath a thin layer of sawdust and everybody cramped too close together and shouting over the too-loud music. I caught a blast of cologne that smelled like hot piss and held my breath until we cleared the crowd and he opened a door along the far wall.

"Welcome," he said, then made a show of his politeness as he stepped inside and offered me a seat.

"It's not a social visit and I don't need a seat, Delray. What I need is a boat."

He closed the door behind him, then made his slow way around the desk.

"Why would you need a boat, Rhoda? What's wrong with all yours?"

Delray flopped into his oversize chair and leaned backward. Put his hands behind his head as if he were embarking on some great and very important deliberation.

"They've been sold."

"You sold your boats?"

"I had to."

"My goodness, Rhoda. I heard money was tight, but I didn't know it was that bad."

"It's that bad, and worse."

Delray winced. "The Sawbrooks without a boat? It just ain't right, Rhoda."

"I'll bring it back good as new. Just tell me how much."

"What I'm wondering is if this has anything to do with that boat fire last night?"

"I wouldn't know about that, Delray."

"I thought you knew about everything, Rhoda. That's sort of your trademark, isn't it?"

"My trademark is knowing what I need to know and not worrying about the rest."

"Because when I saw that fire," he went on, "the first person I thought of was your boy."

"Why would you think that?"

"Because he was in here yesterday, all angry and up in arms, and because his mother is a little bit of a firebug herself. I'm thinking maybe that gets passed on in the blood. That itch."

"Buckner didn't have anything to do with that fire, and I can promise you I don't have any itches to pass on."

"I was with Edward the night you set Jody Pitowski's car on fire," he said. "Did you know that?"

"What?"

"I was with Ed that night."

Delray leaned forward and put his arms on his desk. Arched his eyebrows at me, as if somehow this was a conversation I might be interested in pursuing.

"I'm serious about this boat, Delray. I don't have time for all this—"

"We were out drinking beers on the beach," he said. "And we could see the flames across the bay. We thought it was the movie theater itself until somebody came over from town with all the gossip and said it was Jody's car. You should have seen Edward's face, Rhoda. He went ghost white. He knew exactly who set that fire and why."

I'd never talked to Edward in my life about that fire and now Delray Harper was telling me something about the man I've loved for over forty years that I didn't know? It was infuriating, but I was not going to give Delray the satisfaction of knowing he had one over on me with Edward. Edward, on the other hand, was going to hear about it.

"Just tell me how much for the boat, Delray."

"So if you add it all up." Delray leaned away from the desk now and started to spin little half circles in his chair. "You've got you and your history, and you've got Buckner all upset and stealing a bottle of whiskey right before the fire, and now here you are the very next day, needing a boat in a hurry. It's basic arithmetic, is all."

"Buckner didn't have anything to do with that fire."

The voice came from behind me and it was loud above the music. I turned around to see a young woman enter the room and then pull the door closed quickly behind her.

"Buckner hates fire," she said.

Whoever she was, she was right about that. Buckner used to worry over the fire every time we camped. He was always getting out of his sleeping sack to make sure it was out and sometimes I'd wake up and see him just standing there, searching the ashes for embers to stomp out.

The woman sat down on the stool that Delray had offered me. She was wearing a hooded sweatshirt and blue jeans and had to be one of the dancers. She was tall and thin and young. A looker, too. You could tell it even in the dark and with her hood flipped up.

Delray stopped spinning in his chair and leaned toward the woman. Talked low and serious.

"Sky, honey, I told you to take tonight off."

"I'm not here to work, Delray."

"Then what's going on, sweetie?"

"Nothing," she said. "Which is the problem."

"What are you saying?"

"I'm saying nothing is going on, because I heard your new muscle didn't get the job done. I heard that idiot went over there to the motel and wound up taking a job with the band as their security. They posted a fucking picture on social media is what I heard. They said they ministered to him and that the Lord works in mysterious ways."

"There's just been a little hitch in the giddyup is all. Bernard didn't work out, but—"

"Delray," I said. "I don't know about giddyups or Bernard or anything else, but I need to know if you're going to help me out on this or not. Because if not—"

"Just bear with me one second, Rhoda. Sky here is Buckner's better half, so this relates to what we're discussing anyway."

That took me by surprise, to say the least. Buckner had a few girlfriends in his past, but none of them were as pretty as this one. For a second I thought Delray was trying to run an angle on me.

"What?" I said.

"Buckner is my boyfriend," said the woman. "It's possible we're in love."

Sky, I guess that was her name, turned to look at me and she had bright-blue eyes and high cheekbones. She was even more beautiful than I'd first suspected.

"You're too pretty for Buck," I said.

Delray looked at me and nodded. "That's what I said."

"I like the way he looks enough," said Sky.

"He's not ugly," I said. "But you're still about two miles north of his league. And I know you're not with him for his money."

"We connected," she said. "It's real."

I looked her in those blue eyes and she was dead serious.

"You're going to break his heart," I said. "My God."

"I won't break his heart if he doesn't fuck up."

"He already fucked up. He was drunk last night."

"I'm not thrilled about that," she admitted. "But that's not the kind of fuckup I mean."

"Well, he's not going to cheat. You're way too beautiful to step out on, and even if you weren't, the boy has a heart of gold."

"I know his heart. I'm not worried about that, either."

"What got him upset last night, then?" I asked. "Can you tell me?"

"I can tell you."

It was my question, but she turned to face Delray when she answered.

"I was attacked, Ms. Rhoda. I was giving a dance in one of the rooms and some motherfucker tried to choke me out. I thought for a second I was going to die. I couldn't breathe and everything got white and blurry."

Delray ran a nervous hand over that ridiculous handlebar mustache of his. He did not contest a word of what had just been spoken and that was more than enough evidence for me.

"What in the world, Delray? Don't you protect these girls?"

"We fucked up," he said. "I admit it. We had a bouncer slip out for a cigarette and he didn't let anybody know. He's been fired, obviously."

Sky turned from Delray back to me.

"Then he sent some dipshit he hired, Bernard, to try and settle things and now Bernard has a new job being security for the band."

"What band?"

"It's a Christian rock band. Their name is some bullshit about sand and footprints."

"Footprints in the Sand," said Delray.

"Whatever," said Sky. "It was the lead singer that strangled me."

"Are they that big?" asked Delray. "That they need security?"

"Hell no, they're not that big. They'll dump him at the next town. They're just trying not to get their asses kicked in the meantime."

"Hell's bells," I said. "What kind of show are you running here, Delray?"

A cheer went up from the crowd in the barn and Delray started to drum his desk with his fat little fingers.

"I just got to figure—"

"You don't need to figure a thing," said Sky. "Because I already got it figured and I just came here to tell you what the plan was."

"You have every reason to be upset, but—"

"But nothing, Delray," she said. "I'm going to get my check from the bar and I'm going to talk to some of the girls and let them know I'm okay. Then I'm coming back, and I'll let you know exactly what's happening."

"Does your mom know you're out?" he asked. "I don't want her worried, Sky."

"I'm twenty-seven years old, Delray. My mom knows I'm out because I told her I was leaving."

She got up and left the room. Shut the door so hard behind her that it rattled the mug on Delray's desk.

I liked her already. I liked her a whole lot, to be perfectly honest. She'd certainly gotten Delray's attention.

"Rhoda, I think I'm going to need to take a pass on this boat situation. You can see we got a lot going on here tonight."

"I'll handle everything," I said.

"No, no," he said. "I need to focus. My girls don't feel safe. And they can't work if they don't feel safe. Hell, they shouldn't have to. They need to know they're valued professionals."

"How about this—"

"I'm sorry, but we're through here, Rhoda. That's just how it's got to be."

Delray karate-chopped the air, as if his tone and timing hadn't been rude enough. I didn't take issue with his histrionics, though. He was rattled and there would be no gain for me in correcting his manners.

"Let's just take five minutes and figure out this boat, then you deal with what you need to deal with."

"I don't have five minutes, Rhoda! I'm under siege here."

That was dramatic, but I could tell by the way his eyes were bouncing from one side of his skull to the other that it was how he felt. The way he felt was ridiculous, he was a small child in an old, bloated body, but he was going to carry on for a minute and I was going to have to pretend to care because I needed his boat.

"Rhoda, all I have is the sanctity of the private spaces where my girls work and the moment somebody violates one of those spaces they have threatened my entire way of life. I got some skittish girls back there and they all know they can drive a few hours and work the Déjà Vu in Lansing if things get rocky here. And these rich boys are not going to come in here and pay just any girl. I have pretty girls and they feel safe here and respected. It's my entire brand. Did you know they did a special on me on NPR?"

I don't listen to the radio, but if I did, I damn sure wouldn't listen to any channel that saw fit to have Delray on there blabbering about God knew what, but I didn't say any of that. I just shook my head.

"The host was a woman named Mary Beth Hollins and she's basically famous. She's got a podcast, too, and she described my club as a sex-positive environment. She said people have taken notice of the way I do things and that I have created an erotic oasis set against the underpinnings of northern Michigan's harsh rural landscape."

"Oh for God's sake," I said. "Does she know it's a fucking pole barn?"

Delray hunched at his desk now. I'd tried. I really had tried to humor his fragile ego and delusions of grandeur but it was something about the word *oasis* that sent me. There were pigeons in the rafters and I just couldn't abide pretending any longer that there weren't.

I'd insulted his club, offended him, and he was altogether done with me now. I could see it in his rheumy eyes. Even worse, I'd waited until the end of his ridiculous lecture to do it and suffered needlessly as a result.

I didn't have a backup plan and couldn't stand that I'd wound up reliant on the whims of a man like Delray Harper. I might have died right there in the room from pure spite had Sky not walked back in and saved me.

"Ms. Rhoda will come with me," she said. "You get her the boat in the meantime and we'll call it even."

Sky stood beside me, slapping her open palm with her paycheck envelope.

Delray looked up from his desk.

"What are you talking about?"

"I'm talking about what's going to happen next. I've been thinking about it all day, and while I can't deny that I want their asses kicked, it wouldn't be enough. Let's say your goon didn't turn chicken shit and find the Lord. Let's say he goes over to the motel and breaks teeth. I mean, beats them bloody. Then what?"

"I don't know," said Delray. "They're in excruciating pain and never come back to my bar?"

"Then what?"

"They become martyrs," I said.

"That's exactly right, Ms. Rhoda."

She pointed the envelope at Delray now, for emphasis.

"They become martyrs and the whole church community comes together to make sure they are still able to carry their message to the masses. Every church they go to from here on out will stuff their pockets and hold them up as examples of the Lord's strength and perseverance. Their numbers on the internet will go through the roof. They'll be on the cable news by six o'clock tomorrow."

"That's how they do it." I nodded. "That's exactly their playbook."

"I keep thinking about their bus," Sky went on. "And how it's parked over there at the church. How obnoxious it is, with the painting on the side and the big jacked-up tires. But what would happen if I were to get ahold of that bus and bring it over here? Park it out front and let people take some pictures with it. Have the girls out there posing. Put it up on social media."

"That's a good idea," I said. "Shit, that will do more damage to their career than any punch."

Sky smiled at me.

"Thank you, Ms. Rhoda."

"Well, I'm not just saying it. It's good thinking all around."

"Excellent," she said. "Because you're coming with me, and once we get back with the bus, Delray will have that boat you need. Won't you, Delray?"

Delray turned to me. "Can you hot-wire a bus, Rhoda?"

"I can't hot-wire a car, let alone a bus. That's not in my skill set."

"Is it different between a bus and a car?"

"I don't know," I said. "I don't know the first thing about it."

"How'd you do it back in the day, then? I know you all were involved with those stolen cars in the nineties. Some of that farm equipment, too."

"I had people."

"Well, could you get one of them to do it?"

"They're not around anymore. They haven't been around for years."

"She doesn't need to hot-wire anything," said Sky. "That's not part of the deal."

"How are you going to do it, then?"

"It's going to get done. That's the only thing you need to worry about, Delray."

"And the boat," I said.

"And the boat," said Sky. "You need to worry about the boat."

Delray sighed. Leaned back in his chair.

"You'll tell the girls I did right by you?"

"The girls will know when the bus is sitting outside, won't need to be told."

Sky turned and walked out the door. I'm not much for following folks, but this was a woman I could get behind and I was right on her hip as she strode for the door.

the siblings

They reached the cabin by evening. Jewell saw it first and pointed to the dark edge of the shingled roof. They could see the bunker beside it, too, and the sandbags stacked to form a makeshift barrier.

"Wow," said Buckner.

They were standing on a rock shelf above the clearing and Lucy stood beside her brother. She could see it well enough through the less-swollen side of her face and was surprised by the little pinprick of nostalgia she felt in her chest.

"It's been a long time."

"Not for me," said Jewell, and hurried past them both. "I was out here last summer."

There was still daylight above the trees, and it found creases in the canopy and banded the valley with soft light. There was a hare among the wildflowers and Harold yelped at it as he shot down the hill.

"There you go," said Buckner. "Bark at it now and make sure it knows you're coming."

"He's just being polite," said Lucy.

Lucy began to follow Jewell and the dog, but Buckner put his hand to her shoulder and said they needed to talk.

"We do?"

"I need to tell you something," he said. "About the four-wheeler."

"The four-wheeler?"

"Your four-wheeler. From the park."

"What about it?"

"I stole it."

"You stole my four-wheeler?"

"Last night," he said. "I don't remember doing it, but it was parked outside my house when I woke up this morning. So yeah, I think so."

"Where is it now?"

"Well," he said.

"Well, what?"

"It's been disposed of."

"Disposed of?"

"I burned it," he said. "Actually, we were going to burn it, but then I got chased and sort of launched it into the quarry out there by my house. Long story short, it exploded."

"Who the hell is 'we'? You and Mom?"

"It was her idea."

"What was her idea, exactly?"

"To get rid of it."

"Why the fuck would she do that? Why wouldn't you just call me and say, 'I have the four-wheeler'? Who the hell would look at that situation and say, 'What we need to do is launch this four-wheeler into the fucking quarry'?"

Buckner shifted his weight from one foot to the other. Lucy had a point.

"There again, the original idea was to set it on fire. The quarry thing just sort of happened. But I did want to get it back to you. That was my first thought—get it back to Lucy. The problem there was, it was banged up and we didn't have time to get it fixed. Plus, the cops were likely heading my way because of the fire and Mom said if they found the four-wheeler, it was going to be bad news all around."

"Who wound up chasing you? The cops?"

"No, no. It was some snot-nosed kids. From the resort, it looked like. They were in their daddy's SUV and out looking for trouble. They saw me on the two-track and wanted to play chicken."

"And you're not worried that they're going to call the police?"

"And say what? *Hey, we just damn near chased a motherfucker off a cliff and killed him?*"

Lucy turned away from her brother. He couldn't read her expression through her swelling, but he feared she may be on the verge of tears.

"I'm sorry," he said. "I fucked up."

"You fucked up, but I mostly blame Mom."

"It's not an excuse, but I just didn't have the energy to fight with her and she can be so damn scary. You know how it is. You're less afraid of her than any of us, but I know that you know that feeling."

Lucy did know the feeling. She knew it exactly.

"She's a master manipulator," she said. "She can make it seem like you don't have any choice in a matter."

"Exactly! She puts a spell on you."

"I wouldn't give her that much power, but yeah."

"Do you think you'll get fired?"

"I suppose I might."

"Shit," he said. "I'm so sorry, Luce."

"I don't know, there might be a way out of it. I could mess with the timeline a little. Make it seem like anybody could have just walked in and stolen it. Which is kind of what happened anyway."

"That's what I was thinking. There's going to be some wiggle room for you, especially with going off the falls and everything. You can just say you were trying to save somebody, got caught up in the river, and that was that. You woke up and the four-wheeler was gone."

"I don't think it can be a person, though," she said. "I'll have to say I was trying to save a dog or something."

Buckner agreed. "A dog is definitely better. People typically prefer dogs to other people. Especially when it comes to heroism. You save a person and it's cool and everything, but save a dog and you're likely to end up on a stamp."

"I was just thinking you can't interview a dog," she said. "No way to prove me wrong if there's an investigation."

"See." Buckner smiled. "Smart. That's what I was saying earlier. And you have to admit, you do think like a Sawbrook sometimes. Whether you like it or not, you do."

"If I do," she said, "I certainly do not like it."

"It's not that bad."

"It's not that good, either."

Buckner, relieved the matter had been settled, at least for now, turned his attention back to the dog. He pointed down to the clearing where Harold was still barking and running in the exact same circle he had been.

"Look at that idiot. He must have found a possum or something."

"Why'd you name him Harold, anyway?" Lucy asked. "I meant to ask you that."

Buckner shrugged and began to make his way down the slope.

"Why wouldn't I?" he said.

Inside, the cabin was just a single room with a concrete floor and leaky walls. The whole place stank like must and mold and when

Buckner pulled his shirt up over his nose, Lucy said she was glad hers didn't work anymore.

There was still some sun through the cabin's window, but Jewell had already lit the two lanterns they kept on a shelf beside the entrance. She was sweeping out the dust with a straw broom and Buckner started to inspect the food shelves.

"There's beans and peaches for days," he said. "Plenty of bottled water, too."

Lucy took it all in—the sleeping cots and the old throw rug and the freestanding apron sink. The sink didn't run, but they used it to do the dishes in water they boiled over the campfire.

Buckner opened up some cans of peaches and beans and brought them out to the porch with a jug of water and they all sat down in rocking chairs to eat. Buckner offered Lucy the water first, but she said she didn't think she could drink out of a jug.

"Just open up," he said, and lifted it to her mouth.

Lucy was able to get some of the water down, then Buckner dabbed at her chin with his shirtsleeve to get what spilled.

They all ate with their hands. Jewell and Buckner scooping everything by the fingers while Lucy could only manage a few beans at a time.

"I want to know more about Sky," Jewell mumbled over a mouthful of peaches. "Tell us everything."

Buckner sucked some peach juice off his fingers and nodded. "Well, her son's name is Frog. Actually, his given name is Dashiell, but I call him Frog."

"What the hell kind of name is Dashiell?" said Lucy.

"A shitty one," said Buckner. "But I believe his birth father was a resorter and suspect he had a hand in the naming process."

"Is the father around?" said Jewell.

"Nah. He just gave the boy a shitty name and took off running."

"God," said Lucy. "That poor woman."

"How do you feel about it?" said Jewell. "About her having a child?"

"To be honest, I love that little dude. He's not really walking yet, but he does stumble pretty good, and I think he'll have some athleticism to him. I think he'll be formidable in that way."

Lucy gave her brother's shoulder a squeeze. "I think it's great. You've always been good with kids, Buck."

Jewell dumped what was left of her beans directly in her mouth and then asked Buckner why he called the boy Frog.

"He just has a froggy way about him," Buckner said. "He's real quiet, but you also feel like he's one that could just hop up and start some shit out of nowhere. Do you know what I mean? He keeps you on your toes, I guess."

"It's a good handle," said Lucy. "I like it."

Jewell set her can of beans down and now it was her turn to lick the juice off her fingertips. Talked over her ring and middle fingers.

"Dashiell," she said. "My God, is she trying to get the boy's ass kicked?"

"She calls him Dash, but my point there was, what if he's slow?"

"That's a name that comes with some pressure," said Lucy. "I could see how they'd tease him either way with that one."

"What did they call you in grade school?" Jewell asked. "Buckner the Fucker?"

"That's the one." Buckner nodded. "It was an insult, right up until it wasn't."

"And how do you feel about her working at the Barn?"

It was Lucy that asked the loaded question. It had been nice to go back and forth and share a little bit about his personal life, to open up about this woman and her son that he hoped might change his life forever, but that didn't mean he wanted to talk about everything.

"How do you think it makes me feel?" he snapped.

"I don't know. That's why I asked."

"Well, it makes me feel terrible. I hate it and if I let myself think on it, it starts to make me crazy."

"Of course it does," said Jewell.

"There's some that might like it," Buckner said. "Those that are into being watchers. Voyagers, or whatever they're called."

"Do you mean voyeurs?"

It was Lucy, of course, that corrected him.

"Whatever they're called," he said. "That's not me."

"What about your work? How's that going?" Jewell asked.

She was trying to be helpful. She was trying to move the subject away from uncomfortable territory, which was considerate but did nothing to change the fact that she had steered them directly into something even worse. He supposed there was nothing left to do but say it.

"I got fired, but it was not performance-related. I was caught up in economic factors and found myself in a last-hired, first-fired situation."

"Shit, I'm sorry," said Jewell.

"When did this happen?" asked Lucy.

"It was just the other day. We were starting to think that I might make enough that Sky could get a job waiting tables somewhere instead of dancing, too. You know, make a little less money because now you're living off two paychecks as opposed to one. She really wants to get out of her mama's house, too."

"Twenty thousand dollars and she can quit tomorrow."

Lucy gave a quick snap of her fingers.

"Don't even," said Jewell, and pointed at her sister.

"Don't even, what? Try to help our brother?"

"Use this situation for leverage. Jesus, Lucy. He's spilling his guts here and you're trying to take advantage of it."

"I'm trying to help him."

"You're trying to help yourself."

"I'm providing a solution, Jewell. I'm giving him options. The same as I did for you."

"I'm not going to lie," said Buckner. "I have been thinking about that money since we talked earlier. Since I found out about Jewell."

"Buckner," said Jewell. "Don't you dare."

"Why not? You did."

"I did it with a plan, though."

"And how'd that plan work out?"

"What are you going to do, Buck? Hand over twenty thousand dollars to a woman you just met?"

"I thought you were happy for me?"

"I am happy for you. I'm just saying, you got to be careful with people."

"I'm not going to write her a check, Jewell. I'm just saying I would have enough to help us through the rough spots if she wanted to switch jobs."

"Exactly!" said Lucy. "It's the smart move, Buckner."

Jewell shook her head, long and slow. Looked at Lucy. "You are so full of shit. Acting like this is for him when it is exactly what you want."

"Speaking for myself only." Buckner held up a hand. "I do not feel manipulated. I feel like I could use the money and it's no more complicated than that."

"See? He needs the money and in this case, it also happens to be the best thing for the property and the family and honestly, the fucking earth."

"Oh my God, Lucy," said Jewell. "Don't even start with that earth shit."

"What earth shit? You got a problem with the earth now, too?"

"No, I don't. I've got a problem with sanctimony."

"It's not sanctimonious if it's true. Facts don't have feelings, as they say. I mean, have you ever really thought about what will happen if we lose this river, Jewell? Not to us, but to the river itself?"

"Of course I have."

"Okay, then tell me."

"I might not have gone to college, but I'm not a fucking idiot. I know what happens."

"I don't think you really do know, because you wouldn't be acting like this if you did."

"Okay then, Professor. Why don't you go ahead and tell me? Since that's what you so clearly want to do."

"I'll tell you this much at least. Harbor North is not the end or even close to the worst thing that could happen to the Crow. You just wait until Nestlé comes to town. Wait until they buy up every tributary to every Great Lake and start selling it by the plastic bottle."

"So that's your big move? The corporate bogeyman? If Buckner doesn't give you his land, Nestlé is going to come and take it from him?"

"He's not giving it to me! It's going into a trust and he's getting paid for that!"

Lucy turned to Buckner for backup, but he'd gotten up out of his chair and left. It must have been some time ago, too, because he was already in the field playing fetch with Harold.

"Oh for God's sake, he's not even listening."

Jewell gave her a smug little look, as if somehow the argument had been won because Buckner was no longer there to participate in it. As if somehow Buckner playing fetch with his dog had proven something.

Lucy couldn't stand to sit there a minute more with Jewell, so she went inside the cabin and sat down at the old rickety table. She was thirsty but wasn't about to go back on the porch to fetch her water. The most important thing now was to rest, and she was not about to risk another tangle with Jewell or Buckner by stepping outside.

There was just enough flicker from the nearest lamp to see some of the old family photos on the wall and she turned to study them. They were weathered and fading. They had chipped frames and spider breaks in the glass, but they were the same ones that had always been there and she knew them from memory just as well as sight.

The one she'd always been most interested in was the one of her mother and her aunt and uncle. Rhoda was the youngest, but she was taller than Wanda in the photo and smiling widely between her and Billy. Rhoda was probably thirteen then, which would have made Wanda fifteen, and Billy just about to leave for the army.

Wanda was short and frail and she looked washed out already, which might have been the booze or the angle of the sun on the day the photo was taken. They were standing on the front porch steps at the main house and Rhoda looked big as life. She was young but solid and strong and standing with her shoulders square and her chin set out. Billy draped an arm over her shoulder and Lucy thought about what a waste it was to lose him and Wanda both. She thought about the stories and dreams that had died with them so young, and all the things she would never know and had never been able to ask.

Lucy could never imagine her mother as a girl, and if she could ask one question of either Billy or Wanda, it would have been this: *Has she always been so damn stubborn?*

Rhoda had told her once that Billy had a girlfriend out in San Diego, and that she used to call the house after he died. The poor girl probably just wanted to talk about Billy, but whenever Rhoda answered and she asked to speak with their mother, she had to lie and say she was out. Rhoda always said she wanted to talk to that girl herself but that she was afraid to defy her mother.

Lucy couldn't imagine her mother being afraid of anything, but by all accounts she had been obedient to her parents and maybe that was why she grew up and defied everything else. Or maybe those two things weren't related at all. Lucy didn't know, because there was nobody to ask but her own parents.

There was so much lost in the blank spaces. She had never been able to shake the feeling that there were answers somewhere about who she was and who her family had been—their absence hovered in all that land around them.

She looked out at the fading sun and the wildflowers and the woods beyond the cabin. She saw Harold bounding through the tall grass and felt the air through the thin walls, cooling now with the coming dark.

This was the last moment, the last flicker of quiet before one of Great-Grandpa Harvard's land mines burst and shattered the stillness with a single, violent compression of sound.

rhoda

S ky rode with me in the Olds. Asked me if it was okay to smoke and I told her that it was and pushed in the car lighter.

"I haven't seen one of those in a minute."

"I don't even smoke anymore, but sometimes I'll pop it in just to pop it back out again."

"I love old cars," she said, and ran a finger along the dash.

"You know they don't even make Oldsmobiles anymore?"

"I did not know that."

"I think it's sad," I said. "I know it's not much of a car, but that doesn't mean it's without any value at all."

It was not yet full dark, but we were moving east and the woods between the Barn and the main road were empty of shadows.

I'd lied to Delray inside. Time was, I could hot-wire just about anything I wanted. Used to be that you could start a bus or piece of farm equipment with a flathead screwdriver and if what you wanted was a car, I could get you one of those with two minutes and a halfway decent jackknife.

Nowadays you can't steal anything with your hands. You need a Russian hacker or an engineering degree to make a living as a thief, which is just another way the world has gotten harder for people like me and I just didn't have the time or energy to explain that to Delray.

I asked Sky what the plan was and she said we were going to break into the church boys' room and steal the bus key.

"Where are they staying?"

"Motel 31."

"And they won't be in the room?"

"They go down to the shore every night to eat at the fish fry. My friend Tonya is a waitress there, which is how I know. They always hit on her and don't tip for shit."

"And you say these are Christian musicians?"

"I wouldn't call them much of either one," she said. "To be honest."

The lighter popped. Sky reached for it, lit up, and then cranked the window down and took a drag.

"So," she said. "What I'm thinking is, one of us distracts whoever is working the desk and the other gets the room key. They have actual keys still at the motel. Got them on that big pegboard with the room numbers written in marker."

Motel 31 was named for the highway where it sat and if Jenkins was still working the desk, we wouldn't need to distract him at all. I'd brought a bottle of Wooripple, thinking I could use it to grease Delray's wheels for the boat, but it would work even better on Jenkins. That man couldn't resist a bottle of our 'shine if he tried.

"We could do that," I said. "Or I could just bribe him with a bottle."

"A bottle of what?"

"Wooripple," I said. "It's our family—"

"Shit," she said. "I know what Wooripple is. You brought some with you?"

"I got a bottle in the trunk right now."

"Why do you call it that, anyway? Wooripple? I've always wondered."

"I could make something up," I said. "But the truth is, nobody knows. That's just what it's called."

"But the desk guy will take it and let us in the room?"

"Jenkins?" I said. "Yeah, he'll take that bottle and give us just about anything we want."

"I just want the bus," she said. "And then I want to park it at the Barn and end these fucking assholes."

"Then that's exactly what we're going to do."

Sky kept her cigarette outside and she was turned toward the trees.

"I'm glad we finally got to meet, Ms. Rhoda, even under the circumstances."

It was a nice thing to say, and I told her so. I told her that I was glad to meet her, too, and then she took a last pull of her smoke and flicked the filter off into the night.

Motel 31 was a white brick building with a fading red roof. The lobby had brown carpet and dark paneled walls and there was a stand beside the door stuffed with brochures for all the local campgrounds and tourist traps. The fun sorts of places that working families used to go to around here before the resort priced them out and pushed them farther north for colder water.

There were bells above the door, but Jenkins didn't bother to look up when they jingled. Jenkins just sat there reading a paperback. It was one of those to do with vampires.

"Now," I said. "Here's a man that can be reasoned with."

Jenkins was in his fifties, maybe sixties, and he was nearly bald but dignified about it. Didn't try to comb his little tufts of hair to make them seem anything more than what they were—refugees and the last remaining survivors of a long-lost war.

"Rhoda Sawbrook," he said. "What in the world brings you here?"

"This," I said, and set the Mason jar on the counter.

Wooripple was Germain's recipe originally and it is not like being normal drunk. Wooripple is sort of a leave-your-body-and-enter-parallel-dimensions experience.

I think it's fair to say that it can take you places that are currently beyond the understanding of science. Some claim it can put you into conversation with loved ones that have passed on, while others say it has allowed them access to profound carnal pleasures. Some people just like to drink it and howl at the moon. Or the sun. Whatever is up there at the time. Edward takes a few shots every New Year but I haven't touched the stuff in twenty years. We've always got a couple of jars on hand, though. The Sawbrooks were built on beaver hides and moonshine and in Cutler County a full bottle of Wooripple still carries a fair amount of street value.

Jenkins set his book down. "Is that what I think it is?"

"The one and only," I said.

He looked at Sky standing next to me. She was wearing shades and still had her hood up. He asked who she was and I told him it didn't matter.

"She's just a friend of mine."

Jenkins nodded and returned his attention to the bottle. Asked if I minded if he had a sniff and I told him I did not.

He held the bottle up to look at in the light. I don't know what he hoped to see, because our shit is as clear as window glass. Finally, he unscrewed the top and had his snort. His eyes sprang water and he leaned back in his chair and laughed.

"Holy shit," he said, and shook his head. "That'll stand your butt hairs on end, won't it?"

Jenkins is a big man. He was wearing athletic shorts and a

Detroit Pistons shirt that said BAD BOYS. I looked at the cover of his book, which suggested the culmination of a romantic affair that had spanned some time. Centuries, perhaps.

"So," he said. "What do you need in return?"

"I need the keys to those church boys' rooms."

"The church boys?" he said.

"The singers," I said.

"I know who you mean," he said. "It's just they only got one room."

"Then we just need one key."

"What if they're in there?"

"They're not," I said.

He leaned up out of his chair to look out the window.

"That's their car right there," he said. "Well, actually it's the preacher's car, from out there to Harbor Light where they're doing their worship concerts. The bus is too big for our lot, so they drive that back and forth."

"They're out to dinner," said Sky. "They walk across the highway, then down to the shore at the same time every night."

"Ah." He nodded. "That makes sense. Maybe hit the Sailor's Knot for some enchiladas. Them are pretty good if you get the cheese con queso."

"Jenkins," I said. "I don't give a shit if they're at the Last Supper. I just need the key."

"I'm just thinking out loud," he said.

Jenkins finally got up from his desk and turned to get us a key from the board.

"Can you cut the cameras for us?" I asked. "We'll need about ten minutes."

"Shit," he said. "We don't have no security cameras, Rhoda. What do you think this is, the Holiday Inn?"

Jenkins handed me the key and then we were back outside on

the narrow sidewalk between the parking lot and rooms. Sky was to my left, walking tall in a pair of high-top sneakers. There was nobody else outside and the rooms were darkened behind the blinds.

"Cheese con queso," she said. "What a dipshit."

"What's that?"

"Jenkins or whoever," she said. "There's no such thing as cheese con queso. *Con queso* means 'with cheese.' *Cheese con queso* literally means 'cheese with cheese.'"

"I believe he made it to the tenth grade," I said. "Which is about twice as far as his daddy did."

"Maybe Jenkins Junior will get his GED, then," she said. "What a day that will be."

"Jenkins doesn't have kids," I said. "He was married for a while, but she left him and moved to Minnesota for a lover she met through Amway."

"Small mercies," said Sky, and pointed ahead to the room.

The church boys' quarters were vile. It stank like feet and sweat and there were clothes and old food wrappers scattered everywhere. There were two key rings on the nightstand and I flipped on the lamp and gave them each a quick look. The first set had a few keys on it, including a fob, and the other was a single key connected to a puffy trinket with a small chain. That one had BUS written on a blue tag.

"Bingo," I said, and held it up for Sky.

She didn't answer me, though. She was looking at herself in the mirror. She had her hoodie pulled back and I could see the brown-yellow bruising on her shoulders at the base of her neck.

She was smart to keep that bruise from Buckner and I was grateful to her for that. Otherwise, he'd already be in prison.

"You okay, sweetie?" I said.

She turned and saw I had the key.

"Is that the one?"

"It is."

"Good," she said. "Let's get the fuck out of here, then."

I thought about taking both sets of keys on principle, but figured they'd be more likely to notice they were gone if I did. Instead I snagged a bottle of cologne for Edward. I don't care about cologne one way or another, and neither does he, but he'd get a kick out of me taking it and consider it a trophy of sorts. I asked Sky if she wanted any souvenirs.

"They probably got something valuable somewhere," I said. "Maybe some jewelry or some music equipment you could find a buyer for."

"No," she said. "I don't want anything."

"Are you sure? You'd be surprised what people will pay for."

"I'm absolutely sure," she said. "I'm going to drop that bus off and then forget about these assholes forever."

———————

I stopped at home on the way to Delray's to switch the Olds out for the truck. I'd need the Ford to haul Delray's boat and I left Edward's cologne on the kitchen table with a note.

Thinking of you, I wrote. *Home soon.*

Sky craned her neck to see what she could of the property as we drove off and I told her she would have to come back in the daylight.

"I'd like that," she said.

I stayed off the highway and took back roads all the way to the church. Sky was quiet and looked out at the night and the dark and the low clouds above the trees. I could feel her wanting to say something, but I didn't press her on it. We just drove in the silence until she finally came out with it about a mile from the church.

"Just so you know, I work for Delray at the Barn, but it's not what I'm going to do with my life."

"Okay," I said.

"And I have never, not once, worked those trailers. In case you were wondering."

"I wasn't."

It was a lie, but a polite one.

"Either way," she said. "I wanted you to know."

"Can I ask you a different question?"

"Of course."

"Back at the Barn, you said you wouldn't break Buck's heart if he didn't fuck up. But you said you didn't mean the drinking."

"That's right."

"So what did you mean?"

"I meant the only way he's going to lose me is if he's not tough enough."

"Tough enough for what?"

"Love," she said.

I pulled into the church lot and put the truck in park. I turned to look at her square-on.

"He's driven me to the ends of my own sanity and I can't say he's particularly good at much of anything, but he's nothing but tough. All three of mine are. They're tough all the way through."

"That's good, then," she said, and opened the passenger door. "Because I'm through with those that aren't."

Delray had called it a bus, but it was actually a panel van with a cross and flaming guitars airbrushed on the sides.

"I believe this might be the single most ridiculous vehicle I have ever seen," I said.

"It's the world's biggest clown car," said Sky.

The charm on the key said WASHED IN HIS BLOOD and I asked Sky if she wanted to drive.

"Honestly," she said, "I'd prefer if you would. I'd like to just sit up here and look out."

"You're the boss," I said, and opened the door.

I started the van and Sky got in the passenger side. I backed out of the lot and while she grew quiet again, it was not the same quiet it had been before. I did not feel her searching for the nerve to try to say something. Matter of fact, it was quite the opposite. She seemed at peace beside me, and I rolled my window down and put on the radio.

I told Sky to pick whatever station she wanted, and she flipped it over to classic rock. I was sort of hoping to catch that song that me and Edward liked, or something else from that time, but it was just a block of commercials and then she switched it to modern music. Those songs were just a bunch of sex sounds and echoes piled on top of one another and I blocked it all out and drove.

Sky texted Delray to tell him we were almost there, and he must have closed the stage because there were a dozen girls outside in their bare legs and summer jackets when I pulled into the clearing. There were customers outside, too, holding their beer bottles to the sky and cheering our arrival.

I parked the van right out front of the club where they'd left us a space, and when Sky stepped outside, they called her by name.

The women rushed over to take pictures with the van and for once the resorters stood at a distance and didn't try to make the moment all about them. Delray came over and led me away from the crowd.

"Where's the boat?" I said.

"Calm down," he said. "It's right out there on the main road. I've got a guy waiting on you."

"I'll need a ride back to my truck," I said. "Then I need to get it hitched."

"Like I said, I've got a guy. We're going to take care of everything, but how about you come inside and let me buy you a beer first."

"You can buy me and Edward both a beer the next time we come in for the comedy night."

"I'll plan on it, then," he said.

I turned and saw all the girls gathered around Sky. They were shooting video with their phones and the sound of their happy voices and laughter filled the clearing. I felt like we'd done a good thing getting that vehicle and I'm not ashamed to say I'm proud of what we accomplished.

I was going to tell Delray to say goodbye to Sky for me, but she saw me getting ready to leave and left her friends to hurry over. She gave me a hug and pulled me in close for it, too. It was a real hug, and we both held it for a moment.

"Ms. Rhoda," she said. "I'm so glad I finally got to meet you."

the siblings

They sat on the cabin porch after the explosion. Jewell had the pistol in her hand and Buckner had grabbed a deer rifle from the closet inside and leaned it on the railing. Buckner said it was probably another bear that triggered the mine, but Jewell wasn't so sure.

"We just had a black bear set one off a few weeks ago, and they're too smart to keep wandering through the same minefield."

"They're bears," said Buckner. "They see berries, they want to eat them. End of story. What time is Mom supposed to get here, anyway?"

"Whenever she gets the boat," said Jewell.

Lucy pointed off into the dark, in the general direction of the minefield. "You know she thinks those explosions are Grandpa Harvard communicating from beyond the grave? Like, she actually believes that."

"I mean, it is pretty uncanny the way things happen after one of those goes off," said Jewell. "Buckner getting sent to Iraq. Our uncle's crash—"

Lucy turned toward Jewell. "Are you kidding me?"

"What?" said Jewell. "Stranger things have happened."

"Have they? Stranger things than a dead man talking through land mines?"

"What's he saying now?" asked Jewell. "Is what I want to know."

"He's not saying anything, because he's dead. My God, Jewell."

"I can see both sides," said Buckner.

"There are no sides," said Lucy. "There's reality, and there's Mom and her crazy bullshit. There's truth, and there's lies."

"It must be exhausting to live like you do," said Jewell. "Everything so cut-and-dried and black-and-white. Everything so goddamn scientific."

"What I was trying to say," Buckner went on, "is both of you have some interesting points and maybe you should just agree to disagree on this particular matter."

"Oh, shut up, Buck," said Jewell.

Here Lucy was in agreement with her sister.

"This has nothing to do with you, dude."

Jewell and Lucy went back and forth a few more times, but the argument tapered off quickly. The sisters' brief alignment against Buckner had taken all the momentum out of their own fight and it was quiet on the porch when Harold began to bark in the distance.

The dark was sprinkled with stars above the porch and Buckner scanned until he found the good boy—combing the high brush at the edge of the clearing. He called to Harold, and Harold barked back. The bark was not weighted or shrill. *I'm here*, is what Harold was saying.

"Hey, buddy," Buckner called back.

The day he adopted him, Buckner had walked the line in the pound and Harold couldn't stop wagging his tail. Lots of dogs wagged their tails, though. The thing about Harold was he didn't bark. Not that day.

Harold just stood there and sort of squeaked and it was the most heartbreaking sound that Buckner ever heard—this dog wanting to call out to him, but also not wanting to scare him off. This dog and his desire to love and to be loved all tight and cramped up in his chest until he couldn't hold it anymore and it just came tumbling out in a few high-pitched squeals that stopped Buckner cold.

They rescued each other that day, was the thing. People said that all the time, of course. It was a cliché, which did nothing to keep it from being true, and Buckner could trace almost every good thing that had happened in his sobriety to the day he found his dog. Harold, for instance, was the one who'd introduced him to Sky.

They were walking the shoreline one day that winter when he saw her in a puffy jacket and knit hat. It was a bright, beautiful morning. February in northern Michigan and everything was frozen and clean—sun sharp as glass as it bounced off the ice floes and the blue water beyond the freeze.

He thought she was from the resort at first because of her bright-blue, waffled coat. It was made from some space-age material that glittered in the sun and had clearly never been worn to work in.

Later, he realized it was probably a gift from whatever asshole had convinced her to name her son Dashiell right before he disappeared and abandoned them both. It was a nice coat, though. There was no denying it.

Harold was off his leash that morning and darted for Sky the second he saw her. It was a good sign right off the bat—Harold being an impeccable judge of character and distrusting by nature.

Sky bent down to greet the dog and Buckner hurried after to corral him. Sky smiled while Harold yelped and leapt at her hands.

"Harold!" Buckner shouted. "Down, boy!"

Sky laughed as Buckner grabbed the dog by the collar and tried to calm him. Harold seemed to settle, but the moment Buckner relaxed his grip he exploded into a sprint and Buckner was about to give chase when he looked up and saw the heron take flight.

Buckner had lived his entire life in northern Michigan and never known a heron that wintered, but he saw one that morning. Watched it rise, then soar. The heron swooped and circled and then turned on a wing and lifted even higher, climbing the bright, blue bank of sky until it was lost in the shine.

"Holy shit," said Sky.

Buckner watched her watch the bird. The dark curls of her hair beneath her hat. The high line of her cheekbones and the marvel in her eyes.

The bird fell then, as if it had been dropped from the sun itself, tucked its wings and dove for a ripple of blue water between ice chunks and plucked out a perch.

There was a flash of wiggling silver and then the heron gulped as it rose and swung wide again and floated. Here it gave a few more showy flaps and then extended its wings as it glided to a nearby floe. The heron landed without disturbing a single flake of fallen snow, shook itself free of water, and then stood there straight and regal as a sentry.

Harold was still running in circles on the shore, barking his fool head off.

"Holy shit," she said again.

Sky turned to him and he smiled. He gave her a little nod to let her know that he'd seen it, too—that it had really happened.

"Unbelievable," she said, then put her hand to her forehead to shield the sun from her shades. That's how bright it was.

Now that brightness was gone and Sky felt so far away from him, it seemed possible that she may have been a dream all along. Harold was still by his side, of course, and Buckner spotted him walking at a strange angle in the distance.

Lucy saw him, too. He could tell by the way she leaned forward in the chair beside him as he stood up and shouted for his dog.

Harold did not come running, though. Harold was moving slow and sort of loping forward and Buckner looked at Lucy and could see that she was concerned.

"He's got something," she said.

Buckner leapt off the porch and jogged out into the field and quickly saw why Harold was moving so slow and awkward. He saw what was in his dog's mouth and yelled for his sisters.

Lucy and Jewell came running, but before they were even halfway to their brother in the field, Harold had dropped the severed arm at Buckner's feet. It was a woman's arm, sliced from her body just above the elbow, but intact from there to an open palm.

part V

rhoda

I got the boat to the launch, unhitched, then drove back to the property for Jewell. I couldn't get all the way to the cabin, but I got close enough that I could hoof it in about thirty minutes and figured we could make it back to the shore by daybreak. I had no reason to expect any luck, but with just a little bit of it, we might be across the border by lunch.

The chopper would still be circling, but I'd just be an old lady driving a boat and there were miles and miles between the same customs outposts that I'd slipped through a hundred times before. I'd keep Jewell in the hold to be safe, but I'd get her across. I told myself the hard part was over.

I brought a flashlight from the truck, but I didn't need it. There was a three-quarter moon and bright stars above the canopy and I knew exactly where I was going. I kept my pace even but brisk. I walked directly to the ridge above the cabin and that was when I saw all three of my children standing in a circle and shouting—like they were fighting over the last piece of blueberry pie.

I called out and hurried down the slope, but they barely noticed when I arrived. Jewell was holding up a lantern and now I saw what all the fuss was about. There was a woman's arm, dropped right there in the dirt.

"Somebody stepped on a land mine," said Buckner, and finally turned to me. "But we don't know who."

"I think it might be a detective," said Jewell. "Somebody that tracked us out here."

"It's not a cop," said Buckner.

"Why not? Because it's a woman?"

Lucy was taking the political angle—surprise, surprise.

"No," said Buckner. "Because of the calluses on the fingers."

Lucy glared.

"Why can't a woman have calluses?"

"I didn't say a woman! I said a detective!"

"Maybe she's a detective that's into woodworking or something," said Jewell. "Anybody can have a callus."

"Nobody actually does woodworking," said Buckner. "That's just something people like to say they do."

"The point is it could be anything," Jewell went on. "Having calluses on your hands doesn't exclude you from being anything in this world."

None of my children had any idea who the woman was or where she'd come from, but that wouldn't prevent them from arguing over it until daybreak. Finally, I couldn't take it anymore and shouted, "We don't know who she is!"

"Mama," said Buckner. "That's what we're saying. That's what we're trying to figure out."

"Well," I said. "Maybe instead of standing around, pissing in the wind, we should all just fan out and see if we can find ourselves another body part or something else along the lines of a clue."

Lucy took a sharp, pointed breath and I braced myself for whatever was about to come next.

"A clue?"

"I'm sorry," I said. "Would you prefer I use a different term?"

"No, actually I would not. What I'd like is for you to explain why a clue, as you call it, would do anybody any good right now?"

"Because if we know who she is, we can start to make some decisions that need to be made."

"Whoever this poor person *was* will change absolutely nothing about this entire fucked-up situation. I mean, at this point, she could be a Jane Doe or Celine Dion and it wouldn't make a difference in the world."

"Who?" said Buckner.

"It doesn't matter who," said Lucy. "Is the point."

"That's where you're wrong," I said. "If it's a Jane Doe, it matters very much."

Lucy shook her head. "No, it really doesn't."

"One step at a time," I said. "Let's just see if we can find anything else and then we can fight about what it all means."

"No more steps for me."

This was from Lucy, who turned to walk back to the cabin.

"I'm going to go sit on the porch and hope nobody else explodes before we all go to prison. Maybe that's the message from Grandpa Harvard, eh, Mom? You're all going to prison. That's my interpretation, anyway."

"Oh, get over yourself, Lucy," I said. "My goodness."

"Get over myself? Are you kidding me right now?"

"I am not kidding. I don't say shit just to say it. I don't have ulterior motives or hide my intentions behind a bunch of lawyers and government bureaucrats."

Lucy was nearly to the porch but she stopped, took a breath, then wheeled around.

"I got a question, Mom," she said. "Since you're so direct."

"Anything you want," I said. "I just told you, I've got nothing to hide."

"What kind of bird is that in the workshop?"

"What?"

This question came from Buckner, who was standing beside Jewell. The two of them on one side of the severed arm, with me on the other. Jewell answered quietly, as if she were only speaking to Buckner.

"She's talking about the scary bird. Remember we used to think it was haunted? The big one in the workshop?"

"What's that got to do with anything?"

Buckner was whispering, too, like all of the sudden discretion was a concern.

"It's got everything to do with everything," said Lucy. "Answer the question, Mom. What was it?"

"It was a cormorant, Lucy."

"Which is funny," said Lucy. "Because I don't remember you ever telling us that. Do you, Buck?"

"I don't know, but there again I can't remember you tasing me last night—"

"I don't remember knowing what kind of bird it was," said Jewell. "But I also don't know why any of that matters right now."

"It matters because that bird was literally going extinct when our grandfather shot it and decided to turn it into a trophy."

Lucy was not whispering. Lucy was saying whatever she had to say with her whole chest. She wasn't quite shouting, but it was close.

"And that's the problem," she went on. "Same as it ever was. This family needing to own something that should never have been ours to begin with. Our mother, thinking her name on a land deed is more important than what happens to everything else that exists here. You think we're protecting this place? The Sawbrooks? With our land mines and trophy birds and burned-down boats and dead people? We're the good guys? That's what you think?"

My chest was tight and hot with anger and with hurt and when I spoke, it all came spilling out.

"I love you, Lucy. You're my daughter and I love you, but I swear to God there's times that I can't see a thread of myself or this family inside of your heart. I don't know who you are anymore, and the sad part is that I can't say I feel it's a loss. I can't say I have any desire at all to know whoever it is that you've become."

I meant those words to hurt my daughter, but if they did, Lucy didn't show it. Lucy didn't flinch or pause. She just stood up straight and answered.

"Jewell put her land in the trust three months ago, Mom. Then she lost the money on a Las Vegas poker stake. She was probably going to take the ten that Van was supposed to pay her and try to win it back at the Eagle. Maybe she would have, too. We'll never know because Van was in the boat she set on fire and now he's dead—just like this poor woman with the callused hands. Just like the cormorant that Granddaddy stuffed."

I looked at Jewell and knew it was true because she could not bring her eyes to face me. Jewell just stood there and stared at the dirt.

jewell

J ewell braced herself for an outburst from her mother, perhaps even a physical attack, but Rhoda left the clearing without a word. Rhoda made her way back up the hill and left them all in the field with the arm and the crickets.

"Where is she going?" asked Buckner.

"There's no way of knowing," said Lucy, and flopped down in a chair on the porch.

Jewell crossed her arms and held them close to her chest.

"I don't think I've ever seen her so upset that she couldn't even yell."

"I'm shaken to the core," said Buckner. "To be honest with you."

Jewell walked back to the porch now, too, but sat in the chair farthest from her sister.

"If you're going to punch me," said Lucy, "do me a favor and hit the side of my face that isn't already swollen."

"I'm not going to hit you."

Jewell's tone was flat and her voice sounded far away. She rocked slowly, back and forth, and stared at the floorboards. Buckner came to the porch himself and took the middle chair between his sisters. After a time, Lucy spoke.

"Why don't you want to hit me?" she asked. "I would."

Jewell brought her eyes up from the floorboards and looked out at the field.

"It needed to be said, and now it's over."

"It doesn't feel over," said Buckner.

"It's not over, over," said Jewell. "But the worst part is. The worst part, I think, was carrying it."

Harold settled himself between Buckner and Jewell. Jewell reached down to pet his head, and Harold gave her a few licks and then moved a little closer to her side. Rested his head against her foot and let out a little sigh.

There were no dogs in prison. She hadn't thought about it until just now, but it was true. God, that was awful. She hadn't had a dog since her Labrador, Pepper, passed and now she might never have one again. She'd been meaning to go down to the rescue, too.

A good dog was like having an extra heart to put all the sadness and joy you couldn't hold on your own, and now she might never know that comfort again.

In the end, that was the thing that made her cry. The fact that there were no dogs in prison. She looked down at Harold and when his big, sweet eyes stared back, it struck her as just about the saddest thing in the world and she finally gave out and sobbed.

"I don't know why I told Mom just now," said Lucy. "I'm sorry. I guess I wanted some of the heat on you and I panicked. I shouldn't have done it, and I apologize."

"That's not why I'm crying."

"Still," said Lucy. "It was wrong."

"Why are you crying?" asked Buckner.

"Jesus, Buck," said Lucy.

"What?"

"It doesn't really matter why. She's upset."

"I know she's upset. I can see that, Lucy. I'm just trying to be helpful."

"I don't know why I'm crying," said Jewell. "I guess it's because I might go to prison and they won't have any dogs there. I was sitting here looking at Harold and thinking about how I might never get to have another dog."

"I shouldn't have said that, either," said Lucy. "About you going to prison. We don't know that yet."

"Nobody's going to prison."

Their mother had appeared suddenly, as if she'd materialized from the night itself, and her voice was clear and certain. She threw a rucksack at her children's feet.

"What the hell is that?" said Buckner.

"It's a bag."

"What kind of bag?"

"The kind that just had an arm attached to it."

"Oh shit," said Buckner.

"Where did you get that, Mom?" asked Lucy.

"Where do you think I got it?"

"I don't know. That's why I'm asking."

Rhoda turned and pointed up the hill. "I got it from there."

"But where, exactly?"

"It doesn't matter, Lucy. The point is—"

"You found it in the minefield," said Lucy. "Didn't you?"

"Who cares where I found it?"

"Jesus, Mom," said Jewell. "You could have killed yourself."

"Well, I didn't."

Buckner shook his head. "You shouldn't have done that, Mom. The girls are right."

"The point is the bag and them patches on the side. The ones with the mushrooms on them."

"So, she was a mushroom hunter," said Lucy. "That's who died. Some poor lady looking for mushrooms."

"Some poor lady who decided to climb inside a barbed-wire fence to poke around for something that doesn't belong to her," said Rhoda. "On somebody else's property."

Jewell had her face in her hands now.

"That's not really the point, Mom," she mumbled.

"It's nothing but the point."

"She was looking for morels?"

Buckner asked the question as if it could possibly matter what type of mushroom the woman was in search of when she exploded. Rhoda paid him no mind.

"There's a driver's license in the front pocket of the bag. She's thirty-five years old. Don't know if she's married or not."

"Doesn't sound like somebody that can just up and disappear to me," said Buckner. "This sounds like somebody that people will want found."

Jewell finally took her face from her hands and looked up at her mother. Her eyes still wet at the edges from crying.

"So I'm fucked?"

Rhoda didn't answer right away. Instead she stood and looked at her children. They were an insufferable pain in the ass, but God, she loved them. She didn't think she could ever love a thing in the world more than she'd loved them as babies, but all her love had done as they'd grown was cut deeper and more broadly into her heart. They were more complicated now, that much was true, but in some ways those complications made their togetherness more urgent. They could have been anywhere in the world, but they weren't. They were right there in front of her.

The sky above the trees was beginning to lighten, but barely. It was the time before the dawn when the black goes steely gray and the stars pale and begin to draw back.

"It's not over yet," she said. "We can still get you out, but we're going to have to move and we're going to have to split up."

buckner

Buckner didn't like that they were splitting up. The idea of being away from his mother and Lucy unnerved him, but he wasn't the one to argue the point. Arguing points was Lucy's thing, or maybe Jewell's in certain situations. But under no conditions would it have been Buckner's job to stand up and say, *Hold on a minute, Mom, because I've got some doubts about the plan that I'd like to discuss.*

Rhoda gave Buckner the keys to the truck and pointed him down an unmarked trail. His job was to get Jewell to the boat, put the boat in the water, and then get the boat a few miles up the coast to meet Rhoda at the gas dock. They'd fuel up and then Rhoda would get aboard with supplies for Jewell when she landed.

This was a new addition to the plan, the fuel and the supplies, but there again it was not in Buckner's nature to question such details and it did make sense that Jewell would not want to arrive in Canada empty-handed.

He wasn't sure what Lucy's role in the escape would be, or why she'd been chosen to stay with their mother, but neither of his sisters seemed bothered by the arrangements and that did put his mind somewhat at ease.

They reached the truck quickly and then Buckner backed them

all the way down the two-track. He meant to find a spot to hit a three-point turn and get the truck pointed forward, but it was too narrow on the trail and so he wound up driving two miles of S-curves and hairpins in reverse.

Normally, Jewell would have been wound up and telling Buckner to slow down and be careful—she was an awful backseat driver—but she was so preoccupied with the prospect of prison that she didn't even notice they were going backward. Harold was asleep in the little half seat in the back of the cab because he was a good boy and his faith in Buckner was absolute.

Once they cleared the canopy and hit the gravel he slammed it into drive. There was no more need for subtlety or deftness of hand. Now it was all gas and no brakes. Six thousand pounds of American steel flying down a flat dirt road. Actually, it was probably Chinese steel, but whatever. Buckner couldn't solve all the country's problems in one morning, now, could he? All Buckner could do was get his sister to where she needed to go, to get her a little bit closer to some-where safe.

He hit seventy, then seventy-five. The tall trees narrowed into a blur and his supposedly anxious dog sat unbothered behind him as quiet as he could be—as quiet as he had been in Rhoda's trunk.

It occurred to Buckner that Harold was only really anxious when he was at their house in Creepy Woods. Maybe he'd just been trying to tell Buckner something all along. Maybe Harold knew they were unmoored and too far from home and didn't know how to pretend otherwise. Or maybe it just stank like mold and piss in that house, and that put Harold on edge because why wouldn't it?

They did not have to take the highway or any paved road at all, and before long there were spaces between the trees on the gravel road and flat, marshy fields where the air smelled of fish and iron.

Buckner caught the turn of a seagull rising in the distance and felt the air grow just slightly damp outside his open window.

"We haven't been out together on a boat in a minute," said Buckner. "I'm trying to remember the last time."

"You know this isn't for fun, right?" said Jewell. "I'm trying to avoid prison here, brother."

Buckner knew it wasn't the point, obviously, but there was part of him that was looking forward to getting out on the water.

He'd always loved a boat. The open air and the sound of the chop. The way boat captains got to stand up when they steered and the way they were called captains in the first place. He didn't know what all the nautical terms meant, but he loved those, too. Everything sounded cooler on a boat, right down to the directions themselves. There was poetry to it, which he was not too obtuse to acknowledge.

But mostly what he loved about a boat was all the memories of him and the family. It was damn near all he thought about in the desert. All that water and all that time together. The soupy sky and still water when they all got up early to fish. His daddy at the wheel while the kids huddled in the back in their sweatshirts and knit hats— teeth chattering as their mother pointed to something on the river and launched into a story they'd heard a dozen times before.

Or a long afternoon together on the bay. His daddy doing donuts and trying to toss them off an inner tube at the end of a rope they trailed behind the Cutwater. His mom always said that tubing was for tourists, but then she'd watch the kids get chucked ten feet in the air and couldn't stop herself from smiling if she tried.

He remembered Christmas mornings on the Crow and smelt dipping in the spring and boat races in the summer. The Chicago to Mackinac and the Red Fox Regatta. Quiet, August afternoons when he and his sisters would paddle the river all the way to the mouth and watch as the bay filled with sails. He remembered the reds and the yellows and the blues—all the bright spinnakers blown out in the wind like azaleas in bloom.

"I know this isn't a joyride," he said. "I'm just saying I miss it is all."

Jewell turned to him then, squinting in the sun.

"I miss it, too, and I don't know how we ever got so far away from it all."

Finally, they had come to the landing where the boat was parked beneath the low branches of a willow oak and Buckner put the truck in park.

"Here we are," he said.

He waited for his sister to say something, but she was already slamming the door behind her and heading for the hitch.

Buckner threw his right arm over the passenger seat and turned to look over his shoulder. Some people used the rearview, but Buckner had always felt at a slight remove when he used the mirror—like something got lost in translation in the reflection. He could have done it either way, it was just that he preferred to put his eyes directly on the target. He preferred to have one hand easy on the wheel and he once again executed a series of short, precise turns as he backed the truck toward the Bayliner.

He stopped when Jewell put her hands up, and then watched her work. Her arms were long and narrow while they turned the crank, but they were still tight with muscle. She might be a poker player and a bartender, but she'd worked plenty with her hands, too. They all had.

She shot him a thumbs-up once the boat was hitched and then she climbed aboard.

Buckner told Harold it was almost time to go, then eased the boat into the water. He unhitched, tied off on the dock, then stashed the Ford beneath the willow where the boat had been. He scooped Harold into his arms and ran for the Bayliner, now idling in the shallows and awaiting his arrival.

Jewell leaned over the siderail to take Harold and then Buckner hoisted himself aboard and went for the wheel.

"Should I get in the hold?"

"I think so," he said.

"Do you want me to take Harold?"

"He'll keep you company down there if you want."

"I think I could use some," she said, and then crouched with the dog and opened the latch to the hold.

Buckner did not drive a boat the way he did a truck or a four-wheeler. He revered the water and its ever-shifting depths and dangers and even this morning, with all the need in the world for haste, he took the shallows slow. Stood on his tiptoes and scanned for big rocks just beneath the surface.

There were small cabins along the shore, rentals and family plots where modest boats were tied off at the end of the old docks. They passed a few fishermen and Buckner gave them a nod as he would have on any other day.

He didn't hammer the throttle when they left the shallows, but he did gather speed enough to cut the low breakers and catch some little skips of air off the waves. The water spread wide and ran flat and far into the distance before him—a line of blue unfurling until it hit the low edge of sky.

They were an hour from the meet and right on time. Maybe even a touch ahead of schedule, and just as Buckner started to believe that they might actually escape, that Jewell might somehow make it to Canada, he saw the US *Mackinac*. It was out there in the ribbon of water between the bay and the wide open and he recognized it on sight—the Coast Guard cutter out of Cheboygan.

He jerked the wheel hard to the right, the starboard side, and then he saw the patrol boat. It was long and lean and it shot out of the *Mackinac*'s shadows like a missile. The patrol was chewing up the chop between them and driving Buckner back toward the shore. Now, on shore, there was a sheriff's cruiser parked behind the truck and another one barreling down the two-track behind it.

Buckner cut his turn short and began to fight his own wake. He was headed back toward the open water and hoping the patrol boat might overshoot him. Then it would just be him against the *Mackinac*. He could cut around it and get out into that open water yet, or at least he could try.

He would have to try. He would fight that behemoth and its advanced technologies and military-grade equipment with everything he had. Sure, it was a long shot, but he would have taken it in a heartbeat over the second patrol boat that had now arrived and hemmed him in on the port side.

He was in a small wash between the two patrol boats and there was a third converging behind them. The *Mackinac* was waiting beyond the patrols and above the *Mackinac* he could see a chopper circling.

Finally, he eased off the throttle and let the motor die.

Jewell opened the hold and stepped out with Harold held against her chest. The poor little bugger was shaking.

"I'm right here, buddy," said Buckner and raised his arms in surrender. "I'm right here."

lucy

Lucy was not glad to be returning to the house with her mother. Rhoda said she needed Lucy's help with the supplies, but Lucy suspected it was more about Rhoda not wanting to provide her unfettered access to Buckner and his parcel of land.

They walked quickly down the hill from the cabin and then onto the footpaths that would lead them home. Rhoda set the pace and it wasn't quite a jog, but as near as you could get to one by walking.

Lucy was tired and every step sent a fresh tremor of pain through her swollen face, but her mother had just plucked a mushroom hunter's bag out of a literal minefield and so Lucy was in no real position to complain.

Her mother had always blurred the lines between courage and insanity and Lucy's feelings about that fact had always vacillated somewhere between admiration and horror. Rhoda would never put the land into the trust. She would lose it to the bank before she surrendered and Lucy knew she'd been a fool to ever hope otherwise.

"I don't blame you for Jewell," said her mother.

Those were the first words either had spoken on the walk, but Lucy did not respond. Her effort was solely focused on keeping pace and she had no idea what to say about her mother's revelation anyway.

"I blame Jewell for Jewell because she's smart enough to know better and she made that call on her own. Obviously, you were there to offer it in the first place, for which you're to blame, but that doesn't let Jewell off the hook. You're both grown-ups and responsible for your own choices. You get to carry your own regret."

Finally, Lucy stopped walking and leaned against a pine tree to gather her breath.

"I don't regret a goddamn thing, Mom."

She half thought her mother would just keep walking, and she would have been fine with it if she did. She wasn't interested in another argument or further discussion—Lucy just wanted it on the record that of all the regrets she carried, not a single one was related to her attempts to save the land.

Her mother didn't keep walking, though. Her mother had never walked away from a thing in her life.

"How do you think that mushroom fucker got back here?" she said.

"I don't know," said Lucy. "But I'm pretty sure you're about to blame the trail."

"You don't think she used your trail?"

"She might have, but it'd be a helluva lot easier if she just parked somewhere on Foster Road and walked in. I know the fencing out that way needs plenty of repairs because I was planning to do it before you kicked me out. The trail, though, has brand-new fencing and let me tell you it's no joke. We built it so that you can't see it from the trail, but its intentions are clear if you stray from the path and decide to test it."

"You taking a run at my fences, now?"

"I'm not doing anything but pointing out facts. Your fences along Foster Road are a fucking joke and you can't tell me they aren't."

"If you haven't noticed, I've had a lot going on. Not everything has been tended to, because I've only got two hands. And I didn't kick you off the property, you earned your way off. You kicked yourself off the land when you sat down with those lawyers and the bank."

"I was trying to help you," said Lucy. "I was trying to help the family."

"If you wanna help, you ought to try being helpful. That might be a place to start."

"The land is going to survive if I have anything to do with it, Mom. That's all I've ever wanted."

"And all I've ever wanted was to protect this family. That's the difference. You put the land above your people."

"I just don't think my family needs so much of the land, is all," said Lucy. "Or more to the point, I don't think we can keep it. I don't *want* to keep it if it means living like this. If it means my sister sits in prison."

The sun had risen and there was light through the canopy. There was so much land around them in every direction, and within each inch a universe unto itself. The ridged bark of the tree at Lucy's back and a line of black ants along the fallen branch at her feet. The damp ground cover and the dew on the tall blades of grass between the skinny birch and pines. Then the chopper blades in the distance—that violent drone and whir.

"Jewell's not going to prison," she said.

Lucy pointed in the direction of the chopper.

"It kind of sounds like she is, Mom."

"Nah," said Rhoda. "That's just a bit of saber rattling."

"Okay," said Lucy. "Forget the chopper and the traffic stops and the arson detectives. Say somehow she does get to Canada, what the fuck is she going to do up there, Mom? Are we just going to drop her off on some little island and tell her to sharpen up a stick for a spear?

Or is she going to go to Toronto and live on the street? What's the actual plan here? What supplies are we going to get that are going to help her right now?"

Rhoda leaned against a tree across from Lucy. She wiped at some sweat on her forehead with the back of an arm and sighed. Looked at her daughter from behind her aviator shades.

"Looks like your swelling is going down some."

"It doesn't feel like it."

"Well, it is. You've always been a fast healer. When you were a little girl, you'd scrape your knee in the afternoon and it would be nearly healed by morning. Like it never happened at all."

Lucy had always taken some pride in her reputation as a fast healer, but she did not want to accept what felt like an invitation from her mother for a quick bit of nostalgia. She let the silence linger instead.

After a beat, Rhoda went on. "You think you're trying to save this family, but all you're doing is running away from it. You can't change what you are."

"Maybe I'm not what you think I am."

"Maybe not, but maybe there's some things you don't know, either. Maybe not everything is exactly like you think it is. Like that cormorant that has you so bothered."

"Oh God," said Lucy. "Now you want to talk about the bird?"

"What? You don't want to hear about what happened?"

"I don't want you to launch into some story while we should be hiking. I don't want you to waste my time with any more of this bullshit."

"You were right about a lot of it, but there's pieces to that story you're missing."

"I don't think there's really anything you can say to make it better, so maybe not trying to justify it would be a start."

"I'm not trying to justify anything. I'm trying to tell you the truth."

"Right now?"

"Yes, right now."

"Why?"

"Because my father didn't kill just one cormorant," said Rhoda. "He killed dozens. Probably more. Smashed up their nests, too. Stomped on their eggs and everything."

"Is this a joke to you?" said Lucy. "Are you trying to upset me?"

"It is not a joke and I'm not trying to upset you. I'm trying to tell you what happened."

"I think it's pretty clear what happened."

"The cormorant was on the endangered list, you're right about that. They were protected and they were a predator and they made a rookery out on Tin Island in the bay. Fed on trout and perch and after a few summers there were so many of them that they looked like clouds above the water when they went out to feed. I'm sure you know they live on roe, primarily, and after a few years they'd just about cleared the county of game fish. Of course, this was before the resort so the only tourism we had was fishing and camping. Problem there was, no more fish."

"There were fish."

"Not enough," said Rhoda. "And people lost their livelihoods because of it. Restaurants and stores went belly-up. Motels closed. People packed their shit and left and others got stuck here in land debt with the bank. One night, Margaret Stephens came to the house and she was a sobbing mess because her husband, Tom, swallowed the barrel end of a shotgun and blew his brains out on their bedroom walls.

"She came to see my mom because she was the only person she knew that lost somebody that way. She wanted to know what you did when somebody you loved had killed themselves. She asked it just like that, too. I was eating dinner at the table and Mrs. Stephens was in the living room with my mother and she just looked at her and said, 'What do I do now?'

"She was worried the church wouldn't let her bury him in their plots because it was a suicide, and she couldn't afford a new one somewhere else. She was worried he was going to go into the county grave and wouldn't get to heaven.

"They weren't even friends. Your grandmother said they might not have had a single conversation before that night, but she put on some water to boil for tea and did her best to comfort Mrs. Stephens. What your grandfather did was tell me to get a jacket."

Lucy looked off toward a glade where the sun was brightening the tall grass. Everything had been so urgent. Her mother had steamrolled through the brush, only to stop now and tell a story she'd never bothered to share over the past thirty years.

"We went that night," she went on. "It was just me and your grandfather and we took the boat out to a little island about half a mile from the rookery. We set up a tent and that was our home base for the two days we spent clearing Tin Island of birds. You could hear the shooting back on shore, of course, and that first day the sheriff sent a pair of deputies out, but they weren't there to arrest us. They brought sandwiches and pops and they shook your grandfather's hand.

"He told me that night, and I've never forgot it; we were sitting around a little campfire and he looked at me and said, 'Baby girl, there is nothing more dangerous in this world than a predator that the law won't let you near.' I believe that truth has been borne out by the entire history of the world, and certainly the history of this land right here."

Lucy looked at her mother. The dark skin and the pinch of

wrinkles above her shades. The straight-backed posture and square shoulders. Her infuriating, unshakable conviction in herself.

"Shouldn't we be walking?"

"No," said Rhoda. "We shouldn't. We've come far enough now and the truth is we need to burn a little time."

"We need to burn time all the sudden?"

"That's right."

"Then why were we just sprinting?"

"We weren't sprinting. We were walking quickly."

"The point is, why?"

"Because I didn't know," said Rhoda. "I wasn't sure. I thought I knew, but because I wasn't certain, I needed to go fast and leave myself another option."

"What the fuck are you talking about right now?"

"I'm talking about what happens next," she said. "And I'm surprised you haven't figured it out yet. You've always been the smartest in that way. Jewell is smart in other ways. Buckner isn't smart in any ways, but he has other strengths."

Lucy cringed at her mother's view of Buckner as the bumbling but goodhearted drunk. Somehow Buckner was credited for the fact that he'd never devoted any time or energy to how to best protect the land. That was old news, though. A deeply worn groove and utterly pointless to discuss.

"Mom," she said. "Can you just tell me what's going on? Can you tell me—"

Rhoda held up her hand for Lucy to hush and she did. Instinctively, as if she were once again a child.

Rhoda turned slowly to the left and when Lucy looked, she saw the buck not fifty yards away. He was spectacular, an eight-point with big, budding antlers and broad shoulders. He was standing by one of her daddy's old bait piles.

Her father's stand was still there, even now—right behind the animal at the edge of the clearing. She remembered mornings in the stand with her father and mother both. Steam from a coffee thermos and the autumn cold and clear. The birch leaves all red and orange and their misting breath. The snap of a twig as a deer approached.

Finally, this buck scattered and Lucy returned to the moment. Rhoda was staring at her now.

"You know how your daddy always says that seeing a deer in summer is a good omen?"

"Yes," she said. "Dad might have mentioned that one or two thousand times."

"Do you remember when you were little what you asked him?"

"I asked him lots of things."

"We were out hiking along the road. Foster Road, actually. Right there where my shitty fences are."

Lucy braced herself, but it was just a playful swipe and Rhoda went on.

"I can't remember what we were doing, but I think Jewell was a baby and back at the house asleep. Anyway, we saw a dead deer, road-kill, all torn up and flies everywhere and you looked at your daddy, I mean you were so serious, and you said— You really don't remember this?"

Lucy thought of her father. Not of her sick father, with his frail body and thin wisps of hair, but of the way he'd looked back then, with his dark beard and bulk. She tried to conjure the day her mother was referencing, but she could not.

"I don't," she said. "What did I ask him?"

"You asked him if a dead deer was a good omen. You were so pie-eyed and sweet."

"And what did he say?"

Rhoda wiped at a tear that had slid out suddenly from beneath her shades. That tear startled Lucy, and she waited.

"He said, '*Not for the deer.*'"

Her mother laughed when she said it. She laughed loud and from her belly and Lucy laughed, too. She laughed as quietly as she could, but only because it hurt.

Her mother seemed to have decided something. Everything had been so hurried, and then, suddenly, it was not. Lucy was frightened about what that decision might be but knew better than to ask. Her mother wasn't likely to tell her, and it wouldn't matter if she did— once her mind was set, it was as good as done.

rhoda

I didn't decide what had to be done so much as perform some very basic arithmetic. That's what it usually comes down to in the end. People like to make it seem more than that, but the truth is there isn't much choice to anything when you're a parent. You do what needs to be done and you can either accept that fact or ignore it, and that's really the only decision you'll ever have to make.

I've never believed for a minute that people don't know the right way forward. That the truth is some distant, glimmering mystery. Divining the path isn't the issue; the issue is how difficult that path can be, or, even worse, how goddamn mundane. But you know. You always know. Everything else is just pretend.

Jewell had her ruck from the fire stashed in a hollowed-out portion of her bedroom closet, which was the first place I looked. She'd been stashing stuff in that little hole since she was a child and thought I didn't know because I'd never felt the need to bust her over a couple of wine coolers when it was far more valuable to know where she hid things. That's where a lot of parents go wrong—they don't play the long game. Now I took the ruck into the workshop and tossed it on the table where I'd stitched up Lucy the other night.

I checked the pockets and the liners of the bag and they were empty. There were matches in the main pouch and the bag still stank like river and gasoline. I put my library card in the main compartment and then stood at the door for a moment before I turned out the lights. I looked at the cormorant and shook my head. It was an ugly sonofabitch and I said so, then shut the door behind me.

I stopped in the pole barn for Edward's hunting rifle and left it on the front porch before I went inside to rouse him. He was already up, though. He was moving around the kitchen in some sort of hurry.

"What are you doing?"

"Shit," he said.

"What? You sneak some woman in here while I was gone?"

"I wish."

"I bet you do."

"No," he said. "I was going to surprise you, but I couldn't get it hooked up in time."

He was standing at the counter, fiddling with his cell phone.

"Get what hooked up?"

"This," he said, and then I heard a blast of music on the porch.

"What the hell is that?"

"Connie set it up. It's a Bluetooth she brought for a present. She came up last night to check on me, figuring you'd be gone."

"Well, that was nice."

"It's a music speaker."

"I can hear that. You said it was a Bluetooth?"

"That's what she called it, yeah."

"You're telling me you got a speaker out there on the porch?"

"Can't you hear it?"

"Of course I can hear it! It's about making my ears bleed."

"You don't like it? It's Bobby Seger."

"I think it's fine," I said. "It's just so loud."

Edward tried to turn it down but wound up making it louder. I had to plug my ears and then he just stood there cussing and jabbing at his phone until he finally got the thing quieted.

I looked outside but couldn't see any speakers.

"Where is it?"

"On the porch, just like I told you."

"I was just out there. I didn't see anything."

"It's tiny is why."

"Is it?"

"It's just a little thing," he said, and held up his hands like he was describing a brook trout.

"Well, it sounds real nice, now that you got it turned down to where I can hear myself think."

"What are you doing back here already, anyway? I figured you'd be gone until night at least. How's Jewell?"

"She's fine," I said. "But we need to talk."

"Is everything okay? I keep hearing on the news that they're still looking for leads."

"Pause that music, and let's have a sit."

He was moving well. He had color in his cheeks and he didn't need the chair or the tank to make it to the porch. I think he was riding high from all the excitement.

It was ridiculous, but I did have a moment—it was just a flash—where I wondered if maybe he had snuck some hussy in through the window while I was gone. Maybe one of the cancer nurses we met. There was one with a big chest he liked to eyeball and thought I didn't notice.

Once he was settled in his rocking chair, I went into the living room and flipped on the television.

Local news was reporting live from the river. They had it set up so you could see a burned patch of grass behind the reporter because they're all about the drama. The reporter said that local and state authorities were working together to apprehend the suspect and that the Coast Guard was involved, too. The news said the Coast Guard had cutters and patrol boats on the task and there was the number of an anonymous tip line flashing on the bottom of the screen.

I put the TV on mute but left it running. Went to the kitchen for the phone and called down to Connie Becker's house. Her mom answered and I asked her to give me Rick Pico's phone number.

"What in the world for?" she asked.

"I just need it is all."

"Well, tell that sonofabitch his daughter twisted her ankle at soccer, which he didn't bother to mention or probably even notice."

"I'll tell him," I said.

I busied myself with one last detail while I spoke with Rick and it was good to have myself a little preoccupied, digging through drawers and bins for a little box I needed. I thought a few slammed cupboard doors in the background might help sell the idea that I was in a panic.

I did what needed to be done, but more than anything I said it *how* it needed to be said. Then I hung up. He called me right back, but it only rang once and that was when I knew my story had taken and went to join Edward on the porch. He nodded at my rifle.

"You going hunting?"

"I am not."

"What's going on, then? There some sort of plan afoot?"

"There is."

He took a gummy from his shirt pocket and popped it in. "I got the cologne, by the way. That was a nice little prize. Where'd that come from?"

"I stole it from a Christian rock band."

"Did you, now?"

253

"I sure did."

"That sounds interesting," he said.

"It's a long story."

"Do we have time for it?"

"No, we do not. But I'll tell you that I had Buckner's girl along with me at the time and she is as good as gold."

"Buck's got a girl?"

"She's not a girl. She's a full-grown woman and the best thing to ever happen to that boy."

"Good Lord," he said. "I feel like I missed everything."

"I'm getting you caught up now. Another thing that happened is we had a mushroom hunter get blown up last night on a land mine."

"Do what?"

"One of Harvard's land mines blew. It was one of those ecotourists, trespassing. She was blown to smithereens."

"Goodness grief," he said. "I must have slept right through the blast. What happened to the body?"

"I just told you—it got blown to bits."

"But after that? Did you bury it?"

"Hell no, we didn't bury it. It's just out there in the woods."

"Are you kidding me?"

"No, I am not. They're going to find that woman dead on the property one way or another. The last thing we want to do is look like we were trying to cover it up. She was trespassing on our property and stepped on a land mine. It is what it is."

"What it is, is illegal. You can't just have land mines buried about—"

"I understand that."

"Well, I don't understand anything you're saying. Where are the kids?"

"Buckner and Jewell are trying to get to Canada, but they won't make it out of the bay."

"Why not?"

"Because they got the Coasties out there."

"They called out the Coast Guard?"

"I just flipped on the TV and saw it. I told Lucy to go to Mabel's house and sleep and I imagine she was out like a light the moment she hit the pillow."

"So, what's the plan? How the hell are we going to wriggle our way through this one?"

"It's not one we can wriggle."

"Is that so?"

"But it is under control."

"I'd like to know how."

"I need to tell you something else, first."

"There's something else?"

"It's to do with Wanda."

"Your sister?"

I nodded. "I've been thinking about her a lot lately. I been thinking about how it felt right after, how everything felt empty. Like the whole world got spilled out and run dry."

"I still wish I'd have been here when it happened," he said. "That goddamn war—"

"My point is, and what I wanted to tell you, is about that empty feeling. I think I've been afraid of that feeling. I think that's why I couldn't let you go."

"Rho—" he said.

"Just let me finish."

He held up his hands. "Okay."

"I know you've been in so much pain. I know you've been suffering and I know you've held on because you know I wanted you here."

There were shadows in the grass off the porch, but they were short along the edge of the pines. It was full morning, but not yet too warm.

"I should have let you go," I said. "It was selfish."

"Are you about to shoot me with my own hunting rifle?"

I laughed and I could hear him laughing, too. Then my laughter rose until it rolled into tears and then somehow I was laughing and crying and it was all disappearing into the same sound.

He asked me if I was okay, and I said that I was. I wiped at my eyes with a fist and tried to gather myself.

"I am not going to shoot you," I said finally.

"You know I wouldn't mind if you did."

"Hush."

"What?" he said. "It's true."

"Have you been hearing the helicopters?"

"How could I not? They were circling like buzzards."

"I was worried that you'd hear them and get frightened."

"Frightened of a helicopter?"

"No, frightened for us. About getting caught."

"I don't worry about that. Not anymore. Not for a long time."

"Really?"

He shrugged. "Maybe I didn't stop worrying. Maybe I just stopped paying so close attention to it. I worry about the kids, but not as much when they're with you. You love them too fierce. If you can't protect them from something, nobody can."

"That's a helluva nice thing to say."

"Nice has nothing to do with it. It's just a fact is all."

"I feel like things are going to happen fast now for all of them," I said. "They're coming into the busy time of life and for some reason I believe they're going to be okay. I feel like they have a real chance to make it. They're coming together. It may not seem like it on the surface, but it's happening. I can feel it. They're going to be there for each other, despite it all."

"Are you going to tell me what's going on now? 'Cause I'd say my curiosity is pretty piqued at this point."

"We've got about ten minutes," I said. "Maybe twenty. Thirty at the most."

"Ten minutes for what?"

"They'll send a goddamn battalion, probably."

"Who will?"

"Sheriff's department. Staties. Fucking National Guard, I don't know."

"And who will they be looking for when they do?"

"They'll be looking for me."

"Is that right?"

I nodded. Pulled out my pistol and set in on my lap.

"And why will they be looking for you, and not Jewell?"

"Because everything is going to point to me. All of it. The land mines and the dead woman. Van Hargraves, and everything else. Everything that happened gets put on me and not the kids. I moved some things around, made one phone call, and I think that's enough to sell it."

"Who did you call?"

"I called Rick Pico."

"You did?"

"I did."

"And what did you say?"

"The first thing I did was apologize to him for yesterday."

"What did you do yesterday?"

"Nothing," I said. "But he was the cop in my line at the traffic stop and we talked a few minutes. I told him on the phone that I was sorry if I was acting strange and that I hadn't been myself lately. I started going on about the different pressures I was under and then sort of let it slip about the boat."

"What about the boat?"

"That I was the one that burned it but didn't know anybody was inside."

"You said that?"

"Not in so many words. I just made it seem like I was trying to tell him that I wasn't really guilty of what they thought I was. I said something about how doing one thing doesn't automatically mean you meant to do the other. Then he got real quiet and I hung up the phone."

"You think he'll bite?"

"I'd say I'm certain of it."

"You sprang him a trap, didn't you?"

"It means a lot to me," I said. "That you appreciate that element of it."

"Alfred would be proud."

"I'd like to think so."

"And when the cops get here, you're probably not going to be too interested in a surrender, are you?"

"I will not be interested in that," I said. "No."

"Are they going to buy all this?" he said. "Afterward?"

"They're going to have to. Otherwise, they're going to have all sorts of mess on their hands."

"Because of what happens next?"

"That's right."

"Is the paperwork in order?" he said. "On the property?"

"The paperwork has been in order for five years," I said. "You know that."

"Shit," he said.

"What's that?"

"I forgot the whole reason for all this Bluetooth business."

All of the sudden, he was pecking at his phone again. I couldn't imagine what was so important at that exact moment, but then there was a pop of sound in the speaker and there was music. I looked at him and he smiled back at me. There were tears welling in his eyes.

"God," I said. "I haven't heard this in years."

"It sounds good, doesn't it?"

"How'd you find it?"

"Connie did," he said. "She found it and put it on my phone. I got it right here to where all I have to do is press the button."

I saw the speaker now. It was sitting on the porch rail, no bigger than a tube full of tennis balls.

"All that sound out of that little bitty thing?"

"Modern technology," he said.

"I guess it's not all bad, is it?"

"Did you tell the kids what you're doing?"

"Hell, no."

"They're going to hate you for it."

"Only for a while," I said. "Eventually, they'll understand."

The woman was singing her part of the song now and it was so beautiful and so clear.

"What's her name again?" I said.

"Ronnie Spector."

"Ronnie Spector." I nodded. "That's right. Is she still alive?"

"She is right now," he said. "Right now on this porch, she's alive as she can be."

I nodded. He was right about that.

"That poor woman," he said. "The mushroom picker. I hope she doesn't have a family."

"I don't know what to hope about her," I said. "I think it would be better if she did have one. I think that'd be worth having for her."

"You're probably right."

"Shakespeare said it was better to have loved and lost," I said. "Isn't that right?"

"I don't think it was Shakespeare, but that's the poem, yeah."

"Whoever it was," I said, "had a point."

Before long, I could hear the sirens. They were downriver but drawing closer. They had the chopper up, too—that foolish helicopter, flying its foolish circles and swirling its blades. *Chop, chop, chop.*

"You don't have to come with me," I said. "If you want to stay and help the kids make the transition, I totally understand."

"Fuck you," he said. "And hand me my rifle."

I set the rifle across Edward's lap and realized then he might not have the strength to hold it and aim.

"Do you want the pistol?" I asked. "And I can take the rifle?"

"I can lift it fine," he said. "You just worry about your own situation over there."

"Are you sure?"

He'd already lifted the rifle, though. He hadn't set it on his shoulder, but he was ready.

"I love you," I said.

"I love you, too."

"I always have."

"Sometimes," he said, "it feels like I've loved you since before I was born."

"Delray told me something pretty interesting last night. When I went to see about the boat."

"Oh yeah? What was that?"

"He said he was with you the night I set Jody Pitowski's car on fire. Said it scared the shit out of you."

"So what?"

"So what? So why didn't you ever tell me you knew about that?"

"Why didn't you ever tell me you did it?"

"Because I didn't want you to think I was crazy."

"Shit," he said. "I've been knowing that my whole life."

"But you married me anyway."

"Hell yes, I did. I was always going to marry you."

"Why were you messing around with Jody, then?"

"I wasn't," he said. "She was after me and I was just too polite to know how to tell her to get lost. To tell her I was spoken for. If anything, you did me a favor."

"You didn't answer the question, though."

"What question?"

"Why didn't you tell me you knew?"

"Because I liked knowing something you didn't, goddamnit. Why should you always get to be the smart one?"

The first time I really noticed Edward was on a blustery day in autumn. He was walking through the front doors of the high school and I saw him with his hair combed back and his coat collar turned up. He was talking with a friend and smiling and there was nothing in that moment any different from the moment that came before it, or after, except that it changed everything. I saw him and he saw me. We saw each other and it was all it ever took.

His eyes were still as bright and brown now as they'd been that first day. Two tours in Vietnam hadn't snuffed out his brightness, and neither had a hard life in a bootlegging family. Not even cancer had taken his light. It had dimmed it sometimes but never snuffed it out entirely.

I fell in love with him in a glance in 1965 and over forty years later we were sitting together on the porch and I am here to tell you that the first day and the last day occurred in the very same time and place. That autumn morning and this one in the distant summer were not two separate places on a line, but a single, unified point.

That point was the land around us, too. It was the shadows on the grass and the tall pines that cast them. It was the vervain along the bend of the road and the birdsong in the trees. It was my sister and my brother and the blue cut of the river I could still see in the far away.

The sirens were very close. I could hear them coming from the road and figured they'd probably dispatched a few dozen officers by foot as well. They were going to hem us in on all sides. The chopper was low above the trees and I could feel the gusts from the blades and they were so loud that they drowned out the music.

I didn't care, though. I could still hear the song ringing out inside me.

I put my hand on my weapon and I raised it and I looked at Edward and he had his rifle pointed.

There was somebody shouting at us through a bullhorn now and the first vehicles had arrived in their angry clouds of dust.

We did not fire. We just held our aim and when the man with the bullhorn demanded we drop our weapons, I stood up off my chair and took a step in his direction and I could feel Edward rising with me.

A woman sang beautifully. I was with Edward on Lake Huron and I felt the wind in my face and everything around me was blue and bright.

part VI

the siblings

They were heartbroken and they were angry and they were plagued with regret and self-doubt, but the one thing they were not, was surprised.

Their mother had always gotten what she wanted, and not even the terrible violence and suddenness of her death, and their father's, was enough to change the fundamental fact that it would have made perfect sense to Rhoda.

People like to describe tragic events as unimaginable, but that is almost always a lie. There are very few horrors on this earth unimagined, and the Sawbrooks were not willing to take a note of false comfort in the idea that they could not have seen their mother's death coming.

She got them all, one last time. Jewell's poker table savvy, Lucy's college education, and Buckner's purity of heart and instinct—all of it was utterly useless in the face of their mother's guile. Once again, she had won.

She won because her entire life had been a single, straight arrow fired with great purpose at the same target and she had never once even considered the possibility of failure.

Buckner moved into an old trailer on the property and brought Sky and Frog with him. He put his land in Lucy's trust and Jewell got Sky a job tending bar at the Sailor's Knot. Jewell went back to the poker tables at the Soaring Eagle and Lucy was moving back into Mabel's house.

There were questions from the cops, of course. Detectives and arson investigators. They focused on Jewell and Buckner, who both took public defenders and stuck to their stories.

Buckner's story was the truth. At least parts of it were. He'd gotten drunk at the campground and got in a fight with Ray Tomshaw, and yes, his own sister had tased him and knocked him unconscious, but both Ray and Tammy could confirm that he'd been sitting right there with them when the fire started across the river because how could they forget? His alibi was his own foolish drunkenness and it was rock-solid.

Jewell's side was shakier. She said she'd been at home and had no idea where her mother was that night and that all she'd done was care for her sister when she showed up at the house all beaten and bloody from her fall. Lucy, as everybody knew, had seen a dog drowning in the river and jumped in to try to save it.

It was probably all too tidy by a half, except for the fact that nobody wanted an investigation that ended with the police killing two innocent people on their own front porch. Which was why, of course, Rhoda had done it.

Buckner was the one that went to Franklin for the money. They let the dust settle, but ten thousand dollars was not something they could walk away from and it was owed.

They met on a park bench on the river trail about a month after everything went down. The birch were starting to hue and there were cold snaps folded inside the late summer air. The marching band was practicing at the high school in the mornings and when the wind gusted just right, he and Sky could lie in bed and listen to the snare drums through the pines.

Buckner brought coffee for them both and they sat together and watched the runners and the cyclists and the parents pushing strollers.

"Some days I wake up," said Franklin, "and I still don't know what's happening. It's like I forget he's gone all over again and then I have that terrible moment where I remember."

Buckner nodded. "It's the same way with my parents."

"I still can't believe what happened," said Franklin. "The way they went up there and just—"

Buckner looked straight ahead. Sipped from his coffee.

"Gunned them down?"

"Yes," said Franklin quietly. "Of course, I can't believe what Van did, either. It's all so sad and fucking gruesome. I hate how gruesome it all was, Buckner."

"That part doesn't bother me as much. In their own way, they all had a choice in how they went."

Franklin wore a sweater and blue jeans. He sat hunched forward and peered out from behind a pair of amber-tinted shades. His hair looked thinner on top, and it seemed to Buckner that he might be losing it at a higher rate of speed now.

"I just—"

Franklin paused and for a moment it seemed as if he might cry. He didn't, though. He took a breath and gathered himself instead.

"Some days I just don't know what to do about anything. Some days I just can't even hold a thought in my head for more than two seconds."

"I know," said Buckner. "It's a terrible thing."

"I'm so mad at him that I can't see straight. And part of why I'm mad is because of how much I miss him."

"He was sick. It doesn't make it any better, but he was."

"I don't even want the fucking insurance money. I wanted him."

"I know you did."

"A year ago, I told him it was me or the booze. I gave him an ultimatum. Surprise, surprise, he chose the booze."

"He didn't choose the booze," said Buckner. "He just tried to have you both."

"What's the difference?"

Buckner took that in.

"Maybe there isn't one," he said.

"The worst part is, I didn't even care anymore. I mean, he was such a lousy drunk. It was exhausting, but it was still good enough. I never would have left him and I should have just told him that and maybe this wouldn't have happened."

"It was nothing you could control," said Buckner. "It wasn't your fault."

"I had a feeling something was wrong. More wrong than usual, anyway. He bought me a ticket to see Billy Joel in Interlochen but said he couldn't come."

Franklin brought his hand to his mouth and Buckner was certain he was going to cry now and he reached for Franklin and put his arm around his shoulders. But still, Franklin didn't cry. Franklin just took another breath and went on.

"He said he had to work, but then I came home and he was gone. I came home and there were fire trucks and sirens and he was fucking dead."

Buckner gave Franklin's shoulders a squeeze. He was so tiny he was worried about hurting him, but he also wanted Franklin to know that he was there. That he was still listening.

"He texted me during the concert and something about it felt off. I keep thinking if I would have gotten up and driven home, then maybe I could have stopped it."

"There was nothing you could have done," said Buckner. "Inter-lochen is a ninety-minute drive, and that's in ideal conditions."

"I know, but it doesn't change the way I feel. I keep feeling like I could have stopped it and the truth is that text was his suicide note. He couldn't leave a real one, so he texted me instead. He said, *I hope he plays 'Highland Falls.'*"

"That's a song?"

Franklin nodded.

"It was our song. Not officially, but it was in the conversation. We had a few songs that were important to us and that was one of them."

"Did he play it?"

Franklin looked up at Buckner and now his cheeks were wet with tears.

"He played it," he said. "He played it, and it was beautiful and I swear that I could feel Van there with me. It was like he was sitting right beside me for a moment and I wonder now if maybe he was already gone by then. If he was just stopping by to see me one last time. It's probably just some stupid, romantic fantasy but I swear it felt real and it doesn't matter either way because he's gone now. I can feel how gone he is. Everything is just—"

"Empty," said Buckner.

"Yes," he said. "Empty."

"I know that feeling, too. I've lived in that feeling for whole years."

"I know you have," said Franklin, and patted Buckner's arm. "And you've come so far. How long is it now?"

"Just thirty-two days."

"Just nothing," said Franklin. "That's a lifetime and I'm so happy for you."

Buckner took his arm from Franklin's shoulder and put both his hands on his knees and leaned forward. Now he felt like he might cry.

Franklin put a gentle hand against his back.

"You'll want to know about the money. I'm assuming that's what we're doing here, right?"

"It's not only the money. I consider you a friend."

Franklin straightened himself on the bench. "And I, you."

"I hate that I have to bring it up," said Buckner. "I really do."

"Please. I am so angry at him for dragging you all into this on top of everything else. How much was it?"

Buckner sighed. "It was ten thousand."

"My God," said Franklin. "That man. What a fucking scoundrel he could be."

"I didn't know him well," said Buckner.

"He offered ten because that's how desperate he was to go, and because he knew I'd have it to spare with the settlement money."

"The other bit," said Buckner, "is that it would really help if it was clean money."

"What does that mean? Clean money?"

"It just means it's not dirty. It means we don't have to clean it ourselves. It's free and clear and we can use it."

"I literally don't understand anything you're saying right now."

"It means it's not money that you shouldn't have."

"I only have one kind of money," said Franklin. "I do my job and they pay me money for that, and then I pay my taxes and still have plenty left over."

"That sounds good then," said Buckner.

"That's the thing. We always had so much. We had so much more than enough and he could never just sit with that and be happy. There was always something else, just beyond his grasp."

———

Buckner married Sky that October. It was a small service on the property and Lucy and Sky's mother handled most of the planning. Lucy kept saying there were certain things, colors and foods, that were most appropriate for an autumnal wedding and that drove Jewell crazy. Not the planning itself. It was that word, *autumnal*.

Jewell didn't know why Lucy couldn't just say it was a fall wedding. Actually, she knew why. Lucy had to seem smart every chance she got and when Jewell complained about it to Buckner, he just shrugged.

"If I knew those words, I'd say them, too," he said.

"You're just in love," said Jewell. "You don't care about anything right now."

That was true enough. Sky and Frog were Buckner's world and it was more than he deserved or ever had nerve enough to wish for. Sky was as happy as he'd seen her and she marveled about something on the property every day. She took long walks in the woods and would always come home with some new discovery to share. A little bit of creek where she'd seen deer tracks, or the sudden sight of a circling hawk. She would stumble upon a place that Buckner had described—some cut in the pines where the sun fell just so—some vantage that had sounded too lovely to be true until she saw it for herself.

"There's so much of it," she would say. "It just keeps going."

Lucy was back in Mabel's house, but she was moving her things slowly. She still had a month on her rental in town and was sleeping there most nights. She was saying goodbye, she supposed, to another life that she almost lived.

The scarring from the fall was not insignificant, but Rhoda had done an admirable job, considering. Lucy was left with a raised line of whitened skin that spanned most of her left cheek. She was still startled by her reflection, but not in a way that bothered her as much as she might have imagined. She looked different, but she felt different, too.

It was Jewell who found the box that Rhoda left her. She'd put it on the kitchen counter with a piece of paper taped to the lid. *Lucy*, it said.

Inside was Germain's flask. She would have had to put it there during those last few moments before the end came and she pictured her mother taking the flask from the nightstand and walking it into the kitchen, where she would have searched for something to put it in.

Knowing her mother, the box would have been in the last place she looked and Lucy could hear her exasperated sighs as she slammed drawers and cupboard doors behind her. She could see the sunlight streaming in through the big window above the sink and imagined her father outside waiting patiently on the porch.

The flask would have been one of her final decisions, the thing she did right before the last thing, and now when Lucy held it, she felt as if she were cupping her mother's strange and complicated heart in her hands.

The flask was not just an heirloom or a testament to the family's past. It was not just the engravings. The flask was the inset compass, too—the arrow and the pull of a single, cardinal point. It was a history, and it was a map.

———————

Jewell moved quickly into the main house and she did not discuss it with her siblings or ask permission.

She painted walls and patched holes and came home from a card game one night with a brand-new coffee table strapped to the Ford.

She swept out the dusty corners, took some pictures down, and put some others up in their place.

She missed her mother and her father and she still cried most days, but sometimes those tears felt a little bit less salty—some days they started to feel a little bit like healing.

She sat on the porch with her coffee in the mornings and watched the sun edge up over the pines and sometimes Lucy would join her and sometimes Buckner and Sky would come up from the trailer to visit.

Other times, she would sit on the porch with nothing but the coffee in her hand, but she never felt alone. She could feel her father and mother right there with her, and sometimes she could feel other people, too. Germain and Mabel and her aunt and uncle that she never met and sometimes she swore she could feel Alfred himself. She suspected that Lucy and Buckner felt them, too. They were all there together and she knew they would never lose the land or one another. They had known this place for so long. Their lives were just beginning.

acknowledgments

Thank you to Lyssa Keusch for her vision, belief, and guiding hand. Thank you to Lauren Bello and all the talented folks at Grand Central for putting so much into this book. Seth Fishmann—thank you for believing in me, for your patience, and for being so great at what you do. Huge, huge thank-you to Jack Gernert, who is an absolute dynamo, and everybody at the Gernert Agency.

Thank you to Cassy for remaining the best decision I have ever made and thank you to Leo and Edie for being, by far, my favorites. And thank you to Spoon for being the best dog.

A special thank-you to my Dad for being a relentless supporter of my work, and my most tireless salesman. If you sit next to this man on any form of public transportation, you will almost certainly find yourself ordering one of my books before you reach your destination.

Thank you to the booksellers and advocates who have been so awesome to me along the way. There are too many to name, but I want to give a special shoutout to McLean & Eakin, the world's best bookstore, and the Library of Michigan. Huge thanks to the Weymouth Writers-in-Residence program, an incredible resource for writers in Southern Pines, North Carolina, where portions of this book were written. And to the North Carolina Arts Council: thank you for your tremendous support and advocacy.

Finally, thank you to Eamonn Donnelly and Jeff Stiefel for the perfect finishing touches.

Onward!

about the author

Travis Mulhauser was born and raised in northern Michigan. His novel *Sweetgirl* (Ecco/HarperCollins) was listed for The Center for Fiction's First Novel Prize, was an Indie Next Pick, and was named one of Ploughshares' Best Books of the New Year. He is also the author of *Greetings from Cutler County: A Novella and Stories*. Travis received his MFA in fiction from UNC Greensboro and is also a proud graduate of North Central Michigan College and Central Michigan University. He currently lives in Durham, North Carolina, with his wife, two children, and dog.